G000153132

Outreach

Outreach

SHELLY BERRY

The Book Guild Ltd

First published in Great Britain in 2019 by
The Book Guild Ltd
9 Priory Business Park
Wistow Road, Kibworth
Leicestershire, LE8 0RX
Freephone: 0800 999 2982
www.bookguild.co.uk
Email: info@bookguild.co.uk
Twitter: @bookguild

Typeset in 11pt Sabon MT

Printed and bound in the UK by 4edge Limited

ISBN 978 1912881 703

British Library Cataloguing in Publication Data.
A catalogue record for this book is available from the British Library.

For Moira

1

From the other side of the high street, I watched. I had been sitting in the café for nearly an hour, sipping slowly at my juice to try and make it last, and I hadn't seen a soul enter the building. I pulled out the crisp envelope from my bag and checked the letter again. Yes, I had the right address, and, according to my phone, I was there on the right day at the right time. I tried to push the ridiculous notion that the promise of an interview was some kind of practical joke out of my mind as I slurped up the last of my drink. It was quarter to, and whilst an hour early was obviously way too keen, ten minutes showed willing, discipline and professionalism – traits I hoped would make up for my lack of experience.

*

"Yeah?"
The informality of the greeting made me hesitate.

"Oh, hello. It's Emily. I'm here for an interview?"

The door buzzed open without further instruction from the hissing intercom. The stairwell inside was long and narrow, a naked light bulb offering little comfort. I took a deep breath and began to climb. As I got closer to the woman silhouetted at the top of the stairs, I looked up and smiled expectantly. She was tapping into her phone with manicured nails. I swallowed down my rising irritation and opened my mouth to introduce myself again, hoping to prompt the blonde flake in front of me into action.

"Wait in here." Without looking up she gestured towards the door opposite and stalked down a corridor. I let my mouth hang open, hoping that some unseen authority would pull her up on her tardiness. Resignedly I walked into the room in front of me. The kitchen area to my left was empty of people but strewn with the remains of someone's breakfast – a teabag dumped on the worktop and a globule of peanut butter surrounded by a liberal sprinkling of crumbs. I resisted the urge to clear up the mess and turned to the utilitarian sofas to my right. Perching on the edge of the nearest one, I scanned the newspapers scattered across the coffee tables in front of me, hoping to find a copy of *The Guardian* to pose with for when my interviewers finally emerged. The selection of freebies and tabloids filled me with doubt. Was I in the right place?

"Emily."

I jumped up from my seat, almost knocking my battered satchel onto the floor and thrust out my hand. I nearly started again when I looked at my welcomer. An overweight man with a ruddy complexion looked back at me with amusement.

"Hello, I'm Eric, the service manager. Sorry, didn't mean to startle you." I felt my face flush as he shook my hand firmly and chuckled. "Now, can I interest you in a cup of tea before we start?"

I shook my head rapidly in reply. Eric's smile broadened.

"A glass of water would be nice," I managed. He nodded before turning towards the kitchen cupboards behind me. As he searched for a clean glass, I took a deep breath. My nerves were already getting the better of me and the interview hadn't even started. "*It's all very well knowing the theory, Emily, but you'll never cut it in this line of work if you can't even sit through an interview without turning into a gibbering wreck,*" my dad had chastised after my last failure in this situation. Of course, he was right. As a social worker, he knew what he was talking about, and he was acutely aware of his daughter's shortcomings too.

"I promise we'll be gentle with you."

Eric's words hauled me back into the room. I looked at his eyes, strangely small in his fleshy face, and could see them glazing over. He had written me off already. I took the glass he was holding out and smiled my surrender.

"Okay, folks, are we ready?"

The voice at the door took me by surprise. I looked over to see another man smiling broadly at me.

"This is David. He's one of my team managers and will be interviewing you with me today."

I smiled back my hello. David was younger than Eric and had yet to succumb to middle-age spread. In fact, if it wasn't for the sprinkling of greys at his temples and the laughter lines around his blue eyes, he could have still been in his twenties.

"Shall we put you out of your misery?"

He stood back and gestured me out of the door. I grinned at him, stupidly relieved that Eric wouldn't be grilling me alone. Obediently I followed him out of the kitchen and let him usher me down a short corridor. Ahead of me I caught a glimpse of rows of desks occupied by staff tapping away at laptops and talking into their phones. Relief swept through me when he steered me into a small office to the left, safe from their scrutiny.

3

"Please, take a seat."

David pulled out a chair for me at a round table. I slid into it, my eyes low. His chivalry was putting me at risk of a girly fit of giggles. I arranged my bag at my feet and allowed myself to look around the room as my interviewers settled into chairs opposite me. The glass wall through to the corridor was shrouded with blinds, but the window at the back of the room boasted rooftop views of Camden.

"Nice, isn't it?"

David was smiling at me again. I grinned back and nodded.

"Emily, are you ready? Shall we make a start?"

I sat up straight in my seat and nodded again, this time at Eric. His smile was firm with resolve, but the confidence I had lost several interviews ago seemed to be returning.

"So, Emily, an easy one to start with. What motivated you to apply for a job at Drug and Alcohol Action?"

I took a deep breath and closed my eyes for a moment. Opening them, I exhaled and began.

"I think I will gain a lot from working with people who have spent their lives being judged by others. There are a lot of injustices in this world and I want to help those who have been marginalised to turn their lives around and prove to society that they are worth something."

I sounded like a missionary as I talked, gushing ideas and opinions I had picked up from *The Guardian* and the various professional publications my dad brought home from work. I had started dipping into them as an early teen, hoping my interest in his life would be reciprocated. Whilst the knowledge I had gleaned from them had failed to impress him, it had helped me out no end when it came to my job applications. As the questions kept coming, I smiled self-righteously at the panel as I talked, watching them carefully as they scribbled down my answers and tailoring my responses to their reactions. Eric nodded whenever I finished making a

4

point, his jowls wobbling dangerously, his arm curled around his papers like an oversized schoolboy sitting an exam.

"Emily. We work with people with a range of support needs. They are often very vulnerable, however, many have a history of violence. How would you ensure your own safety when visiting our clients in the community?"

This enquiry came from David, his eyes smiling encouragement as he spoke. I smiled back.

"I think the key to working with vulnerable people who may pose a risk to the health and safety of themselves and others is risk assessing. This should be done in advance and reviewed regularly..."

I had rehearsed the answers to some of these questions so many times I was almost reciting them on autopilot. As I chirped away David watched me, his eyes shining with life whenever they met mine, his face full of interest as he jotted down the odd key phrase. His shirt sleeves, rolled up to the elbow, revealed toned bronzed arms and his jaw line was still firm and angular. When I finally stopped talking, he looked at Eric, his eyebrows raised before turning back to me.

"Well, thanks for that, Emily. We've run out of questions for you, but do you have any for us before we let you go?"

I rattled off another set response and nodded enthusiastically as Eric responded to my enquiries about career progression and training. The pair exchanged glances again.

"Thank you very much for your time, Emily. We're interviewing a few more people today but hope to let everyone know by the end of tomorrow. Can I just check we have your phone number down correctly?"

I nodded confirmation of my details, trying hard to ignore the fruitlessness of the exercise. I thought the interview had gone well, but the exchange of glances and comment about the competition were warning signs I was starting to recognise. David showed me out of the office, making recommendations of things to do in the area before I headed home as we walked over to the door. I put on my perma-smile, nodding along to his suggestions and shaking his hand vigorously before bolting down the stairwell to the high street below. Turning right, I walked with purpose in the direction of King's Cross, discarding the notion of spending any more time than I had to in London without a second thought.

*

Hunched over my laptop, I jumped when my mobile rang. After another round of fruitless job searches, I had immersed myself in the worlds of my acquaintances as they shared their successes on Facebook. I peered expectantly at my phone's screen, wondering if one of my many "likes" had prompted an invite out for coffee – a date even. I didn't recognise the number.

"Hello?"

"Er, yes, hello, is that Emily?"

The male voice sounded familiar.

"Yes."

"Emily, it's David from DAA."

It took me a second to figure out the acronym. My heart sank a little. It was the call. Another thanks, but no thanks. Another failure.

"I'm calling to thank you for coming along to meet us yesterday and showing an interest in working for us."

I closed my eyes as he waffled, already wondering how to tell my dad that he would be stuck with me for even longer.

"Although you clearly lack experience in the field, your knowledge on working with the complexities of our client group really impressed us, and we'd like to offer you a job."

My mouth dropped open.

"What?" I whispered. David's laugh crackled down the phone.

"Let me rephrase. Would you like to join our team as a support worker?"

I looked around the pink walls of my bedroom, blinking disbelievingly at my posters of seals and otters. I had done it. I'd got a job.

"Yes! Yes, of course! Oh, thank you!" I gabbled. David laughed again.

"You're welcome. Now, we need to contact your referees and send off for your DBS check but, all being well, I was hoping we could look at a start date in, say, six weeks' time?"

*

I was in the kitchen preparing dinner when I heard the front door slam shut. I looked at the illuminated numbers on the oven door next to me. 17.57. He was home early. I listened to his footsteps as he walked through the hallway, trying to gauge whether this was a good thing or not. I looked down at the onion I was thinly slicing as he walked in.

"Hi, Dad. Good day?"

He grunted as he walked towards the kettle. The vocalism was inconclusive. I'd had a similar response when I'd told him what A levels I was taking, which university I was going to, my decision to follow his footsteps into a career in social care and, eventually, become a social worker. Whilst he had forwarded me the odd job alert, his motivation was more likely to get me out of the house than to support my decision. I watched him out of the corner of my eye as he dropped a teabag into his favourite mug. His cheeks were as sallow as ever, the grey stubble that threatened to become a full-blown beard almost matching his complexion. But his choice of tea over Scotch was a good sign. I cleared my throat.

"Dad, I've got some news."

He took a long, weary breath.

"And what would that be?"

I waited for the usual list of sarcastic suggestions, but it didn't come.

"Well, I've been offered a job."

"A job? Where? Did you decide to apply for one down at Tesco's after all?"

I hadn't earned his congratulations yet.

"No, Dad. It's in London. At Drug and Alcohol Action. It's a floating support service for…"

My voice trailed off as my father snorted.

"Let me guess. Drug and alcohol users."

He mashed the teabag against the side of his mug before dumping it in the bin and walking out of the room. I followed him to the lounge and watched him as he settled into his armchair with the Society supplement of his daily. Hovering by the doorway as he peered at the type through inadequate glasses, I waited for further acknowledgement. A minute must have passed before he looked at me again, catching me inspecting his ever-expanding bald patch.

"Well, Emily, I can't say I think you have it in you. They are a tricky lot, junkies. I saw you working with little old ladies or something, to be honest."

He turned back to his paper. Silently I returned to the kitchen. There was no point arguing with him. My dad was usually right about these things. All my great hopes and ideas never came to anything. When I was six I wanted to be a ballerina. He had eventually given in to my high-pitched whining and sent me to a class. I was so excited, but once I got there, my enthusiasm waned. My dad dropped me off outside the crumbling church hall and I had scrambled out of his brown car, bursting with excitement. All the other little girls had their mummies drop them off, fluffing up their pink tutus and tying up their shoe ribbons. In my plimsolls and cheap nylon flap of a skirt, I immediately became the outsider, the freak. After three classes of humiliation, the disapproval of my teacher and the sniggering of my peers, I refused to go back. My dad said nothing. But then, he didn't need to – the slight shrug of his rounded shoulders and the flick of his eyebrows said it all. I closed my eyes against the memory and leant heavily against the kitchen worktop. Taking a deep breath, I opened my eyes and turned back to the pile of vegetables before me. I had to show him that I would see this through, that I could accomplish something. And I would.

2

I shut my eyes as the door slammed in my face. Keeping them closed, I tried to focus on the sounds coming from the other side. Shoes scraped along the path towards the old Fiesta my father insisted on driving, his keys rustling as he fished them out of his pocket and jammed them into the lock. I released the breath I had been holding as the car door opened and snapped shut. I remained motionless as the engine sputtered to life and disappeared into the chaos of London traffic.

A throat clearing brought me back to the dark hallway. For a moment I thought it was my father, still standing on the other side of the door, wanting to say goodbye properly, take me out for lunch and buy me a few groceries to get me started. But the sound was behind me. It was Matt, my new flatmate, a plate of toast slathered in Marmite in one hand and a mug of black coffee in the other.

"You alright there, Em?"

I attempted to disguise a wince at the shortening of my name with a smile.

"Yeah, fine thanks," I said way too loudly, and instantly blushed. I turned to trudge up the stairs, trying my best to ignore the dust clinging to the edges of the beige carpet. The door to my room was open, revealing the boxes and bags overflowing with my worldly belongings. My father had insisted I move all my stuff out and the thought of unpacking it all sat like a dead weight in my stomach.

Matt coughed again. I looked over my shoulder to see him standing motionless at the bottom of the stairs, his mid-afternoon snack still in his hands. I studied him from my vantage point. His wavy hair was ill-advisedly slicked back and shadows of angry acne crowded his face. Teamed with his slim frame, he looked like an overgrown adolescent.

"Good luck with the unpacking. Give us a shout if you fancy a cuppa later?"

His blank smile was less than convincing.

"Yeah, thanks."

I closed the door behind me, terminating the conversation before he could extend it any further. I looked around my new home. Light streamed in through the large window, highlighting every crack in the painted walls, every smear of grime, every chip in the furniture. I sighed my irritation. My new landlord had blatantly failed to have the room cleaned or repainted, let alone replace the dubiously stained mattress. But it was too late to do anything about it now. I turned to the box nearest me and tore off the packing tape. I would be starting my new job the next day and needed to have at least my essentials to hand in the morning. Matt's telly blared from the room below me. I felt myself flush at the thought of our earlier interaction. Meeting new people wasn't one of my strong points, especially those I didn't really care for. Unfortunately I knew it was something I was going to have to do a lot of the following day.

A knock at the door made me start. I stood motionless for a moment, a pile of clothes dangling from my arms.

"Hello? Is anyone there?" a female voice sang from the hallway. I dumped the clothes onto the unmade bed and blinked. A stray tear was running down my cheek. Quickly wiping my face with the sleeve of my cardigan, I stumbled through the jungle of boxes and pulled the door open. I was greeted with a wide lipsticked smile. The woman's black hair hung easily over her shoulders, accentuating her enviably petite frame and cream skin. Her laugh was melodic.

"Sorry, Emily isn't it? Did I startle you?"

Gripping onto the door handle, I realised that I had been standing with my mouth slightly open without speaking for far too long.

"Um, yes. Sorry, I was... busy."

The woman's smile shrank slightly in response. I stuck my hand out awkwardly.

"Yes, I'm Emily. I've just moved in."

The woman laughed again and peered around me into my room.

"So I can see. Matt told me your name. It was clearly too much to ask of the landlord to share that with us." She rolled her eyes before taking my hand. Her grip was light but firm.

"I'm Beatrice. I live downstairs in the front room. I'm afraid I'm away quite a lot with work and stuff, but I hope we can be friends?"

I studied her face carefully. Her large brown eyes were wide and hopeful. My eyes burned with ridiculously grateful tears.

"Yes, that would be nice," I managed with a small smile. Her face lit up.

"Great! Well, I shall leave you to get on with your unpacking. But I'll be in most of the afternoon if you fancy a break. I have a bottle of Malbec begging to be opened." She squeezed my hand slightly before letting it go. I let it fall limply against my thigh.

"Maybe later," I managed. I didn't really like red wine. My friend Lorraine had bought a couple of bottles to warm us up for our graduation ball over a year ago. I hadn't wanted to disappoint her by turning it down and drank half a bottle before even attempting to do my make-up. The photos of me splattered all over Facebook the next day cruelly illustrated my poor judgement.

The sound of Beatrice padding down the stairs brought me back to the present.

"See you," I called out, raising my hand in a static wave. She looked over her shoulder at me and smiled, a hint of confusion in her beautiful eyes. As she reached the bottom of the stairs I shut the door and rested my head against the rough paintwork. My new life in London had not got off to a smooth start. I swallowed down panic as it rose in my throat and took a deep breath. So maybe I could have made a better first impression with my housemates, but Lorraine was already in London, and I was about to start to work and make new friends, start a new life.

Everything was going to be fine.

3

I pressed the buzzer and took a step back. Behind me people scuttled along, their heads bent against the world, their minds focused on getting to wherever they needed to be. I looked up at the front of the building but couldn't tell if the lights were on in the office. I looked at my watch. 8.37. I was early – my sleepless night and anxious rush to get ready once my alarm finally went off had seen to that. I had spent a good hour last night deciding what to wear. My meagre wardrobe was not the smartest or the most exciting, consisting mainly of black trousers and a selection of brown, black and grey tops. I had opted for a pair of black bootleg trousers, faded with age, a black T-shirt and the long grey cardigan I had picked up from a charity shop back home last week. I had disguised the scuffs on my black ballet pumps quite effectively and, despite the absence of an ironing board anywhere in the house, had managed to get most of the creases out of my outfit.

"Hello?"

I took a deep breath.

"Hello, this is Emily? It's my first day today."

Despite the unconvincing squeak in my voice, the door buzzed open. The dark stairwell seemed much longer than I remembered. As the door clicked closed behind me I slowly began to climb, fumbling to find the handrail and cursing myself for not wearing my glasses. The door at the top of the stairs opened. I squinted as light hit my face.

"Okay, so let's start this induction by pointing out the light switches, shall we?"

I felt my face flush at the throaty chuckle that followed. I looked up again and tried a smile. It was Eric, the head of the service who had been one of the party of two to interview me. From his elevated position his stomach looked even bigger than I remembered, hanging over the waistband of his chinos. As I reached the top of the stairs I looked at his face. His small eyes were studying me carefully from below thick white eyebrows.

"So, Emily, you decided to take us on, did you?"

I shifted the weight of my bag and looked at my hands. Anything but staring at his bulbous red nose.

"Well, I received a phone call offering me the job…"

"And you said yes, so I hear? Well, I take my hat off to you. I should warn you now, you'll be working with some difficult people here. And that's just the management team."

He turned and walked into the staff kitchen behind him. I followed, clasping my satchel in front of me, and watched silently as he flung open a selection of cupboard doors. With a grunt he fished out two uniform white mugs.

"I don't know about you but I'm in need of some caffeine. Tea? Coffee?"

His stare made me colour again.

"Um, I'll have a tea, please," I stuttered. He looked at me blankly for a moment before turning to the packet of PG Tips on the counter in front of him.

"Good choice. Sugar? Milk?"

"Just milk, please," I managed.

"Very good. I'm afraid I need a bit of something to sweeten me up," he said as he dropped three generous spoonfuls of sugar into his mug. He glanced at me as he turned to the hot water urn above the sink.

"Nervous?"

I shrugged.

"I guess."

He smiled as he poured water into the second mug.

"Please don't be. I know it's easier said than done. I was certainly nervous when I started working here as a volunteer all those years ago, but we're not a bad bunch. And, like a nice chunk of Stilton, we've got better with age." He passed me my mug and winked. "Just in case you've forgotten, I'm Eric, the service manager. I've put you in David's team. He's the other guy who interviewed you, and a thoroughly nice chap. Although I doubt he will be in for at least another hour – he's been a bit all over the place since his missus dropped another sprog." He chuckled again. "So I'm afraid you're stuck with me for now. Shall we go into my office and I can start to fill you in on what we're all about?"

I smiled at my feet and nodded.

"Good stuff."

He strode past me out of the kitchen. I followed him obediently, being careful not to brush against his stomach as he held his office door open for me. He ushered me towards the seat next to a sprawling corner desk covered with post-it notes and other scraps of paper.

"Organised chaos," Eric explained as he eased himself into his chair. "Although they do say that messiness is a sign of creative genius or something. Either way, it works for me." He smiled at me, managing to catch my eye before I could avert my gaze. He nodded at the chair. "Well, sit down and make yourself comfortable. There's a hook on the back of the door if you want to hang your cardy up. It gets a bit warm in here, especially as the sun moves around." He pointed his head towards the large window as he bent to switch on his computer. Outside, the sun was already bright, managing to find its way into the room despite the best efforts of the surrounding tall buildings to stop it in its tracks. Eric cleared his throat.

"Now, whilst this stupid machine wakes up, why don't you remind me a bit about yourself?"

I still had my spiel fresh in my mind from hours of careful interview prep. He listened intently as I talked, his beady eyes trying their best to penetrate mine at every opportunity, his jowls wobbling slightly every time he nodded his understanding. My performance complete, he gave me a potted history of Drug and Alcohol Action. I nodded along, sipping at my too-strong tea, making a mental note not to accept a brew from Eric in the future and trying my utmost not to stare at him whilst trying to appear interested. Nothing he told me was new – I had researched the organisation thoroughly before even applying and could easily have given his talk myself. I felt myself relax as he went on to talk about the more technical side of working with drug users and alcoholics. Again, I had done my homework.

As Eric wittered on, more and more people filtered into the building, passing his office noisily as they chatted on their mobile phones and caught up on each other's weekends. I nodded along to Eric's monologue on procedures and protocols, interjecting examples of how to manage volatile situations and support our clients through various crises.

"At the end of the day, it's all about managing risk. Risks to yourself and risks to the client, and being able to react accordingly when they change by adapting your behaviour and the support offered," I concluded as I sat back in my chair, smiling at Eric with new-found self-assurance. He blinked at me with his small piggy eyes.

"Indeed, I agree, Emily." He took a deep rasping breath. "You clearly know your stuff. Although I should warn you that until you've found yourself in these situations it's hard to know how you will react – and how you'll cope."

I smiled again.

"Well, I feel confident that with your guidance I'll be absolutely fine."

He nodded slowly as he turned back to his computer.

"Yes, I'm sure you will. And you have some very experienced people in your team who I'm sure you'll learn a lot from as you shadow them this week – and who will no doubt offer you some very valuable feedback when they accompany you on your first visits."

I looked at him dumbly, the smile slowly slipping from my face. He didn't think I could do it, just like my dad.

"I don't need that. I'll be fine on my own."

Eric looked at me, his shaggy eyebrows raised at my sullen tone. With a smile I shrugged, desperate to disguise my growing dislike for him.

"I mean, I don't want to be any bother. I'm sure everyone here is really busy and I'd just be a burden if they have me trailing after them all week, then having to tag along with me until God knows when. I'll be okay."

Eric looked at me for a moment, the grooves in his pudgy forehead deepening with concentration.

"Emily, it will be no bother. Shadowing and joint visits are a part of everyone's induction and an absolutely essential part of it too. Even for staff with five, ten, even twenty years of experience working with this client group." He turned back to his computer and clicked something with his mouse. "They are a very vulnerable group but, when they are using, they can become manipulative and slippery customers. It's important that you see how to deal with them first hand before we let you loose on them." He rested his hands on the arms of his chair and hauled himself up.

"Now, I've printed out our staff handbook for you to read for a while until David gets here." He glanced at his watch. "Which he better do pretty damn quick."

I looked at my watch too. It was quarter past ten. I felt irritation rise in my chest. I was sure I'd read somewhere that, although the place was pretty flexible about when you worked your hours, you had to be there by ten. Clearly Eric didn't run a very tight ship – and someone who was supposed to be my line manager couldn't even be bothered to get to work on time when he had new staff starting.

Eric was at the door.

"Now, let's collect this for you from the printer and find you somewhere to sit until your manager gets his arse into gear."

He pulled open the door to the man himself. He was panting heavily, his floppy brown hair sticking to his forehead with the beginning of a sweat. His deep blue eyes widened when he saw Eric.

"Oh shit, Eric, I'm really sorry. Had a bloody nightmare of a morning with the kids being sick and all. Then the fucking tube was delayed…"

Eric held up his hand.

"It's okay, Dave. Now take a deep breath and pull yourself together. Emily's here."

David looked at Eric blankly before realisation hit his face. He caught my eye before pushing past the older man, his hand extended towards me.

"Oh shit, Emily, I'm so sorry. It's your first day and I didn't even remember. Shit."

He pushed his hair out of his eyes as I took his hand. I felt myself colour again as he pumped it vigorously. Eric cleared his throat and laughed nervously.

"Less of the language please, David, or I really will have to introduce a swear box in this place. Emily doesn't need to listen to that."

I watched my manager's face as it dropped. He clearly hadn't had a chance to shave that morning – or all weekend, for that matter. Suddenly I felt a bit sorry for him.

"Oh no, it's okay, I swear all the time." A fake laugh betrayed my white lie. "In fact, don't get me fucking started."

David stared at me for a moment before a smile burst across his face. Long dimples appeared at either side of his mouth as he laughed, making him look quite handsome. The burning in my face intensified at the thought, my gaffe not helping the situation.

"Emily, I'm so glad you have a sense of humour. It will help you out no end here, I can tell you."

"Well, why don't you two go have a laugh somewhere else and leave me to get on with some work."

David looked back at Eric, who was still holding the door open. He threw me another grin before turning back to his boss and offering a salute.

"Right away, sir," he laughed as he almost jogged out of the room. Eric stifled a sigh.

"I've printed off the staff handbook for Emily. Can you collect it for me? Maybe she can read it whilst you check your emails. Oh, and when you get a moment, I'd like a word."

The smile momentarily slipped from David's face before he regained his cheerful composure.

"Sure thing." He looked at me. "Well, come along, Em, and I'll introduce you to the team."

I tried to smile back and nodded as I followed him out of the room and into the bright open plan office. It was just as I remembered. As I walked past the rows of plywood desks, heads popped up from behind laptop screens, mouths smiling at me as they chattered into standard issue Nokias.

After the relative quiet of Eric's office the sound was almost overwhelming. I felt my head start to thump as my heart sank. So many new faces, so many people waiting to find out if I was a fraud. My pace dropped, instinctively reacting to my rising panic. David slowed too and turned to face me. He smiled softly, his dimples appearing again.

"Don't worry, their bark is worse than their bite."

He winked before turning to the nearest desk and rubbed his hands together.

"Okay then, let's start with some introductions. Anna, this is Emily, Emily, this is Anna. Emily's just started today. Anna's not fortunate enough to be in my team but is pretty much part of the furniture."

Anna groaned at David's little joke and rolled her eyes at me with a smile before turning back to her work.

"And the chap next to her on the phone is Des. He's one of the other managers, but sadly no way near as good as me. And opposite him is Charlie..."

David rattled his way through the rest of the habitants of the office, striding from desk to desk with an ease that only comes with the knowledge that those around you like you. I watched him carefully as he introduced me to face after face, throwing in the odd bit of personal trivia and engaging in a bit of banter with anyone who wasn't on the phone. He was quite tall and athletic and, despite his age, still looked pretty good. Based on his performance, he knew it too.

After what felt like an age, he finally dropped into a chair near the front of the office and flicked on a computer.

"And this is my little home from home," he grinned, gesturing for me to sit in the seat next to him. "I'm afraid not many of my lot are around yet but I'm sure you'll meet them in due course. Now, if you don't mind, I'll just check my emails before I get you set up with a laptop and a mobile. Then we can get down to business." He grinned at me before focusing on his computer. I watched him for a moment before looking down at the handbook on the desk in front of me. I turned to the first page. With the chatter and clacking of keyboards around me, it was almost impossible to concentrate. I took a deep breath as I tried to decipher meaning in the words dancing in front of my eyes. I'd never been very good in noisy environments and had much preferred studying in my room rather than the university library where, to my irritation, people seemed to think it was okay to talk and giggle to each other in hushed tones despite the disapproving looks of the librarians. Right now, I would have done anything to have been there.

"You struggling a bit?"

David was staring at his screen, a small smile on his lips. I sat up quickly from my hunched position over the page.

"Um, yeah. I guess I'm just not used to working in this kind of environment," I managed. He laughed.

"Don't worry about it. It just takes a bit of getting used to, that's all. And these guys are a noisy lot." He looked at me quickly. "Look, I've still got a shitload of emails to work through here. Why don't you go out for a long lunch and take that stuff with you to read somewhere a bit quieter? There's a French café just down the road that does great coffee and paninis."

I hesitated for a moment, suddenly self-conscious. I'd only been there five minutes and my manager was already sick of the sight of me.

"I don't mind it here, really. I'll be fine," I stuttered. David rapidly finished typing a sentence and hit the send button before turning in his chair towards me.

"I'm sure you will be. But as your manager, I'm ordering you to go and have a break. Besides, our Eric wants a word with me too, so God knows how long I'm going to be." He leant back in his chair and fished a fiver out of his pocket. "Now, if you can be back here at two that would be perfect.

And if you can bring me a cappuccino and us both something sweet and calorific to get us through the afternoon that would be even better." He held out the crumpled note and looked at me, an eyebrow raised. I looked at it for a moment before plucking it from his hand. His smile widened.

"Good lass. Oh, and by the way, if you find the staff handbook less than riveting, feel free to break up your reading with something a little more exciting. I promise I won't be making you sit an exam on it or anything when you get back."

He swivelled his chair back to position and clicked his mouse onto another email. Silently I picked up my satchel, scooped up my cardigan and crept towards the exit.

"And one more thing," David called after me. I whirled around.

"Yes, David?"

He glanced at me again, his face warm with another wide smile.

"You're gonna be fine here. Trust me."

4

"I said, excuse me, please!"

I looked at the chest of the Suit as it shoved past me. Behind me someone tutted as I stumbled with the force of his irritation.

"You know, there'd be a lot more room if you took that rucksack off your back."

I didn't bother looking around to see who had spoken, or to whom. My hot face burned even more as I slid my bag off my hunched shoulders and let it hang between my legs. The weight of my new laptop pulled at my fingers, but there was no way I was going to let it rest on the floor. One of the first things my dad had said to me when I told him I was moving to London was how high the crime rate was, and I refused to fall victim. It was exactly what he expected of me.

I shifted my satchel to my lower back and grabbed at the rail above my head as the train lurched. Someone muttered behind me again. Lorraine certainly hadn't been lying when she said how rude Londoners were – and how unbearable the Underground can be during rush hour. Despite having stripped down to my black T-shirt, I could feel sweat trickling along my spine and pooling at the waistband of my trousers. Choosing to live in South London whilst working north of the river had clearly been a flawed plan.

Finally, the train came to a stop at Camden Town. A surge of commuters forced me onto the platform before the doors had fully opened. I paused to catch my breath and rearrange my bags, but a wave of bodies pushed me along the platform towards the escalators. Feeling my composure waver, I swallowed and bit my lip as I paused at the barriers to fish my Oyster card out of my bag.

"For fuck's sake."

The hoodie barged past me, sending my card to the floor. I watched it as it was passed from foot to foot like the puck in the ice hockey games my dad was so fond of watching. It came to rest on the other side of the river of people, safely wedged at the bottom of a notice offering service updates. I took a deep breath and waded through the crowded station to retrieve it before pushing my way back into the stream of human traffic. People tutted and swore around me, but by the time I felt the sun hit my clammy face, I was past caring.

*

"Blimey, did you run to the office today?"

Eric shook his head and chuckled as I strode past his office. I was really starting to dislike him, even if he was the head of the service. I dropped my bag onto the first desk I came to and flopped onto the chair. My head was thumping and my body ached with exhaustion, and it was only just 9.30.

"Morning, Em."

It was David. He was sitting at his desk across the office from me. His smile made no attempt to hide his amusement. I tried to smile back.

"This is Fran. She was too busy bombing around London yesterday to pop in and say hello, but has decided to grace us with her presence today."

The woman perched on the desk next to him playfully punched him on the arm before striding over to me, her arm outstretched. I smiled up at her as she shook my hand, trying not to show my awe at her appearance. Bleached blonde hair hung in dreadlocks down to her flat chest. Her ripped jeans and vest exposed milk-white skin, which looked even paler in contrast to her dark eye make-up and cherry red lips. Despite my distaste, my envy at her unnatural beauty and obvious ease threatened to seep through every pore of my body.

"Pleased to meet you, Em."

Her grip was firm and her Scottish accent so thick it took me a moment to figure out what she had said. She raised an eyebrow, scarred from an old piercing, as I decoded.

"Lovely to meet you too," I finally managed.

"Well, Emily, I'm going to leave you in Fran's hands today. She's got a few visits planned so you'll get to see her in action. And, don't worry, she isn't as scary as she looks. Well, until she's had a couple of pints, anyway."

Fran placed her hands on her delicate hips and shook her head as she rolled her eyes.

"Well, at least I can hold my drink, unlike some people around here," she said, tossing her head in David's direction. "Now, I've got to log on to my computer and check a few things first, so why don't you grab yourself a drink and freshen up in the ladies. Looks like your journey into work was as bad as mine."

She smiled and turned to scoop her bag up from David's desk before heading to the back of the office. I watched her as she set up her laptop, transfixed by the red rose tattoo that slid over her shoulder blade as she moved. She turned to shoot a retort back at some office banter and caught my eye. I looked away from her smile as I hurried towards the ladies, my bag clutched tight to my chest. Safely out of sight of my new colleagues, I splashed my face with cold water. I studied my reflection as I dried myself with a coarse paper towel. Murky green eyes stared out from a pale face, the shadows beneath them making them appear all the more gormless. I averted my gaze as I pushed my lank hair back into a ponytail, trying hard to fight the urge to compare my own mousy appearance to Fran's. Fran, who despite her outlandish style, managed to look... well, she stood out anyway. Taking a deep breath, I glanced at the mirror again before pushing my way out of the toilets.

*

"... so, really, I should be looking at closing this case soon. I mean, I do worry that he might relapse but he's been doing really well since he moved to his new flat. And, when he's actually sober, he's really good at keeping on top of things, you know, his money and stuff. I reckon he could teach me a thing or two, I tell you."

Fran hadn't stopped talking since we left the office. She had decided that we should walk to our first visit and had gone striding off down the high street before I had time to object. She had given up on asking me about myself by the time we got to the first of what seemed like a ridiculous amount of markets and had taken it upon herself to give me a short biography of all the clients she had arranged for us to visit that day. Why she couldn't have done so in the office where I could have made notes I didn't know, and was finding it a challenge to hide my annoyance at her slap-dash approach.

By the time we reached our first destination my mind was swimming and my face slick from the grimy heat. Fran grinned at me from behind her oversized sunglasses as she jabbed at the intercom of the concrete tower.

"So, hen, are you ready?"

A voice cracked at us from the speaker before I could respond. It didn't sound happy.

"Morning, Ian, it's Fran. Can you let us up, please?"

The door buzzed irritably and Fran pulled it open.

"After you."

It took my eyes a moment to adjust to the unlit lobby. The faint smell of urine grew stronger as the lift doors creaked open. Fran stepped in first and held the doors open with a booted foot as I followed. As the doors closed I inhaled through my mouth before holding my breath. Fran rested her sunglasses on top of her nest of dreads before turning her attention back to me, her head cocked to one side.

"So I take it you're not used to inner-city council estates then, eh?"

My face flushed in response to her perception. She smiled.

"Don't worry about it. I wasn't either when I first moved to London. But it isn't so bad once you get used to it. Just be careful when you're wearing sandals. And carry some hand sanitiser with you too, especially if you're going to be out and about all day."

She looked at me and wrinkled her nose as the doors slid open. I followed her past several standard green doors to the flat at the end of the balcony. The open door exposed a dark hallway littered with post and ignored takeaway menus. I watched Fran as she disappeared into the room, seemingly unperturbed by the flaking walls and filth that clung to every surface. I took a deep breath and followed her in.

The air was thick with sickly-sweet smoke. I tried to suppress a cough as I stepped into the living room. Bright sunlight poked through gaps in the threadbare curtains, exposing particles of dust as they swirled in the air like unseasonal snow. Fran was perched on the edge of a sofa, her notebook already open and her pen in her hand. The man sitting opposite her looked less than pleased to see us. The huge armchair, surrounded with piles of books and empty lager cans, looked like it was about to swallow him whole.

"Who's she?" he muttered as he fished in his grubby jeans pocket and pulled out a lighter.

"This is Emily. She's just started and is hanging out with me today whilst she learns the ropes. Remember, I told you she'd be coming last time I visited?"

His pale eyes flicked from Fran back to me.

"Yeah? Well, if she's staying, can she sit down? She's making the place look untidy."

He cackled softly at his own joke. Fran rolled her eyes and smiled before beckoning me over to the sofa. I picked my way through the chaos towards my seat. Resisting the urge to check that it wasn't damp with my hand, I settled onto the edge, my bag on my lap. Ian was still watching me.

"So, you're new, eh? No shit."

He snorted another laugh as he stubbed out a roll-up in a mug precariously balanced on the arm of his chair.

"Now, Ian, be nice," Fran scolded. "So, shall we get on with it?"

Ian shrugged his consent and folded his bony arms across his chest.

"Well, I guess it goes without saying that you're drinking again?"

Ian stared at her.

"Jeez, Fran, you're good. I mean, how did you figure that one out? You should join the Old Bill with your investigative skills, eh?"

He looked at me and laughed. I tried a smile back before returning my gaze to the floor.

"Very funny. Now, Ian, you know as well as I do that you drinking isn't a good idea. You don't need me to tell you that your liver is fucked. And don't you think you're tempting fate? I mean, do you really want another relapse?"

Ian sucked his teeth.

"Do we really have to talk about that whilst she's here?"

"Ian, Emily works for the same service as me. She knows the score and nothing we discuss will be new to her. There's nothing to worry about. Everything will be kept confidential…"

"Yeah, yeah. Tell me something I haven't heard before."

Fran took a deep breath.

"Look, Ian, I know you find it difficult to trust professionals. But I promise we have no interest in sharing anything you tell us with anyone else, especially anyone who might use information about you to your detriment. Okay?"

The room became quiet, the only noise coming from the rumble of traffic from the street below and a muffled television from a flat somewhere above. I looked up from my hands, still clasping my bag, to find Ian looking at me with cold eyes. I stared back, feigning the confidence that was so desperately absent. His gaze slid back to Fran before returning to me.

"Okay. But I'm warning you, don't fuck me about…"

"Great. Now let's move on…"

Fran started to scribble on her pad. I turned in my seat to face her, hoping to shift the focus from myself to my colleague.

"So, the drinking. When did this start again?"

Ian sighed and rubbed his eyes with the heel of his hand. The dirt under his nails and nicotine-stained fingers turned my stomach. I swallowed quietly and tried to focus on the conversation. Fran seemed to maintain eye contact with ease whilst making the occasional note, nodding empathically from time to time. I felt myself become invisible as they became engrossed in their conversation. My mind started to wander as Fran probed Ian further. I just hoped that not everyone who we worked with was this difficult. And dirty. And why hadn't Fran said anything about the way he spoke to me? Was everyone going to be so hostile, even threatening? My eyes began to prickle. I could hear my dad now, telling me what an idiot I was for thinking I could ever do this kind of job.

"Em?"

Fran's voice cut through to my consciousness. My head jerked in her direction and I blinked. She was standing and looking at me with her crooked smile. I glanced at Ian who was still sunk in his chair, busily rolling another cigarette.

"Yes?" I stammered.

"Are you ready to go?"

"Sure."

I winced at the enthusiasm in my voice as I got to my feet and swung my bag over my shoulder. I smiled brightly at Fran before heading to the door.

"Er, what's yer name?"

I stopped in my tracks and turned slowly towards the enquiry. Ian was staring at me, his gaze not quite high enough to meet mine. I cleared my throat.

"Um, Emily."

"Emily. Right." His eyes roamed around the room for what felt like an age before they rested on the pile of books nearest him.

"So, do you read?"

I frowned and looked at Fran. She opened her eyes wide and nodded her encouragement.

"Er, yes. Yes, I do."

"Have you read any of the *Millennium* series?" he fired back at me. Shit, another test I was bound to fail. I hadn't even heard of it.

"You know, *The Girl with the Dragon Tattoo* and all that," Fran prompted.

"Oh, yes! I mean, no, I've not read it, but I've heard of it. It's supposed to be pretty good," I gushed, enthused more by my recognition of the name than my desire to read it. Ian's face softened.

"Good? They're fucking excellent," he said as he leant forward in his chair, carefully extracting a paperback from the bottom of his nearest stack. Stiffly he stood up. His T-shirt hung loosely from his bony shoulders. He was even skinnier than I had imagined. Popping his roll-up in his mouth, he held out the book towards me. He glanced up at my face before looking back down at his offering.

"Here. Take it."

I looked at the book blankly before glancing at Fran. Instinctively I stepped back.

"Oh no, it's okay. You keep it. I'll borrow it from the library."

Ian snorted.

"Well, why not save yourself the bother and take this one. I've got no use for it now. Go on."

I looked at Fran again. Another test.

"Um, we're not supposed to accept gifts from service users," I muttered.

Fran smiled warmly.

"It's okay. It's just a loan, isn't it, Ian?"

Ian shrugged.

"If you want to call it that, sure." He looked me again. "Look, just take it, yeah? It's only a book. It won't give you AIDS or anything."

He coughed a laugh, whether at his own joke or my reddening face I wasn't sure. I hesitated before stepping forwards and taking it from his hand.

"Thanks," I whispered. Ian's frame relaxed.

"Welcome," he muttered as he wandered back to his chair. Fran watched him for a moment before turning to me.

"Right. Well, let's go." She smiled at me and winked. "See you, Ian," she called over her shoulder as she strode out of the room. I followed her silently, my eyes on the carpet. She let me pass her on the balcony and shut the door behind her. I breathed deeply as I walked towards the lift, glad of the air which, although not fresh, was certainly an improvement on the stale atmosphere inside Ian's flat. As I pressed the button for the lift, Fran trotted up behind me.

"You okay?"

I turned to look at her. The shadow of a line had appeared between her brows and her deep brown eyes were wide. Her concern made me want to cry.

"Sure," I croaked. She smiled warmly.

"Okay then, hen. Well, I don't know about you but I'm parched. Shall we grab a quick drink before our next visit?" Her smile turned into a frown. "Strictly non-alcoholic though. Even I don't drink this early, and an hour with Ian is enough to put anyone off their beer."

She playfully poked me with her elbow as she stepped into the lift. A wave of exhaustion hit me as I watched her fish her mobile out of her jeans pocket. She glanced up at me and grinned.

"So are you coming? Or are you taking the stairs?"

*

"Cheers."

Fran tapped my plastic cup with hers and took a long sip through the wide straw. Tentatively, I sipped at mine. Squidgy balls danced with sweet milky liquid in my mouth. Fran grinned at me.

"So, what do you think of bubble tea, then?"

I swallowed my mouthful. The tapioca tickled the back of my throat.

33

"It's okay."

Fran laughed, her eyes sparkling.

"Well, I've gotta say, you look less than convinced." She took another gulp of her drink and sighed. "Ah, that's better." Dumping her cup on the Formica table between us, she leant back in her chair.

"So, tell me what you thought of Ian, then."

I chewed at my tea slowly as I frantically searched my mind for something intelligent to say. Once I had rejected numerous negative adjectives there was very little left. Eventually I swallowed.

"Well, he likes to read."

Fran smiled at me gently.

"Yes, he does. I think it helps him escape from his demons." She dropped her head to one side. "It was nice of him to give you that book, wasn't it?"

I nearly choked as I suppressed a laugh.

"Yes. I thought it was a bit weird, though."

Fran nodded thoughtfully.

"Maybe. Why do you think he did it?"

I shrugged. Fran twisted her mouth and looked up at the ceiling.

"Mmm. I wonder if it was some kind of peace offering?"

This time I couldn't suppress my laughter.

"A peace offering? Why would he do that? He doesn't strike me as the kind of person who would bother. Especially with someone he so clearly dislikes."

Fran reached for her drink and took another slurp. She swirled the remaining bubbles absently as she studied my face. I took another sip of mine, hoping to disguise my unease.

"Emily, I doubt very much that Ian disliked you. He's just very suspicious of people he doesn't know. He's had some bad experiences with workers who've said they were trying to help him so it just takes him a while to trust people. And, for him, attack is the only form of defence he knows." She chuckled a smile. "Trust me, he gave me hell when I started working with him. But we worked through it and now we get on just fine. I've learnt to read between the lines when he gets verbal and he's figured out that I really do have his best interests at heart."

She shrugged and drained the rest of her drink, chasing the last of the tapioca pieces with her straw. Finished, she stood up.

"Right. Now I'm going to pop to the little girls' room. Then shall we make our way to visit number two?"

"Great," I enthused, smiling up at her. She grinned back before heading to the back of the tiny café. I watched her disappear into the ladies while I sipped my drink. My encounter with Ian ran through my mind. Maybe Fran had a point. And maybe I needed to stop being so sensitive if I was going to be able to do this job. My cheeks burned as I silently scolded myself.

"Shall we?" Fran was at my side, pulling her rucksack onto her back. I jumped out of my chair, bashing my thigh against the table in my haste.

"Sure," I smiled through my pain. Fran glanced down at the table.

"You gonna finish that?" she enquired, nodding at the remainder of my bubble tea. Instinctively I grimaced.

"No, I've had enough, thanks. It was nice, but I think I'm a bit full after all those bubbles."

Fran smiled at me as she scooped up the cup.

"Waste not, want not," she quipped and bounded out of the door, oblivious to the open-mouthed stares of a group of tourists queuing at the counter.

*

"So, the wanderers return. I thought we'd lost you for good."

David grinned at us from behind his monitor, his hands resting on the back of his head. The muscles of his forearms flexed visibly.

Stiffly I removed my satchel from my shoulder and dropped it onto the desk opposite him. To my left, Fran already had her notebook open and laptop switched on, ready for action. She had offered to get me started on DAA's database by showing me how to input case notes from our day's visits. Secretly I suspected that her plan was to get me to do her administration whilst she flirted with David, but I didn't see how I could possibly challenge her without looking like I wasn't willing – or a prize cow. Taking in the reams of notes dancing across the double page exposed, I felt my heart sink. That was an awful lot of information that needed transferring onto the computer and, with my pedestrian typing, it was going to be an arduous task.

"Ah, David. You're really funny, you know that? Maybe if you got your arse out of the office and on a few visits with your support staff once in a while, you'd remember that walking across Camden and actually getting any meaningful work done with our client group takes time."

Fran was looking at David from over the top of a pair of black-rimmed glasses, her hands on her hips. Laughing, he released his head and threw his hands into the air.

"Okay, okay. Jeez! I was only making an observation. Can't a manager even show concern that one of his most valued team members, along with his newest recruit, seemed to have gone AWOL for most of the day?"

Fran shook her head as she bent down to type something.

"You are such a cheeky fucker. Isn't he, Emily?"

Suddenly, both their eyes were on me. I looked from Fran to David, desperately trying to read their expressions. I hesitated.

"Oh, I don't know. I mean, we had a really busy day. I guess we didn't realise how long we were out for…"

My voice trailed off as a smile spread across David's face. His cheeks gave way to his dimples as he looked over at Fran, his blue eyes sparkling mischievously.

"You see that, Fran? It's called respect. R e s p e c t. Aretha Franklin sang about it once. You should look it up sometime."

Fran cocked her head to one side and poked her tongue out at him before turning back to me.

"Now, hen, did you want to get your laptop out of your locker and I'll get you started?"

"Okay," I said, jumping out of my chair. In my haste to escape being the brunt of yet another joke I almost ran into a steaming cup of coffee.

"Whoa!" It swerved out of my way, the scalding liquid held at arm's length whilst another hand at my elbow steadied me. I stared at it dumbly for a moment before looking up. A pair of blue eyes peered at me from behind a curtain of long eyelashes. A smile spread across the man's freckled face as his look of alarm morphed into one of relaxed curiosity.

"Well, that's quite a way to introduce yourself, isn't it?"

I looked down at the floor, helplessly searching for something to say.

"Don't worry, Em, I think you missed his trainers. Good job too, they look like another new pair. How much did those ones cost you, Jim? Ninety quid? A hundred?" I heard David jibe from his desk.

"Ha ha, very funny. At least I can say my footwear isn't a relic from the nineties." Jim turned back to me, his smile even brighter.

"I'm so sorry. I didn't spill your coffee on you, did I?"

Jim looked down at his clothes, releasing my elbow to inspect his Superdry T-shirt more closely.

"Nope, I think you missed me. What about you? You're not scalded or anything are you?"

Lines gathered across his forehead as he looked at me. I made a fuss of checking myself. Anything but to have to meet that piercing gaze.

"No, I'm fine. Thanks."

Jim looked at me uncertainly. My smile clearly had not been very convincing.

"Well, thank goodness for that. We don't need to take Emily down to A&E on her second day and Jim won't be dipping into her first pay cheque to pay for his dry cleaning bill," David said. I looked over at him. He was staring at his monitor as he typed, a small smile on his face. He glanced up at me and winked.

"Well, I better go get my laptop. I've got work to do," I murmured and began to walk away, trying to hide my hot face beneath my hair.

"So, you're Emily, are you?"

I stopped and turned around. Jim was still staring at me. From my new viewpoint I could see that he was actually quite short for a man, not much taller than me, but clearly made up for his lack of stature by working out. He caught my eye and grinned. I had been blatantly checking him out and he had noticed. My cheeks burned even more.

"Um, yes. Pleased to meet you." I tried to sound casual and gave what I hoped was a nonchalant smile before hurrying to the toilets. Safely behind the cubicle door I sat down, not even bothering to pull down my trousers. I dropped my head into my hands. My pulse throbbed through my temples, the heat from my face warming my palms. I took a deep breath and released it slowly. It wavered with emotion. Swallowing, I tried again, ignoring the mocking voice at the back of my head telling me how pathetic I was. My breathing back under control, I looked at my watch. 4.20. I had no idea when I had disappeared into the toilets. In fact, the day had been such a whirlwind that I had lost track of time soon after leaving the office with Fran. Either way, I had a job to do, and I couldn't let my stupid social inadequacies get in the way of it. I put my hands on my knees, pushed myself up and strode out of the ladies.

"You okay there?"

I could feel Fran studying me closely as I switched on my laptop.

"Yep." I turned to her and smiled, straightening my back as I did so. "I just felt a bit queasy for a minute. Think I must have a touch of heatstroke or be a bit dehydrated." I shrugged and turned back to my computer. Fran's gaze didn't budge.

"Okay, hen. Well, you know we can leave this until tomorrow if you're feeling a bit under the weather. I'm sure David won't mind."

I looked at her again. The little line between her brows had reappeared. Despite the heat outside, Fran's make-up was as sure of itself as it had been seven hours ago. I smiled bravely.

"No, honestly, I'm fine. I just needed to freshen up and drink some water, that's all."

Fran searched my face for a moment longer before pushing herself out of her chair.

"Okay, hen. But I'm going to get you a glass of squash and some sunflower seeds from my locker. And you're not allowed to argue."

I watched her as she walked purposefully to the kitchen. She didn't even look back to wait for my response. As I logged into my laptop I couldn't help but smile. Okay, so Fran wasn't my usual cup of tea, but she was nice, really nice, and knowing that someone like her was around to look out for me was a real relief. Getting started with my new life was proving to be more of a challenge than I'd expected, and I needed all the friends I could get to see me through.

*

39

Something warm firmly pushed against my leg. My spoon disappeared into the pan of lentil and bean stew as soon as I dropped it. I looked down to see Beatrice's cat curl its tail around my leg and sighed. After another long day at Drug and Alcohol Action, my nerves were frayed, and the journey home had done little to repair the damage. Gingerly I rescued my spoon with the help of a spatula, cursing under my breath as I burnt my fingers on the hot metal whilst simultaneously turning down my rice before it boiled over. I'd taught myself to cook on my dad's electric cooker and, thankfully, the ones in my halls at uni had been almost identical. Gas hobs made me nervous at the best of times, and the way things were going tonight, it would be a miracle if my dinner would be at all edible.

"Hello? Who's there?"

I heard the front door slam and the thud of heels along the hallway carpet. I looked around to see a woman fill the doorway with an array of carrier bags from shops I wouldn't even dare enter in fear of being laughed out. She was tall, black, and wore her curves with a self-assurance that I instantly envied. She arched a perfectly shaped eyebrow as she looked me up and down.

"Oh. So you must be Emily."

She flicked a lock of ebony hair behind a fur-clad shoulder before offering me her hand. I stepped forward and shook it gently. Her grip was firm.

"I'm Rebecca. I live upstairs. Sorry, I've not had a chance to introduce myself before now. I've been crazy busy revising for my exams." She rolled her eyes. I pulled my hand away and smiled. I could smell my dinner catching.

"Oh, so you're a student?" I asked casually as I stirred my stew and fumbled to turn down the heat. Rebecca laughed deeply.

"Oh God no. I graduated years ago. I just have exams to take at work. I'm an accountant."

"Oh really? That must be, um, interesting."

Rebecca laughed again and looked behind her.

"Er, yeah, really interesting. Well, the potential earnings are anyway." She looked at me again, eyeing a splodge of tomato sauce on my grey jogging bottoms with distaste. Pointlessly I tried to cover it with my hand.

"Anyway, I'm done in. Oxford Street was a killer tonight and I'm afraid I'll be ordering a takeaway rather than following your good example. Goodnight."

She turned and walked to the stairs without waiting for my reply. In awe I watched her hips as they swayed seductively beneath her coat.

"I've made enough for two if you want some stew?" I called after her.

She hesitated at the bottom of the stairs and turned to look at me. It was too dark to read her expression.

"No, it's okay. It smells really, well, wholesome, by the way."

I watched her as she disappeared up the stairs. So, Rebecca was flatmate number three. I felt my stomach sink. I had hoped she might have been more like, well, me. Beatrice had seemed nice enough but had admitted herself that she was never home, and Matt was, well, a guy. Loud Salsa music began to thump through the ceiling from the room above. Behind me my rice hissed as it boiled dry.

5

"Surely it can't have been that bad?"

Fran shook her head at her pint as she raised it to her lips. I took a sip of my wine and carefully placed my glass back on the table. I could feel the alcohol swimming through my veins and loosening my tongue.

"I don't know. But I got the feeling that she didn't like me. At all. And then that music…"

I shuddered at the memory. In reality, Rebecca's music had kept me awake two nights running and I was hoping that Fran might be able to offer some advice on how to deal with it. I glanced at her as she supped at her beer.

"So, do you have flatmates? Or do you live with your boyfriend?"

Fran looked up at me with surprise as she slammed her glass back onto the table.

"Boyfriend? Fuck no. In fact I avoid them at all costs, let alone live with one. No, hen, I live with my friends."

"But do you ever fall out with them?" I pushed, mentally noting her reaction to the boyfriend question. Fran shrugged.

"Well, we all kinda get on fine. We're all quite laid back, you know, and we've known each other for years." She looked at me and cocked her head to one side. "Don't get me wrong, though. When I first moved to London, it was hard. I didn't know anyone and had no money. I had to make friends quickly just to find a sofa to sleep on and to keep a roof over my head, you know what I mean?" She looked beyond me into the past, smiling as she shook her head.

"Some of the people who helped me back then will be friends forever. I tell you, there are some nasty people out there who will take advantage of a young woman like yourself. You should thank your lucky stars you've got yourself somewhere decent to live. The rest will come with time, believe me."

I nodded and sipped my wine as I tried to decode what she had just said. The fog of alcohol made my task even harder. Desperate to keep the conversation flowing, I took a stab in the dark.

"I guess so. I just wish my flatmates were a bit more... welcoming? They just seem a little distant."

Fran put her hand over her mouth and quickly swallowed a mouthful of beer. A choking cough stifled her laughter.

"Welcoming? Hen, you know you're in London, don't you? Londoners don't do friendly. They do what will benefit themselves and nothing more." Her laughter stopped abruptly. "Oh gawd. Don't look now but the boss has just walked in."

Automatically I turned around. David was walking towards the bar, deep in conversation with Jim. I watched him as he ran his long fingers through his already mussed hair. His pale blue shirt hung loosely over his jeans, creased from a day of restraint under his waistband.

"Hey, Emily! How you doing?"

Blinking, I looked at Jim. He was smiling at me widely, no doubt in amusement at my apparent fascination with my manager. On cue, David turned to follow his gaze. His eyes widened as he grabbed at Jim's arm.

"Oh, no. Jim, we're going to have to do something. Fran's already trying to corrupt the newest member of our team. Bloody hell, Fran, give her a chance, she's only in her first week."

Fran sat back in her chair and folded her arms across her chest.

"Ha ha, very bloody funny. Anyway, what are you doing here? Haven't you got a wife and two bairns to go home to?"

David mirrored her stance.

"Erm, yes, actually I do, but after a particularly long day I thought I'd grab a swift pint with my old mate Jim here, if that's okay with the Queen of Glasgow?"

Fran shrugged.

"Fine by me. I just hope your missus doesn't mind you going out having fun whilst she's running around after two kids, that's all."

A slight frown betrayed his act of indifference.

"I'm sure that she will be very understanding about it."

He turned to look at me. My face automatically burned.

"So, Emily, having lumbered you with the lovely Fran all week I owe you a drink. What will it be?"

I looked down at my glass. It was almost empty. And we had only been in the pub half an hour.

"Oh, no, it's okay. I've had enough, thanks."

David snorted.

"Yeah, sure. I know you young people. Really, there's no need to stand on ceremony. Now tell me what you want or it'll be tequilas all round."

"Get her a red wine. That's what she's just had," Jim suggested. He was looking at me intently again. He caught my eye and smiled. Instinctively I looked away.

"Right, red wine it is. Fran, I'm assuming you'll be having another pint. Jim, care to join me at the bar?"

I studied the chipped polish of the table as they walked away, my hands in my lap.

"Well, well, what do you know?"

I looked up so see Fran smiling at me, her chin resting on her hand. My flush deepened. She had clearly seen me staring at David.

"What?"

She lifted her head from its resting point and leant across the table.

"Well, forgive me if I'm wrong, but I think you might have a secret admirer." She jerked her head towards the bar. I looked past her. Jim was talking intensely, emphasising the point he was making with wildly gesticulating hands. David was leaning on the dark wood, nodding periodically as his gaze wandered around the pub. He caught my eye and smiled. I looked back at Fran, my mouth slightly open. She was draining the last of her pint.

"You really think so?" I whispered.

She dumped her empty glass on the table and looked me in the eye.

"Emily, I don't think so. I know so."

"But... he's married!" I exclaimed, hoping my expression of horror would hide my excitement. The thought of a man like David finding me attractive made my stomach flip. Okay, so he was a bit older than me, but he was still really handsome and, well, attentive – something I had never experienced with a man before.

Fran was looking at me blankly. Suddenly she clamped her hand over her mouth, her laugh mocking me through her fingers.

"No, not David, honey. Jim."

She sat back in her chair again. I stared at her for a moment before looking over to the bar. David and Jim were walking over, drinks in hand. Jim was a good four inches shorter than David, and, although he made up for his height with his strong build... I couldn't help but feel disappointed. In comparison to his younger friend, David didn't need to make up for anything.

"Okay then, ladies, one pint of Amstel, one large Merlot," Jim said as he carefully placed the glasses on the table. He looked at me as he slid my wine across the smooth surface. "I figured a large would be in order," he grinned.

I smiled at him briefly before busying myself with a large gulp of the heavy liquid.

"Ladies? I don't know about that," David said as he pulled a stool up to the table. Looking at me he raised his hand apologetically as he sat down. "No offence, Emily, I'm sure you fit the bill, but our Fran?" He winced and shook his head. "I'm not so sure."

I looked down at my glass as Jim joined in with his laughter.

"Yeah, I get it, guys. Now how about you stop being arseholes or leave me and Em in peace, eh? We were having a perfectly pleasant evening before you two clowns showed up."

Without looking up I couldn't be sure how serious Fran was being.

"A thousand apologies, Fran. Listen, I tell you what, why don't you two just carry on as though we weren't even here."

I looked up to see David looking at me, his hand on his chest. I looked at Fran. She was watching me with impossibly dark eyes, her face expressionless. I turned back to David and smiled weakly.

"Oh, we weren't talking about much. Just about me moving to London. Pretty boring really."

Fran nodded enthusiastically.

"Yeah, that's right. And I was warning her about what some people are like around here too."

I glanced at David. He studied his pint as he swirled it gently before lifting it to his lips. His hair fell onto his forehead as he swallowed deeply. He pushed it away as he returned the glass to the table.

"Very wise, Fran, very wise."

I took another sip of my drink. The room around me was beginning to blur around the edges. I wasn't sure if the tension around me was real or the alcohol was making me imagine things. Eventually, Jim cleared his throat.

"So, where are you living, then, Emily?"

I looked at him dumbly. He was sat next to me, his elbows resting on his knees. I had almost forgotten he was there.

"Ah, yes, Emily, tell us a bit about yourself. You're an out-of-towner, aren't you? What on Earth possessed you to come to this dump?" David added almost too enthusiastically.

I looked up at Fran. She smiled at me and nodded her head once. I smiled back uncertainly, confused by the tightness around her lips.

"Um, well I came here for my career really. I wanted to work with this kind of client group and there wasn't really much going on where I am from. You know, it's quite a small town…"

I looked around the table as I spoke. Jim was listening intently, smiling and nodding as I talked. David also seemed to be listening as he worked his way through his pint, but his gaze remained low. Fran alternated between looking at her watch and the door. Mentally I cursed myself for drinking so much as I chattered on. I must have done something to offend her. I scanned through the evening's events in my mind, pausing the re-run at the point when Jim and David arrived. She had said I had an admirer. I had assumed she meant David, but had been wrong. Majorly wrong. Or had I? I looked at Fran and smiled as I started to tell our little group about my time at university. She smiled back, the earlier rigidity softening, perhaps with the help of her second drink. Or maybe in the belief that she had thrown me off the scent.

Perhaps David did like me, but she didn't want me to know.

"So, what about your folks? What do they reckon about your career choice?" Jim asked as he took a sip of his drink. I noticed he had hardly touched his half of lager, whilst Fran and David were nearing the end of their pints.

"Oh, well, my dad's a social worker, so he's fine with it. In fact he helped me a lot, you know, looking for jobs and preparing for my interviews."

It wasn't a direct lie.

"What about your mum?" David prompted.

I looked at my hands.

"Oh, she died. When I was a baby. So I never knew her. Obviously," I added, laughing a little too loudly.

"Oh, hen, you poor thing." Fran instinctively reached over and touched my hand. I resisted the urge to pull away and shrugged.

"It's okay. I mean, I never knew her to miss her, if you know what I mean. And my dad more than makes up for not having a mum around." Another lie. The reality of the situation made my eyes prickle. I hadn't heard from my dad since he dumped me here on Sunday. Swallowing back my emotion, I smiled brightly around the table. Three blurry faces stared back.

"So, what about you guys? Are your folks still around?"

Fran and Jim exchanged glances and simultaneously inhaled through their teeth.

"Do you want to go first, Jim?" Fran asked. Jim smiled and shook his head at the floor.

"Well, what can I say? My folks always had high expectations of me and were bitterly disappointed when I decided to train as a teacher, even though I turned out to be a damn good one."

"What do they think now?" I blurted out. He shrugged.

"Well, they don't. They died a few years ago. It was quite sudden." He glanced at me, uncertainty in his eyes. "Don't get me wrong, I miss them terribly and would do anything to bring them back. But I feel a lot less pressure to be someone I'm not now, you know?"

I didn't know, but I smiled and nodded enthusiastically before turning to Fran.

"What about you?"

Fran pulled a face.

"Staunch Scottish Catholics. Didn't get on with them at all. Left home as soon as I could and never looked back."

David laughed.

"And there you have it. Why Fran is so, well, Fran-like."

Fran sat back in her chair, one leg lazily crossing the other.

"Well, you know, David, not everyone was as lucky as you when they were growing up."

David shrugged.

"Fair comment." He looked at me apologetically. "My parents were, or rather are, pretty cool. They didn't care what I did as long as I was happy. They weren't even that fussed when I got married young. Just told me to do what felt right and that if I made a mistake I'd only learn from it."

"Did you make a mistake?"

My question was out before I had chance to veto it in my mind. David stared at me blankly for a moment before his face creased into a smile.

"Emily, you don't hold back, do you?" he managed, laughter lines crinkling around his eyes. Shaking his head he drained the rest of his drink and stood up.

"Okay, kids, I'm going to leave you to it. I've got a family to go home to, whether I like it or not. Laters."

He nodded at Jim and threw me a wink before striding towards the door. He was still shaking his head as he disappeared from view.

"Wow, Em, we're going to have to watch you when you've got a few drinks down you, aren't we?"

I looked around to see Fran grinning at me. Realising it was hanging open, I snapped my mouth shut.

"Oh God," I muttered. My face was burning with embarrassment. And the wine wasn't helping. I looked at Fran helplessly. "I can't believe I just said that."

"Neither can I. But it was bloody hilarious," Fran laughed. She picked up her glass and emptied it of its contents. "Okay then, you, let's get you home. You've got another day to get through before you can get completely legless and have the luxury of a weekend to recover."

"It's alright, Fran, I'll walk her back to the tube. I'm going that way."

I almost jumped at the sound of Jim's voice next to me. I looked around to see him quickly finishing his drink and standing up. Fran shrugged.

"Okay." She jumped out of her seat and swung her bag over her shoulder before looking at me.

"Right then, missy. Our first visit tomorrow isn't until 10.30 so no need to rush in if you want a bit of a lie-in. I'll tell David I asked you to drop something off at the benefit office or something. Jim," she pointed an accusatory finger at him, "I'm leaving her in your care. Behave."

She looked at me, her eyebrows raised pointedly, before bounding towards the door. I watched her leave in silence.

"Shall we?"

I looked up to see Jim extending his hand towards me, a wide smile planted across his freckled face. I smiled back feebly as I gingerly stood up and took his hand, more out of necessity than desire.

6

"Hello?"

The phone had been ringing so long I had almost given up on my dad answering.

"Hi, Dad, it's me," I gabbled. I heard him take a deep breath before he exhaled loudly.

"Emily. How are you?"

"Oh, I'm okay. Really good actually. I've had my first week at work now..."

"So you have."

The first twenty-two years of my life had taught me that it was best to ignore the natural dryness of his tone.

"Yes, and it's been going really well. Everyone in my team is really nice, and I've been doing a few home visits with this girl called Fran..."

"Really? You're doing visits already? Surely they're going to offer you some training first?"

I took a deep breath.

"Well, accompanying Fran on her visits is part of the induction, Dad. I've had to read up on a lot of handbooks and stuff too…"

My dad snorted.

"Is that it? Surely you need to do a course or something?"

I hesitated.

"Well, you learn on the job. And they wouldn't have taken me on if they didn't think I could do it. Next week I'll start taking the lead, though, and Fran will be there just in case I need her."

"Really. Well, I hope this Fran knows what she is doing…"

"Oh yes, she does, and she's really lovely too, Dad."

"Well, it all sounds very irresponsible if you ask me, having young women going out visiting druggies when they haven't been properly trained."

I hesitated, unsure what else to say. I didn't want to get into an argument with my dad over the phone. Besides, it was pointless. He always won.

"So, what is the management like?"

His question filled me with relief.

"Oh, they're really good. Eric, the service manager, is a bit funny, but my line manager, David, is really nice. I mean, really supportive," I added quickly.

"Funny how?"

"Well… he's a bit, I don't know, judgemental. Serious. I feel like he's almost waiting for me to do something wrong."

My dad tutted.

"Well, Emily, someone has to keep an eye on you to make sure you know what you are doing. And of course he's judging you. He needs to know that he can trust you to do your job, especially as it will probably be his head that will roll when you mess up."

"*If* I mess up, Dad," I corrected automatically. Immediately I regretted it.

"Of course, Emily. You know best. I've only been working in the field for over thirty years."

"Dad..."

"Look, Emily, I've told you from the start, I don't think you're cut out for this kind of work. You're far too naive and seem to have some romanticised idea about what it's going to be like. I'm just being honest with you. If you don't change your attitude you could find yourself in serious trouble."

I sat on my bed, my eyes closed, as my father lectured me once more about my poor career choice. His tirade over, I counted to ten and took a deep breath.

"So how's work for you, Dad?"

He sighed down the phone.

"The same as always, Emily. Look, I'm going to have to go. I want to get the lawn mown and take Barney for a walk before it rains. I'll talk to you soon."

I sat dumbly for a moment as I took in his words.

"Okay then, Dad. Say hi to Barney for me. I love you."

The phone had already clicked dead.

7

"Can I get you another?"

I looked up to see the barman leaning on my table, his hands spread wide on the chrome surface. He raised an eyebrow as I took in his shabby appearance. He didn't belong in a bar like this any more than I did, but whereas as I was no way near cool enough for its mirrored surfaces and black leather seating, he made it look ridiculously pretentious. I tried to meet his gaze and smiled.

"Oh, okay. Yes please."

I watched as he sauntered back to the bar before casually looking around at the other clientele. Most of them were Suits talking loudly over the bass of the music. Perched on my stool in my grey trousers and black shirt I felt even more conspicuous than I did at work. At least there you could pretty much wear what you wanted and, even though I was decidedly more conservative in my dress than most, my clothes didn't look, well, cheap.

I smiled my thanks as the barman placed another glass of red in front of me. He walked away without an acknowledgement. I looked at my watch. It was gone 6.30. I had arranged to meet Lorraine over an hour ago but she had texted to say she was running late. That had been forty minutes ago. I pulled my phone out of my bag and sighed irritably at its silence.

"Emily! Hi!"

I looked up to see Lorraine wobbling towards me in an impressive pair of heels. Her hair, once a mousy cascade of waves, was pulled back into a platinum ponytail. Black-framed glasses and red lips completed her formidable look.

I slipped out of my seat and hugged her tightly as soon as she got to my table. She felt tiny, even skinnier than I remembered, her ribs poking me through her razor-sharp suit. I pulled back and looked at her, unable to hide my surprise.

"Jesus, Lorraine, you've lost weight."

She smiled as she hopped onto the stool opposite me.

"Yeah, I know. It's this job. It's better than any diet going if you want to lose a few pounds."

I stared at her as she settled in her seat and studied the cocktail list. Her pale skin looked almost transparent around her dark blue eyes despite a visible application of foundation. I wondered what she looked like without her mask. Glancing up at me, her smile faded.

"What?"

I averted my gaze to my wine and took a sip.

"Nothing."

"Em…"

I took another mouthful and shrugged.

"You just look so… different, that's all."

Lorraine's smile slowly returned.

"Thanks. I guess London has given me a bit of a makeover."

I watched her as she effortlessly caught the attention of the barman and waved him over. The combination of my wine consumption and his puppy-like obedience made me snort with laughter. Lorraine glanced at me with a frown as she placed her order. As he walked away, she turned towards me and placed her elbows on the table.

"Something funny?"

I put my hand over my smirk and looked at her. She didn't smile back. Dropping my hand back to the table I tried to keep my amusement under control.

"No. It was just, well, interesting to see how that barman reacted to you. When I arrived he hardly even acknowledged my existence. But you…" I gestured at her grandly before bursting into another fit of laughter. Lorraine watched me in silence until my laughter subsided.

"Emily, Jason knows that I am a valued customer. I often bring my clients here and, with them, their money and influence. He shows me nothing but respect," she hissed across the table. Spotting Jason approach with her Cosmopolitan, she sat back in her seat and smiled at him sweetly, touching his arm unnecessarily as he left. Her mouth was a flat line when she turned back to me.

"Just don't embarrass me here, okay?"

I nodded dumbly and watched her as she sipped her drink. Her face relaxed again.

"Oh, that's better. I've had a hell of a day. I was starting to think I would never get away anywhere near on time."

Resisting the urge to point out that she had still managed to be over an hour late, I smiled sympathetically as I sipped my wine.

"Sounds tough. No wonder you're losing weight."

Lorraine looked at me sharply. I held my breath, berating myself for clearly saying the wrong thing yet again. I hadn't seen Lorraine since we had left uni and, as my only friend in London, I really didn't want to piss her off. But I'd forgotten quite how prickly she could be.

Lorraine hesitated for a moment before taking another glug of her cocktail. She looked at my blouse as she swallowed.

"Well, in my job you have to look good. And working twelve-hour days means that you don't always get the chance to eat regular meals."

I gaped at her, my mouth open.

"Twelve-hour days? You're kidding me!"

She smiled smugly.

"That's PR for you."

I shook my head.

"Well, I don't know how you can keep going. Especially when you aren't eating properly."

Lorraine rolled her eyes.

"Jeez, alright, Mum. Look, I have my coping mechanisms and am doing just fine. Besides, it's not forever. As you move up the chain the pressure to prove yourself slackens off a bit."

I stared at her in silence as she pulled her make-up bag out of an expensive-looking handbag.

"Anyway, I'm just going to nip to the ladies, then shall we get another drink? I have a meeting 7.30 so it will have to be a swift one."

I looked from her empty glass to her face.

"A meeting? Tonight?"

She rolled her eyes again.

"Yes, Emily, tonight. Look, I did warn you that I was really busy."

She looked at me warily before striding over to the bathroom, gesturing Jason towards our table as she passed the bar. I felt the heaviness that had been growing in my chest tighten as she disappeared behind the padded door. I had been looking forward to a night of girly fun and it looked like I was going to get barely an hour of Lorraine's time before she had to leave. I sat in silence as Jason put another glass of wine in front of me, trying desperately to keep my disappointment to myself. Before I had a chance to fully dismiss the emotion rising in my throat Lorraine was back, her lips even redder and her eyes wider and darker than before. She glanced at me as she tasted her drink.

"So, how's the new job going?"

I swallowed awkwardly.

"Um, okay. I only started last week so I'm still getting into it."

She nodded as she took another sip of her Cosmo.

"Cool. So what's everyone like?"

I shrugged.

"They're okay. This girl Fran has been doing a lot of visits with me, she's really nice."

Lorraine nodded enthusiastically.

"That's really great! I mean, you need to make new friends here, don't you?"

I shrugged.

"I guess." I lifted my glass to my lips and looked at her over the rim as I drank. "It's nice to know that you're here though, too."

"Mmm." Lorraine looked down at her glass. She was slowly running her fingers up and down the delicate stem. "But, you know, I'm really busy so it's good that you're getting to know other people too. You know, people who are a bit more like you."

I felt my forehead crease.

"What do you mean?"

Lorraine sighed as she looked at her watch.

"Well, Emily, we work in very different environments. I work in a cut-throat agency where you have to be tough to get ahead, whereas you're trying to help people and have to be nurturing and kind. You want to be hanging around people who understand your job and are a bit more, well, sympathetic, don't you?"

I studied her face carefully. She was watching me with saucer-like eyes.

"Don't you want to be my friend anymore, Lorraine?" I whispered.

She tutted and shook her head as she drained the last of her drink.

"Oh God, Emily, don't be so melodramatic. I'm just saying that we have become very different people with very different lifestyles, and it's good for us to have other friends who appreciate us. Besides, I'm so busy at the moment I don't have much free time to meet up with you anyway. Especially as you live south of the river."

"I don't mind coming up to see you if it makes it easier?" I knew I sounded pathetic, but my wine consumption had ensured that any attempts to hide my feelings would fail miserably.

"Emily, come on. Don't be like that. We'll still see each other, just not all the time, okay? I have my life to get on with, you know?"

I looked up at her through watery eyes. She was already standing up, her bag on her shoulder. Her frown was hard to read.

"Now, take care of yourself. I'll call you when I can."

She briefly hugged me with one arm before heading to the door. Through the din of the music I heard her tell Jason to put our drinks on her account. I looked around the bar. Clusters of laughing people mocked my solitude. I downed the rest of my drink and slid off my chair. Blinking back my tears I dumped my glass back on the table and walked unsteadily towards the door, my head bent against the revellers surrounding me.

8

My hand hesitated before knocking on the door. David pulled it open almost instantly, his mobile clasped to his ear. I stared at him for a second as he looked at me blankly, his eyebrows raised. I looked down at my watch in silence as the female voice on the other end of the line continued to chatter away. It was two minutes to eleven. When I looked up again he had stood back and was waving me into Eric's office. It was nearly two weeks since I had walked into the very same room on my first day. I watched him as I carefully sat at the round table and opened my still-crisp notebook. David was pacing around the office, his free hand cupping his mouth in a vain attempt to maintain privacy.

"Yeah, okay then, Gill... I'll pick them up on my way home... Of course I won't forget... Okay, look I have to go now...Okay... You too. Bye."

He puffed out his cheeks and exhaled slowly as he terminated the call. Shoving his phone into his pocket he looked at me and grimaced.

"Sorry about that. Just had to sort out a few things at home."

I looked from his sincere blue eyes to my notebook and shrugged.

"'S okay."

Hearing him turn away I glanced up again. He was rummaging through a pile of papers on Eric's desk. His hair, already a mess from too much nervous tousling, had fallen into his eyes. His white shirt, clearly freshly ironed at the start of the day, was starting to crease. As my gaze wandered below his waistline to his jeans he straightened up and turned to the table. I looked down at my blank page quickly and scribbled down the date as he sat opposite me. He smelt of laundry liquid and a clean, citrusy aftershave.

"Okay then, Emily, let's make a start."

He looked up from his notes and smiled warmly. The dimples at the sides of his mouth deepened.

"So, this is your first official one to one. We try to meet with every member of our team at least every four to six weeks, just to touch base with them to see how they are getting on and to discuss any difficult cases. This kind of work can be quite challenging, mentally and emotionally, so we like to make sure people have a chance to get the support they need. Okay?"

I nodded, my hands clasped on my lap. He nodded back.

"Cool. Well, as you're new to the service and new to working with this client group as a whole, I thought it would be useful for both of us to meet more often, say once a fortnight, just whilst you get into the swing of things?"

My face dropped. His smile softened as he held up his hands.

"Look, Emily, don't worry about it. The management team just want to make sure you're getting the support you need. I mean, you did a really good interview and clearly know your stuff. But, you have to agree, being able to talk the talk is very different from being able to walk the walk."

My mind whirled frantically. I had been on at least half a dozen visits with Fran that week. Okay, so they had been a challenge, but I had got through them. What had she said?

"I'm doing my best," I muttered, my eyes returning to the table. David took a deep breath.

"I know you are, Emily. We all do, and you're doing fine. We just want to make sure that you're going to be comfortable carrying out visits on your own and feel confident to deal with our more challenging clients."

My mind snapped back to a visit I had carried out the previous day. I had thought it was going well. Fran had introduced me to her client and explained that I was going to review their support plan. I had been almost halfway through when he had kicked off.

"For fuck's sake, what the hell is all this, anyway? You're sat here asking me all these questions and making all these notes, but it isn't helping me, is it?"

I had gaped at his angry red face for a good few seconds before being able to utter a response.

"It's, it's for y-your support plan. So we know what you need help with," I had stammered.

"Look, I've already told you what I need help with. I need a new fucking flat. How is asking me what drugs I'm currently using going to help me with that, eh?"

Next to me Fran had cleared her throat gently.

"Sorry, Alan, we maybe should have explained a bit more about it before we started. We just want to touch base with everything that is going on for you so that we make sure we haven't missed anything. Also, there might be something else going on in your life that might be impacting your housing situation, or vice versa. Do you know what I mean?"

Alan had muttered something under his breath before letting me continue. By the time I had got to the end of the form I had been exhausted. When Fran decided to conclude the interview for me I hadn't objected.

"Emily?"

I blinked. David was peering at me, his brow mapped with lines. I blinked again, mentally shaking myself.

"Um, okay."

He took a deep breath and reached across the table. The skin on the palm of his hand felt dry and warm on my forearm. I looked up at him with surprise.

"Look, Emily, you're doing a really good job. Fran said that you come across as very professional and knowledgeable, and she said that your notes and stuff are really thorough. Which is really important, especially when it comes to risk assessing and more official reports. But we just need to work on the small stuff like conflict management and building rapport, okay?"

I looked up at him and nodded. He smiled again and sat back in his chair, removing his hand from my arm. Immediately my skin prickled, seeking his warmth. He looked down at his papers.

"Anyway, we've managed to pull a few strings and squeeze you onto a course about dealing with difficult people next week on Tuesday. Does that sound okay?"

"Oh, I think I have visits arranged with Fran that day…"

David held up a hand.

"Don't worry, it's all sorted. Fran will go along anyway and arrange a handover visit in a couple of weeks' time. Okay?"

"Okay."

David grinned at me.

"Great. Now, shall we take a look at the cases you've been allocated already and you can tell me how your first visits went?"

I sat up straight in my chair and flicked to the notes at the front of my book. Clearing my throat I started to recite what I had written down during my handover with Fran. He stopped me as I began the summary of my second client.

"Sorry, Em, before we move on, have you visited Stacey yet?"

I looked up from my notes.

"Um, yes. We saw her on Monday."

He nodded enthusiastically.

"And? How did it go?"

I shrugged.

"Okay. She seems pretty stable. Fran talked to her a bit about AA as she's stopped going. She said that there are too many people there who still drink so she'd rather not go anymore, you know, in case they tempt her back."

"And is she going to any other abstinence groups or anything?"

I scanned through my notes again.

"Um, not anymore. She just finished a twelve-week course on it, though."

David nodded again.

"Good stuff. So does she need any support with anything else?"

I frantically searched my already frazzled brain. It was starting to feel like I was being tested.

"I don't think so. Maybe we can close her case?" I offered tentatively. David twisted his mouth and frowned.

"Maybe. But I would keep her open for a couple more months and just touch base with her a few more times. Maybe start to talk to her about work and training?"

Silently I berated myself. She had mentioned wanting to retrain as a nurse.

"Sure."

David smiled again.

"Good stuff. Now, let's move on to Alan, shall we?"

By the time our supervision had finished my forehead was throbbing. David seemed to sense my fatigue and opened the office door for me.

"I'll send you an invite via email for our next catch-up and get back to you about that advanced drug awareness training, okay?" He smiled down at me. I tried to smile back.

"Okay. Thanks."

"No problem. And remember, you're doing good, kid."

I laughed feebly.

"I guess it's just a bit more difficult than I thought it was. You know, getting people to like me."

He laughed loudly. I looked up, surprised. He shrugged apologetically. His sparkling blue eyes reminded me of the sun glistening on the sea. The ridiculous romanticism of the thought made my cheeks burn.

"It just takes a bit of time to get to know your clients and to build up that level of trust, Em. I mean, why wouldn't they like you?"

He winked at me before turning back to the table to collect his notes. I resisted the urge to watch his long fingers as they worked through the pile of papers and scurried back to my desk. Sitting heavily on my chair I let my head drop into my hands and sighed. My mind was a jumble of clients, support plans and… David. Images from the last two hours flashed into my head like a slideshow. David running his hands through his hair. That smile and those dimples. His sea blue eyes sparkling as he winked at me. The warmth of his hand on my skin.

"You okay, hen?"

I lifted my head almost too quickly. Fran was looking down at me, a single line between her eyebrows betraying her concern. I pushed my hair away from my face rapidly and smiled brightly.

"Yes, I'm fine. Just a bit tired, that's all."

She put her hands on her hips and let her head fall to one side.

"Really? Because the groan that just came out of you would suggest otherwise."

Once more blood rushed to my cheeks. Oh God. Everyone in the office must have heard me. I heard someone snigger a few desks behind me. They must know what I had been thinking about. The humiliation made my eyes prickle precariously. Fran suddenly crouched beside me, her hand on mine. I looked down at it as I desperately tried to push away the memory of David's touch.

"Oh, honey, was it that bad?"

I looked at her dumbly.

"What?"

Her frown deepened.

"Your one to one. I know David can be a bit of a jerk. What did he say?" she whispered.

I couldn't help but laugh. Knowing Fran had clearly misunderstood my anguish and her sincere face was just too much for me. I felt a tear escape as I tried to control my outburst. Fran stood up and, after a furtive look around the office, pulled me towards the door.

"Jim, if anyone asks we're going to lunch," she called over her shoulder.

We were halfway down the stairs before I was able to speak again.

"Fran, I'm okay, honest. It was just a bit, well, overwhelming, that's all. So much to remember…"

My voice trailed off as the brightness of the sun hit my face. Fran let go of my hand and linked her arm through mine as she led me across the high street.

"I know. But you clearly need to get out of there. Two hours locked in a room with David is enough to drive anyone to distraction."

The irony of Fran's misinterpretation forced another bubble of laughter out of my mouth. She looked at me quizzically as she pushed open the door of the café.

"Jeez, Em, what did he do to you?"

*

The sweetness of the tea was strangely comforting, almost calming. I looked over the top of my mug as I took another sip. Fran was watching me closely, her cappuccino untouched. Her dreads, scraped back into a loose bun at the nape of her neck, made her head look too big for her delicate body.

"Better?"

I smiled appreciatively.

"Yes. Thanks."

"I'm afraid I'm a bit of a traditionalist when it comes to handling a crisis. Tea and sympathy never fails to help if you ask me."

A smile touched the corner of her mouth. I smiled back, this time managing to prevent it from spilling over into near hysteria.

"Well, the tea is certainly doing the trick. I feel much better now."

Fran's smile disappeared.

"Well, you weren't for a moment back there, I can tell you. So what happened in there that upset you so much?"

I took another slurp of tea as I mulled over my response. Fran was still staring at me. I couldn't tell her that I... what? Had a crush on my boss? Was that what it was? The cliché was almost as embarrassing as the situation itself. Carefully I settled my mug on the placemat in front of me.

"Oh, it's nothing, honest. I just, well, this work isn't quite what I thought it would be. I think I'm struggling a bit and am worried that David and Eric don't think I'm any good at it."

Fran studied my face carefully. I looked back at her as steadily as I could.

"That's it?"

I shrugged.

"Pretty much, yes."

I fought the urge to look away. When she finally looked down at the table to pick up her coffee I was exhausted from the effort.

"Okay. Well, first of all, David and Eric were both on your interview panel, yes?"

I nodded.

"So they are both perfectly aware of your lack of experience. They would be pretty stupid to expect you to know exactly what you are doing straight away."

I looked down at my tea as Fran folded her arms. Her frown had spread to every corner of her face.

"It's not that, Fran. It's just, well, David said I needed to do more training and stuff. And he said that he'd heard I was struggling with some of the clients and needed to learn how to deal with their anger."

I looked at her through my eyelashes, waiting for a reaction. Fran shrugged her shoulders and tightened her arms across her flattened chest.

"Okay, well, training is always good, especially when you have to deal with people like Alan on a day-to-day basis."

Slowly her frown evaporated as her eyes widened.

"Oh, hen, you're not upset because I told David about that visit, are you?"

I averted my eyes back to my tea and laced my fingers around the mug handle.

"Well, no, but…"

Fran released her arms and let them fall to her sides as she laughed. My face flushed with a mixture of embarrassment and anger.

"Oh, Emily. David wants to know how you are getting on and just asked me if there was anything you're struggling with. I think anyone can get stuck when it comes to Alan and his moods but there are ways that you can prevent a confrontation with him. Learning a few techniques for dealing with people like that sounds very sensible to me." She leaned across the table and stilled my hand as it rocked my tea into a gentle whirlpool. "And give yourself a break. You've only been doing this for two weeks. Experience is a great teacher, you know."

I pulled my hand away and let it fall on my lap. Instantly I realised that my action probably came across as sulky. In fact the entire conversation probably painted me as an immature adolescent. I glanced up at Fran. She was looking at me with wide eyes, her mouth slightly open to say words that she couldn't quite find. I smiled meekly.

"You're right, Fran. I'm overreacting. Sorry, I just... I just want to be good at my job."

Fran's face relaxed slightly.

"Okay then, hen. But you know you need to give yourself a break. It will all come to you, you just need to give it a chance – David and Eric gave you one and wouldn't have if they didn't think you were up to it. And you'll learn as you go, and from other people in the service."

"Like you?"

Fran's sharp look almost berated me as much as my silent self. Quickly I smiled, hoping to cover up my moodiness as humour. Slowly the corner of Fran's lips perked up.

"Yes, young lady, like me. And Jim. I'm sure he'd be happy to teach you a thing or two."

I rolled my eyes and giggled.

"Very funny. Or I could ask David?"

I studied Fran's face for any clues to her feelings about our boss. I hadn't forgotten our conversation in the pub during my first week. Instantly she wrinkled up her nose in distaste.

"Well, you could do, but trust me, if he intends for every supervision he has with you to last over two hours, you won't want to spend much more time with him."

I nodded my understanding. Understanding that she clearly didn't want me to get too close to him. But then apparently our first one to one had lasted longer than what was normal. And that he had taken a risk hiring me in the first place.

"So why don't you like him?" I blurted.

She looked at me blankly for a second, then shrugged.

"Well, it's not that I really dislike him, he's just not got a clue really. I mean, he thinks he knows it all, but I don't think he really gets what it's like for some of our clients, you know, what real hardship feels like. Plus," she added, raising an eyebrow along with a pointed finger, "he's an early midlife crisis waiting to happen."

Her smile broadened as her raised hand returned to her cappuccino. I smiled back and looked down at my tea as our sandwiches were placed in front of us. My mind was still swimming, but clarity was starting to emerge about the relationship between my manager and my mentor. And there appeared to be more to it than Fran was willing to admit.

*

"Emily?"

I looked up from my computer screen to see a blurry Jim standing next to me. I squeezed my eyelids together tightly and looked at him again. His smile broadened.

"Tell me about it. I have to use drops these days to keep my eyes from drying out I spend so much time on my laptop. If I were you I'd pop into Boots and invest in some. Trust me, you'll thank yourself."

I smiled at him before turning back to my screen. I stared blankly at it as I tried to remember what I had been doing. Jim had completely broken my concentration just when I was getting to the end of my to-do list for the day.

"Tough day?"

I tried to suppress my annoyance as I turned to him again, a smile plastered across my face.

"It's been okay. I just need to finish off a couple of things then I'm done, I think."

His freckled face brightened.

"Oh, that's good. You looked like you were having a hard time of it earlier, so I'm glad."

I let my head drop. Oh yes, earlier. My eyes rested on Jim's pristine yellow and blue trainers. My colleagues clearly couldn't help but be amused by my meltdown. My face reddened as I waited for the rest of his taunt. He cleared his throat. Here it came.

"Anyway, if you're nearly done, I wondered if you fancied a quick drink? I know it does me wonders after a particularly tough day."

I looked up at his face again. He was still smiling down at me, his blue eyes hopeful. Blue, but not as blue as David's. Or as clear.

"Um, no, it's okay, thanks. I just want to get these things done then go home."

Jim's face dropped.

"Oh, okay. Well, if you fancy one another time…"

"I just have a bit of a headache, that's all," I interrupted. I smiled at him quickly before turning back to my screen. I felt irritation rise in my chest as he continued to hover by my desk.

"Understood. Well, make sure you get away sooner rather than later. I'm sure that can wait until tomorrow if you're feeling a bit rough."

"Okay." I beamed at my screen as I began typing briskly, hoping the action would prompt his departure.

"Cool. Well, I'll see you tomorrow."

"Bye," I piped as he walked away. I glanced up at him as he left, his Billabong rucksack slung over a shoulder sporting another Superdry T-shirt. I watched as he paused at David's desk. He said something and shrugged as David laughed loudly, leaning back in his chair. As he strode to the door I looked back at David. He caught my eye and smiled. Quickly I dived back behind my monitor. Blood pumped to my face, making it almost impossible for me to concentrate on the words I had just typed. Why had he looked at me like that? Did he know that Jim had just asked me out? Was he mocking me? Or... was he just pleased that I had said no? I peered around my monitor and looked at him again. Only the top of his head was in view, his eyes no doubt glued to his work. I looked back at mine. It was no good. My heart was now pounding along with my head. How could a man that beautiful be interested in a little thing like me? But then, that smile, the supervision, the fact that he had given someone with such little experience a chance in the first place. That comment, *"why wouldn't they like you?"*

I sighed as I hit the save button. I glanced over at David again as I shoved my belongings back into my satchel. One tanned arm stretched behind his head as the other held his phone to his ear. His face was almost rigid as he gazed at his computer, his mouth only moving slightly as he spoke. I took a deep breath as I threw my bag over my shoulder and walked purposefully towards the exit. As I walked past his desk I looked over. Our eyes met as I raised my hand to wave goodbye. His face instantly softened into a smile as he tucked the phone under his chin and raised his hand in return, his eyes glinting mischievously. I quickly looked away and narrowly missed careering into a row of lockers as I hurried out of the office, only taking in a breath when the warm evening air hit my face on the street below.

9

I heard the doorbell buzz inside the flat and took a step back. The August sun was behind one of many clouds. Looking up at the ominous sky I pulled my new cardigan around me. Fran had teased me when I had presented the new addition to my wardrobe to her that morning.

"It's only from Primark, but it's cashmere," I had gushed, encouraging her to stroke my arm. She had obliged before looking up at me with one of her crooked smiles.

"It's lovely, Em. But when are you going to inject some colour into your life?"

Coming from Fran, the comment was hardly a surprise. Okay, so today she was almost conservative in a mini kilt with co-ordinated red knee-high socks and a cropped T-shirt, but grey was not really in her remit.

The door flew open. Stacey looked at me blankly. The two-year-old in her arms screamed in my face.

"Oh God, Emily, sorry I forgot you were coming today."

I smiled as sweetly as I could. She was going to cancel and, with a screaming child in tow, I wasn't disappointed.

"That's okay, Stacey. Do you want to re-arrange?"

She shook her head vigorously.

"Oh no. I need to see you today. They've gone and stopped my Universal Credit again, haven't they?"

My heart sank. Having witnessed Fran try to deal with the benefits office on more than one occasion, I knew this was not going to be an easy visit. Plus, it was my first one on my own. I fixed the smile on my face.

"Okay, no problem. Let's see what we can do."

I perched on the edge of the fake leather sofa and surveyed the flat as Stacey searched for her paperwork. The flat was immaculate, and apart from a smattering of toys on the freshly hoovered carpet, tidy too. Fran had warned me that Stacey's pride in her home usually slipped when she had relapsed. I felt myself relax. That was one less thing to worry about, anyway.

"I can't find the last letter they sent me anywhere. Would you…?"

Stacey held the screaming brat towards me. Before I could object it was in my arms and wailing all the more loudly at the sight of its new sitter. I wasn't great with kids at the best of times, let alone when they were in the middle of a tantrum. It wiggled furiously as I tried to sit it on my lap and keep any snot-ridden paws away from my new cardy.

"Here it is." Stacey scooped her child up and replaced it with a piece of paper. I studied it carefully.

"It says you missed an appointment at the job centre?" I offered.

Stacey's eyes widened.

"Well, maybe I wouldn't have if they had sent me an appointment letter."

She flopped onto the matching sofa opposite me and threw her head into her free hand. Locked under Stacey's other arm, the baby wailed as she grabbled at her mother's white T-shirt for a breast.

"What the fuck am I supposed to do now? I've got no money and she needs nappies and food."

I swallowed awkwardly as tears began to roll down my client's face. I took a deep breath as I collected my thoughts.

"Have you told them why you missed the appointment?"

Her laugh was hollow.

"Are you kidding me? I can't get through. I never can. And it's an 0845 number so I'm out of credit now too." She gulped back a sob. "What are Social Services gonna say if I can't even feed her?"

I hesitated at the thought of Stacey's social worker. Should I let her know? The policy around sharing information and child protection was confusing enough on paper. But in practice…

"Look, can I borrow your phone to try and get through to them?"

I looked over at Stacey who was staring at me with wet eyes, her arm stretched towards me. Quickly I dived into my bag and pulled out my Nokia. A smile quivered on her lips as she took it from me and punched in the number. I averted my eyes as she clamped the phone between her ear and shoulder as she lifted her T-shirt for the grovelling child. Desperate for a distraction, I mentally went through a list of options. Crisis Loan, Social Services, charity grant…

The phone clattered to the pine coffee table between us.

"The bastards cut me off," Stacey sobbed as she crumpled back into her seat, dislodging her child from its food source. On cue, it howled. A needle of pain niggled at the corner of my temple. I needed to get out of there.

"Okay, Stacey, you need to calm down. Getting upset isn't going to help the situation, is it?"

She stopped sobbing abruptly and gaped at me. Two spots of colour rose on the cheeks of her deathly-white face.

"Calm down? Emily, I haven't got any money! Have you any idea what that feels like?"

I held my hands up.

"Stacey, we aren't here to talk about my experiences, we're here to help you. Now, if you want I can go back to the office and try to get through to them later this afternoon – it's lunchtime now so we probably won't be able to get through for a while anyway."

Stacey didn't answer for a moment. Even the child had grown quiet.

"Okay. But what am I supposed to do in the meantime?" she asked quietly.

"You go down to the job centre and apply for a Crisis Loan. If that doesn't work, let me know and I'll see if Social Services..."

"I don't want them to know, Emily. They've only just taken her off the Child Protection list and I don't want her to end up on it again."

I took a deep breath.

"Okay then. Well, we'll cross that bridge when we get to it, okay? Now, I need something in writing saying that you give me permission to speak to the benefits office on your behalf."

I pulled my notebook out of my bag and quickly composed the letter, thankful that I had seen Fran write one only a few days before. Satisfied with its content, I passed it over to Stacey along with my pen. She took it from me and signed it in silence. The kid stared at me with huge wet eyes as it sucked on its mother's nipple. I averted my eyes, stuffing my belongings into my bag as I stood up.

"Right. Well, give me a call after you've been to the job centre, and we'll go from there?"

My client didn't return my smile.

"I have no credit. How am I supposed to do that?"

I stared back at her ungrateful eyes.

"Okay then. Well, I'll call you in a couple of hours. Is that better?"

She nodded and looked away, her face crumpling with mounting tears. I walked out of the room quickly and closed the door before they had a chance to fall.

*

"So how did it go with Stacey today?"

I looked up from the fax machine to see Fran next to me, her hands firmly placed on her hips. I wondered if she knew that the pose naturally led a person's eye to her bare midriff.

"It was okay, thanks. Her benefits have been stopped so she's a little bit stressed."

Fran shook her head as she sucked her teeth.

"Bloody hell, again? Why?"

"Missed appointment," I shrugged. "It's okay though. I've spoken to the benefits office and have just faxed over permission to speak to them on her behalf."

"But what is she going to do..."

"I advised her to go to the job centre and apply for a Crisis Loan. And if that doesn't work we're going to talk to the social worker," I interrupted. Fran released her hands from her waist and placed one on my arm.

"Sorry, hen. I just worry a bit about her. She's done so well but I know how worked up she can get when things go wrong."

"Well, everything's under control," I muttered, scooping up Stacey's letter as it slipped out of the machine. I glanced up at Fran's face and tried to read her expression. Her smile didn't give me any clues.

"I'm sure it is, honey. Just give me a shout if you need a hand with anything." She puffed out her cheeks. "You're gonna have your hands full sorting this one out."

She gave my arm a final squeeze before striding back to her desk. In one swift movement she was sitting on her chair, one leg tucked under her bum, the pen she had stuffed into her ponytail now dancing between her fingers. I took a deep breath as I wandered back to my own workstation. I knew that Fran meant well but couldn't help but feel like she didn't think I could manage without her. Exhaling slowly, I reached for my phone and dialled again.

10

Gripping onto the handle above my head, I pulled my sleeve up my arm with my free hand and tilted my head to read my watch. 9.24. I was going to be late. As the bus jolted to another halt, I planted my feet even wider apart and grabbed the pole next to me. I had been on the bus for the best part of an hour now and was more than a little tired of the driver's lack of consideration for his passengers as he lurched his way north. Lorraine had warned me that London grinds to a standstill when the tube falls to pieces, but this was ridiculous.

As another bead of sweat trickled down my spine, I mentally ran through my diary for the day. I had visits pretty much back to back until about 2pm. I had kept my afternoon as free as possible to catch up on my paperwork which, so far, was a system that worked for me.

"Don't you find that you get more out of your visits if you go in the afternoon? I mean, some people get up nice and early like you, but others…"

I had shrugged off Fran's helpful suggestion. As someone whose organisational skills were at best chaotic, I really didn't need advice from her on how to plan my day. Okay, so I had had a few no-shows and a bit of a grumble here and there, but so far it had worked for me. And it worked for David too.

"Jeez, Em, I think you're the only one in my team who has all their support plans and risk assessments up to date. I don't know how you do it, but feel free to share your secret with your poor manager here."

Predictably I had blushed and muttered something inarticulate before scuttling away, but I had received the message loud and clear. I was doing well, and it had been noted.

Absently I released my grip as a fellow commuter squeezed past me towards the door. The driver slammed on the brakes as I grappled for another handle, but it was too late.

"Watch it!"

The buggy to my left stopped me from falling into the row of people standing in the aisle. Scrambling back to my feet, I felt a sharp pain where its handle had embedded itself in my stomach. I felt tears spring to my eyes in response as the child inside it started to whimper. A round woman with hair tightly restricted in a ponytail glared at me before attending to the rising screams.

"Stupid fucking cow."

I didn't catch the rest of her muttered tirade as I pushed myself to the back of the bus, ignoring the irritation I left in my wake, until I had at least something I could lean on. I pushed my damp back against the side of the seat next to me and closed my eyes. I had managed to keep my tears at bay, but my side still throbbed. I was going to have a huge bruise by lunchtime, but nothing more serious. However, the wound to my pride was no doubt going to plague me for the rest of the day. Coupled with the late start and more than one challenging client to look forward to before I could head back to the sanctuary of the cool, clean office, I knew today was going to be tough. As the bus threw me into the Suit next to me, I tried to swallow back the dread that threatened to creep through every corner of my body.

*

"Hi, Alan. Sorry I'm late."

Alan peered at me from the other side of his front door. His eyes were narrow with a combination of sleep and suspicion. I kept my smile firmly in place.

"So, can I come in?"

Alan grunted and gave me a quick once-over before stepping back. I fought the urge to shrink away as I passed him in the narrow doorway and headed to the living room.

"Not in there. In there."

With a start I followed his order and slid into the small kitchen to my left. A pile of unwashed crockery was precariously stacked next to the sink, days-old food crusted onto the cheap earthenware. Tesco bags stuffed with rubbish were dumped next to an overflowing bin. The state of the ancient worktops and peeling floor filled me with a sudden craving for a bottle of bleach and a pair of Marigolds.

"So, what are you here for?"

Alan was watching me from the doorway, his fists hanging dangerously at his sides. I suddenly realised that he had blocked my exit. Panic rose to my throat.

"Well, I brought a medical questionnaire for you to fill in for your housing application. I just need to call the office to let them know I'm here then we can make a start, okay?"

I blindly searched my bag for my phone as I gabbled on. Relief flooded my body as my fingers closed around its plastic case. Alan watched me in silence as I shakily dialled the office.

I smiled at him weakly as I reported in to the duty desk. He didn't smile back. My call complete, I took a deep breath.

"Okay, job done. So, how have you been, Alan?"

His gaze didn't leave me as he moved across the cramped room and pulled out a scuffed chair from under the chipboard table. Slowly he sat down and pulled a crumpled packet of Mayfairs from his jeans pocket. He jerked his head towards the other chair.

"Sit down. I'd be better if I wasn't still living in this shithole," he muttered through teeth clenched around his cigarette.

I hesitated for a moment as I considered pointing out that his flat would be a lot nicer if he cleaned it, but decided against it. Boldly I stepped over to the vacant chair and sat down, deliberately avoiding paying too much attention to its state.

"Well, if that's the case, shall we make a start on this form?"

Lighting his smoke, he gestured at me vaguely with his free hand.

"Sure. If it will help."

"Well, other than trying to do a mutual exchange…"

He snorted.

"Yeah. Like anyone's gonna move here by choice."

I shrugged.

"You never know…"

Alan's eyes slowly travelled up my body to meet mine. His intense gaze made my face burn. Quickly I looked away and busied myself retrieving the form and a pen from my bag. Making a small space on the cluttered table for my work, I cleared my throat.

"Right. Alan, what's your date of birth?"

I could feel his eyes boring into me as I studied the form intently. From the corner of my eye I noticed him flick cigarette ash onto the floor.

"Haven't you got that information on one of your other forms?"

"Yes, but…"

"Well, can we just get onto the stuff you need from me and you can finish it off at the office?"

I blinked at the piece of paper in front of me.

"Yes, but…"

"Let's get on with it, then. I've got stuff I need to do."

I looked up at him. He stared back unwaveringly. I hesitated before picking up the form and flicking through it.

"Alan, I-I'm sorry but I need to know that stuff now to be able to complete the rest of the form."

He took a long drag from his cigarette. His fingers that held it were stained yellow with tobacco. My stomach contracted with revulsion.

"Emily, isn't it? How old are you?"

I looked around the room in search of some kind of clue.

"I'm not sure what that has to do with…"

"My point is you're young, you haven't got a lot of life experience and you clearly don't really know what you are doing. Now why don't you stop wasting my time, run back to your fancy office and come back once you've done your homework like a good girl?"

I gaped at him as he stood up and stalked over to the window. He picked up a rusting tin from the corner of the sill and pulled off the lid before peering inside.

"Actually there is something else you can help with. I've run out of money and I don't get my giro for at least another three days. Can you lend me a tenner?"

I made a show of looking for my diary as alarm bells rang in my head. Eric had made it quite clear that lending money to clients was out of the question.

"Alan, you know I can't do that. But if you want me to support you to apply for a loan or approach a charity for a grant…"

I jumped as he slammed the tin onto the kitchen worktop.

"No, I don't want you to help me do that."

I stared at him as threw his cigarette butt into the sink and took a deep breath. His hand rose shakily to his face and covered his eyes. Quietly I pushed my belongings back into my satchel and stood up.

"I think I should leave, Alan. This is clearly not a good time for you."

Although a little high pitched, I was pleased at how evenly my voice came out. As I stepped towards the door, Alan dropped his hand from his face and turned to face me.

"Look, I'm sorry, okay? I just lent a mate twenty quid last week and he hasn't given me it back. Stupid, I know, but he was desperate, and now I have no electricity left. See?"

I jumped out of his way as he reached for the light switch next to me. Dutifully I watched the fluorescent light above us as it failed to respond to his frantic flicking.

"I just need a bit of cash to tide me over for a couple of days. Look, I know you're not supposed to, but Fran used to do it all the time. There's no way the social will give me a loan for something like this."

I nodded my understanding as I continued to inspect his light. It was true; Fran was forever helping her clients out here and there, buying them something to eat on a whim and giving them old books and newspapers. This was no different really. With a sigh I dived into my bag again and pulled out my purse.

"Okay, Alan. But only this once. And I want the money back when I next see you. Alright?"

Alan's eyes widened as I handed him the ten pound note. Gently he took it from my hand and studied it as he held it in both hands. I looked from the money to his face. His expression had softened from one of extreme irritation to one of huge relief in a matter of seconds. I looked back at the money, suddenly nervous.

"Alan?"

He started and looked up at me. His smile looked unnatural.

"Yes. Of course. Thank you, I really appreciate it."

He held out his hand. Pushing the thought of those stained fingers out of my mind I took it and shook it firmly. Quickly he pulled his hand away and pushed it into his jeans pocket as he looked around the room.

"Well, I'm going to go out and top up my electricity key. When are you coming back?" He shifted his weight from one foot to another and looked at me expectantly. I stared back in disbelief. Was he starting to like me? I debated pulling out my diary again but thought the better of it.

"Well, what about in three days, when you get paid? I'll pop over at about one?"

Straight away I regretted my words. I sounded desperate to get my money back. In reality I was just desperate to keep Alan on side.

"Yep, that sounds fine. And we'll get that form done, eh?"

I shrugged.

"Sure. I'll make sure I'm better prepared next time."

His grin made me feel uncomfortable.

"Yeah. Make sure you do your homework before you come to class."

Gold fillings from the back of his mouth flashed at me as he laughed at his own joke. I smiled back at him awkwardly before backing out of the kitchen and walking quickly to the front door.

By the time I was out of the building I still wasn't sure whether the visit had gone well or not.

*

"David?"

As he looked up I spotted the mobile phone clamped to his ear. I held up my hand in apology and began to back away from his desk. Seeing my retreat he widened his eyes and gestured to the seat next to him. Dutifully I sat down and looked down at my hands as I waited.

"Yes… look, I know, Gill, but if you want to go… of course I'll be fine… oh, okay…"

Out of the corner of my eye I glanced at him. His hand went up to his head, no doubt to run his fingers through that mop of hair. He leant forward and dropped his elbow to the desk as he sighed.

"Look, if you're really worried about it just, just make something beforehand and I'll heat it – no, that's not what I meant, Gill…"

I shifted in my seat. This was a private conversation and I was sure David didn't want me to hear it. Or did he? I let my eye wander to his thigh. The denim that covered it did nothing to hide his athletic physique.

"Okay, well, it's up to you. Gill… look I've got to go now, alright? You do what you think… okay then. Bye."

I averted my eyes back to my own hands as they lay in my lap. David took a deep breath as he terminated the call.

"Sorry about that, Emily. I'm afraid there's no rest for the wicked. Especially when they're married with kids."

I looked up at his face as he laughed wearily. The usual sparkle in his eyes was absent.

"Is, is everything okay?"

Despite the stammer I was impressed with my own boldness. He looked at me, his eyebrows raised. His smile returned quickly.

"Oh, yes. Just the usual. Gill has been invited out tonight but is stressing about leaving me with the kids. You know, it's just one of those cases of damned if I do, damned if I don't." He averted his eyes back to his computer screen and shook his head.

"Anyway, enough about me. What can I do for you, Em?"

I hesitated. I wanted him to carry on talking about Gill, and sensed that he wanted to tell me more, too.

"Oh, it's nothing really. You sure you're okay?"

He turned back at me, his sea blue eyes looking at me with curiosity. Or perhaps recognition of a mutual understanding. His smile widened.

"Honestly, I'm fine. But thanks for asking. So…"

His raised eyebrow was so suggestive I couldn't help but blush. I looked down at my hands again, hoping he wouldn't notice.

"Well, it's just, I went on a visit today and the client asked me for money."

David turned his seat towards me and leant back, his arms folded across his chest. His face was suddenly serious.

"I didn't give him any, I just, well, I wasn't sure what to do." The lie was out without any hesitation. David studied my face carefully. I shrugged helplessly.

"Okay, so what was the money for?"

"Well, he lent a friend twenty pounds and hadn't been given it back yet. His giro isn't due for another three days and he was out of electricity."

David nodded slowly.

"What about a Crisis Loan?"

"I suggested that but he wasn't interested. He said he wouldn't get one for something like that."

"And he was definitely out of electricity?"

I nodded, my confidence returning. David nodded again and stroked his chin. His stubble made a rasping sound against the palm of his hand.

"Who was it?"

"Alan."

Slowly David sat up in his chair, his eyes wide.

"Is he using again?" He stood up and looked around the office. With a frown he sat down again. "Where's Fran when you need her?"

I stared at him blankly for a moment as my stomach flipped. "No, I don't think he's using again. He was just a bit desperate. He showed me and the kitchen light definitely wasn't working."

I pushed the memory of Alan looking so groggy, so angry and frustrated, yet so ecstatic when I gave him the money out of my mind. Anyone would be upset in his situation, but his reaction had seemed beyond everyday irritation. But then, Alan wasn't like most people.

David's face relaxed again as he looked past me towards the office entrance.

"Ah! Fran. Just the lady I was looking for."

Fran shook her head as he beckoned her over. Her loose dreads swung angrily as she strode over.

"David, I know you're my manager and all but I wish you wouldn't summon me like I'm your maid or something." She plonked her bum on the desk next to me and folded her arms. Black and yellow stripy tights peeped through the rips in her jeans. She caught my eye and smiled wryly. "Everything okay, hen?"

"Emily's been having a few problems with your little friend Alan," David interrupted. Fran cocked her head to one side and looked at him.

"'My little friend', eh? Well, I didn't realise me and Alan were chums now, but go on."

"He asked me for money, that's all. He'd run out of electricity and needed to top it up," I explained quickly, determined to be a part of this conversation. I could handle this, and wanted David to see that I was as capable as Fran in dealing with the situation, if not better. If she wasn't always giving clients handouts it would have been a lot easier to handle.

"Electricity? Well, he doesn't have a key meter anymore so I don't see how that could have happened. Hasn't he been paying his bill?"

I looked at Fran incredulously.

"Well, he said he was popping out to top up his key when I left, so I don't see how that can be the case." I knew I sounded haughty, but I didn't care. David had insisted on bringing Fran into this conversation and she clearly didn't have a clue what she was talking about.

"Didn't you say he showed you that his electricity wasn't working?" David interjected. I looked at him and smiled gratefully.

"Yes. He turned on the kitchen light and nothing." I lifted my hands and shrugged. Fran sucked on her teeth.

"That light hasn't worked in about four months because Alan can't be arsed to go out and buy a new light bulb." She shook her head sadly. "He clearly wanted the money for something else. And I'll give you three guesses what."

I looked from Fran to David. He was nodding along with her hypotheses. One that had managed to make me look more than a little bit gullible. Anger began to burn inside my chest.

"Look, there was nothing in his manner to suggest he was going to go and use. Maybe it was for something else but he was too embarrassed to tell me what?"

Fran's laugh did little to extinguish my fury.

"Okay, hen, maybe, but it doesn't look good, does it? Look, let me come along to your next visit and we'll see what's going on."

"No!"

As soon as the word was uttered I regretted it. The entire office went quiet. David and Fran exchanged a glance before turning back to me, their surprised faces a mirror of each other's.

"Look, everything is fine. I just wanted to double check with David what the protocol is around helping clients in a financial crisis, okay? I can handle Alan."

I turned to David, my hands clasped together like a desperate disciple. He studied my face for a moment before looking up at Fran.

"Okay, Emily. But keep an eye on Alan. He's a slippery one, right, Fran?"

I smiled a silent thank you before turning to my mentor. She was staring back at David, her dissatisfaction lining her brow. She glanced at me before returning her gaze to our manager and shrugging.

"Okay then, you two. I shall leave it in your hands. I just hope you know what you're doing."

I opened my mouth to respond but she walked away before I could form the words on my tongue. Next to me, David chuckled quietly.

"Don't worry about her, Em. She just doesn't like being told she's wrong." I turned in time to catch his wink before he leant in.

"I think it's a Scottish thing," he whispered before sitting back in his chair, a wide grin on his face. I smiled back uncertainly and stood up to leave as David turned back to his computer.

"Oh, Em, just one more thing?"

His question stopped me in my tracks. Coolly I turned around.

"Yes?"

David's face was serious again.

"So where did he get the money in the end?"

Blood rushed to my face as I tried to figure out where the trap was hidden.

"Sorry?"

"Well, you said he was going out to top up his key when you left. Where did he get the money from?"

I took a deep breath as I searched for an answer.

"Oh… I think he said he was going to try the social after all. Or borrow some money from his brother or something."

David smiled at me.

"Okay, good. Oh, and Emily?" I turned back to him again, hoping that my desperation to escape this conversation wasn't too obvious.

"Yes?" I managed.

He paused for a moment, letting his eyes settle on mine.

"Any other questions, just ask."

I was still grinning like an idiot when I got back to my desk. I'd just been given a free ticket to talk with David whenever I wanted. Okay, so he was my manager, but he didn't need to offer like that. It was an invitation to spend time with him, and, coming from a man who had made clear his marital problems...

"So, you got it all sorted out?"

Fran's voice disturbed me from my thoughts. She was sitting opposite me, her eyes on her laptop as she typed furiously. My irritation, dissipated by her own, was replaced with amusement. Fran, the coolest girl in the office, was jealous – of me.

"Yeah, all good. I just wanted to check with David I had done the right thing. You know, it can be a bit confusing when other people don't follow the rules."

I couldn't resist making a little dig, but if she noticed it she didn't react.

"Fair enough, hen. So, Alan's sorted it out then, has he?"

"Oh yes. He was going to try to get a Crisis Loan and if that didn't work he was going to ask his brother to lend him the cash."

The lie was even easier the second time around.

"His brother? You mean James?"

"Yep." I tapped my mouse victoriously before looking up. Fran was gaping at me. I met her gaze easily. She held it for a few moments before turning back to her own work.

"Alan's brother James died last year, Emily," she said quietly as she flicked through her notebook and flattened a page open. I stared at her in silence until she looked up again.

"He... he didn't say James. He must have meant someone else, you know, like a friend. A brother in that sense." I smiled at her brightly before looking back at my screen and randomly selected an email to read in earnest. I heard Fran exhale loudly.

"Oh, okay. That's good."

Silently she began to type again. I stared blankly at the words in front of me. I knew she didn't believe me, but then, what could she do? David knew she was annoyed at my competence without her, and if she said anything to him he would assume she was still bitter about the conversation we'd had a few minutes before. Slowly I began to relax and turned back to the database to update my notes.

"You know, there's nothing wrong with admitting you've made a mistake. We all do it, and more often than not they can be rectified if we own up to it. At the end of the day, we're all human and we're learning as we go along."

I debated ignoring Fran's speech. I knew exactly what she was saying, but I wasn't going to rise to it.

"Yes. I guess we are all still learning, aren't we?"

I smiled to myself when Fran declined a response.

She hardly spoke to me for the rest of the day.

11

"Emily? Emily!"

I don't know how long she had been banging on the door, but it was Rebecca's voice that cut through to my consciousness as I stood under the cascade of hot water.

"Emily, you've been in there nearly half an hour. The rest of us have to get ready for work as well, you know."

I rolled my eyes to myself as Rebecca ranted on, her voice muffled by the bathroom door and the hiss of the shower. Slowly I turned the water off and squeezed water from my hair before I stepped out of the bath and pulled my towel around me.

"Just a min," I called as I wrapped my hair into a turban and grabbed my toothbrush. My flatmate seemed to have been developing a problem with me since I had moved in. If I wasn't hogging the bathroom I was leaving the kitchen in a mess or not picking up the post when I came in and putting it on the bottom step like she insisted we all did. I clearly irritated her, but then she quite often had the same effect on me.

When I opened the bathroom door she was there, her arms crossed over an ample bosom covered in a red satin dressing gown that did little to hide the wideness of her hips. Her hair, desperately in need of yet another trip to the salon, was pulled into a tight ponytail. Her lips were shrunken into a tight pout.

"About bloody time," she muttered as she pushed past me and slammed the bathroom door shut. I looked at it blankly for a moment before turning back to my room. Matt was standing at the top of the stairs, watching me carefully. He was already dressed for work in a checked shirt and jeans, his skin angry with a new outbreak of red lumps. His gaze made me blush.

"I don't know what her problem is," I muttered as I padded over the landing to my bedroom.

"I think it's just that you spend so long in the bathroom sometimes, Em. I mean, some days you're in and out in ten minutes but others you seem to be in there for hours."

I felt my blush deepen. What was it to him how long I was in there?

"Well, you managed to use it without much difficulty."

"That's because I've started to get up at 6.30 so that I can avoid the backlog. And you two bickering. You just need to be a bit more aware of other people around you, Em."

My mouth involuntarily dropped open. So, Matt was taking sides with Rebecca. Again. My eyes became as hot as my face.

"Maybe we need to draw up some kind of rota. You know, so we all get an allotted slot in the bathroom. It's even worse when Beatrice is around too."

He pushed his hands into his pockets and eyed me carefully as I opened my door. Beatrice. Why couldn't she be the one who was always here rather than Rebecca and her Salsa music and giggling girly friends? And Matt who, although less irritating, creeped me out with his slicked-back hair and staring eyes?

"Whatever."

I slammed my door shut behind me and looked at the ancient digital clock next to my bed. 7.43. Okay, so after a quick bowl of porridge at seven I guess I had been in the bathroom a long time. Sometimes I just needed a bit of time to think, mainly about David admittedly, but my flatmates seemed hell-bent on blowing an extra minute or two completely out of proportion. I pulled the towel off my head and started attacking my hair with my hairbrush. Of course my leisurely shower also meant that I only had just over quarter of an hour to get ready for work and out the front door, giving me very little time to try out my slowly increasing make-up collection. My hair tangle-free, I threw my clothes onto my still-damp body and grabbed my mascara. I tried to ignore the fact that the gloopy black make-up made my eyes look like I had stuck a couple of dead spiders to them and slicked on some pink lip gloss. Grabbing my bag, I quickly checked my appearance before running out of my room, pausing only to lock my door. From across the landing Radio 1 blared whilst the faint aroma of cigarette smoke mingled with burnt toast drifted up from the floor below. I held my breath as I jogged down the stairs and threw open the front door. Taking a deep breath of London air I strode purposefully towards the train station, picking a stray hair off my sticky lips as I went. The relief of getting away from my miserable flatmates was quashed as soon as I saw the heaving platform. I looked up at the electronic display above the heads of my fellow commuters. The last train had been cancelled, and the next one was delayed by thirteen minutes. I quickly dismissed the option of the bus and resigned myself to yet another nightmare journey to work.

*

"Hi, Stacey. Sorry I'm late."

Stacey's smile was less than convincing. I made up for it by widening my own as I squeezed past her and made my way into her flat. Relief swept over me as I noted that her screaming offspring was nowhere to be seen – or heard. I quickly assessed the state of my client's living area. The living room was as neat and tidy as always. As I made my way over to my usual perch on the faux leather sofa I glanced through the kitchen door. An empty cornflake box stood by the chrome pedal bin, along with a collection of bottles and cans. Her recycling, ready to go outside no doubt. Nothing to worry about there – she was still keeping up with appearances, which was a good sign. As I sat down and opened my bag, it clicked. I couldn't see them now, but I was pretty sure that the cans had been for beer and at least one of the bottles had looked suspiciously like one that had previously contained wine.

*

"Can I get you a drink?"

Stacey's question caught me off guard. I sputtered as my response got caught in my throat. Struggling to get my cough under control, Stacey watched me with mild surprise.

"Maybe a glass of water," she said quietly and walked swiftly into the kitchen whilst I tried to regain my composure. I took the water from her gratefully and took a sip.

"Sorry about that," I croaked as I placed the water on the coffee table between us. Automatically Stacey was up and sliding a coaster under the dripping glass. As she reached over a cloud of stale alcohol hit my face.

"I did warn you I'm a bit OCD," she laughed as her eyes roamed around the room, seemingly unable to find somewhere comfortable to rest. I cleared my throat and gave her my warmest smile.

"That's okay, Stacey. We all have our little quirks, don't we?"

Her response was the tiniest of smiles. I waited for a moment before continuing with my spiel.

"Well, today I'd like to review your risk assessment with you, if that's okay? I just want to go over with you any potential problem areas and see what we can do to minimise any associated risks, for your own and other people's safety. Is that okay?"

She shrugged.

"Okay, but I don't see how I'm a risk to anyone. I mean, even Social Services are happy with me, and God knows they're hard to get on the right side of."

I nodded sympathetically.

"Of course. But I'm sure they wouldn't have got so heavily involved unless they felt that they had to."

As soon as the words were out I knew that they had been a mistake. Stacey looked up at me, her eyes wide. I looked down at my form and coughed, hoping that my client wouldn't notice my rising colour.

"Anyway, that's all in the past now. Let's focus on the here and now, shall we?" I chirped. Stacey didn't reply. "Okay, so the first section is about financial stability. We sorted out that little benefits blip, didn't we?"

I looked up, hoping that eye contact, in a show of confidence, would bring the interview back on track. Stacey was quietly wiping hers with the end of her sleeve.

"Yes, it's all sorted now, although I'm having to pay back those Crisis Loans. They're taking seven pounds out of my money every week, can you believe it?"

I took a deep breath.

"Well, I guess that's the problem with loans. You have to pay them back. At least they don't charge interest like a bank or one of those loan sharks though."

Stacey snorted a laugh.

"Yeah well, but I wouldn't have had to have taken the loan in the first place if they hadn't messed up my benefits." She glanced up at me. "When I had this problem before, Fran called them up and got them to reduce the repayments to about three pounds. Do you think you'll be able to do the same?"

Fran. I couldn't escape her, could I? Well, I refused to let her disrupt my schedule. Risk assessing was essential to reducing harm, although I was sure the likes of Fran just saw it as another meaningless paper exercise.

"Well, I can see what I can do. Maybe we can give them a call next time I visit? We need to update this risk assessment today."

Stacey sighed and pulled her white cardigan around her body.

"So, I'll make a note here that you would like to reduce your repayments. The next section is housing. Is that all okay? Rent up to date?"

"Well, I got a few letters when my housing benefit was stopped, but it's all okay now, other than a bit of arrears for my service charge."

I nodded as I scribbled down some notes.

"Good. Are you making extra payments to clear the arrears?"

Stacey laughed again.

"Well, no, because I'm having to repay the loan at the minute. I'll get onto that once I've paid back the social."

My pen paused. I looked up. Stacey was shaking her head at the ceiling, her lips pressed firmly together. I sat up straight in my seat.

"Look, Stacey, I'm sorry if you're finding this process uncomfortable. But I'm just trying to make sure that you're as safe as possible and reduce the risk of lots of things, like homelessness, poverty, everything. Do you understand?"

Stacey met my gaze for the first time that day.

"Yes I do. And I am trying to reduce risk to myself and my daughter by doing everything I can to keep my head above water. Do you understand?"

I looked at her steadily for as long as I could before returning to my work.

"Of course. Now, let's move on, shall we?" I turned my attention to the next category on my form. My heart sank.

"So, alcohol misuse. Are you still abstinent?"

My pen hovered above the page. Stacey was silent for a moment.

"Well, yes."

I hesitated.

"I have to say I'm a bit concerned about the bottles next to your bin, Stacey."

I hated the school teacher-ish tone of my voice.

"I had a few friends over last night. A friend had offered to look after the baby so I thought I'd have a bit of a party. Nothing major, just a bit of a catch-up with people, that's all."

I looked up again. Stacey had pulled the sleeves of her cardy over her hands and was furiously picking at the cuffs.

"So, did you have a drink?"

"Well, I had a bit, but nothing major. It was a one-off."

I sucked the air between my teeth.

"Okay, but you know how easy it is to fall off the wagon, Stacey. And you have your daughter to think about…"

"You think I don't know that?" The sharpness of her tone made me jump. Stacey was on her feet, pacing in front of the window. The strips of light from behind the half-closed blind haphazardly highlighted her lumpy body. I looked at my form again. I'd made a line across the page when she'd startled me. I'd have to re-write it and get her to sign it next week.

"Sorry, Emily, I didn't mean to snap. I just get nervous about these things." She pointed her sleeve at the papers in my lap. "I worry in case something stupid like having a couple of glasses of wine will make Social Services go berserk and get them thinking about taking away my little girl again." She blinked rapidly. "I just don't think I can bear the thought of it."

I watched her for a moment as she dabbed at her eyes. Her emotional state was doing little to convince me that all was okay.

"Look, Stacey, no one wants to take your little girl away. I just need to know if you are at risk of a relapse so that I can put in place the support that you need to prevent that from happening. It's for the best, for you and your daughter."

Stacey sniffed to herself for a bit before sitting back down opposite me.

"Okay, fair enough. Well, I can tell you now that there is absolutely nothing to worry about. Last night was a one-off. There is no way I'm going to start drinking again, so you really don't need to worry about it. And you certainly don't need to list it as a risk on your form."

I looked from her to my papers.

"I don't know, Stacey, I'm not sure that I'm comfortable with that. And I certainly think I need to make Social Services aware."

"No!" She was on her feet again. "There's no need. You're worrying about nothing. I mean, if a dieter lost loads of weight then ate a chocolate bar, you wouldn't immediately assume they are going to get fat again, would you?"

I was watching her carefully. Although what she was saying made sense, there was something about her desperation that made me uneasy.

"I know you're just doing your job, Emily, but you have to believe me, there isn't an issue here. I know I might seem a bit strung out, but I'm nervous about people poking about in my life again. I've moved on, and I want to be able to continue to move on without anyone holding me back. Do you get me?"

I looked at her round face. Her earnest gaze met mine with ease. I sighed.

"Okay, Stacey. But please tell me if you start drinking regularly again so we can do something about it. Deal?"

Her shoulders softened.

"Deal."

I made a few notes on my form as she sank back into her sofa. When I looked up again she was clicking a message into her phone, her face the picture of calm. Her message sent, she tucked her mobile into her pocket and looked at me expectantly, a smile on her face. Relieved, I smiled back.

"Okay, so shall we move on? Health. Any problems there, Stacey?"

12

"Well, cheers."

I dutifully clinked Fran's pint with my large red wine and took a sip. I noted with amusement the irony that, since working at Drug and Alcohol Action, my dislike of the heavy liquid had disappeared. In fact, rather than seeing it as a necessary evil, I quite enjoyed it.

"So, how was your day?"

Fran was busy ripping into a bag of crisps. I watched her as she carefully tore the packet open to expose its contents. A smudge of red lipstick on her front tooth flashed at me when she spoke.

"Um, it was okay. Spent most of it getting on top of reviewing cases, but managed a couple of visits this morning."

Fran smiled, her lips pressed together as though suddenly aware of her make-up malfunction, and shook her head.

"You're certainly good at keeping up with your paperwork, hen. I wish I was as good at it as you are."

Fran popped a crisp into her mouth before washing it down with a gulp of beer. She pushed the packet across the table towards me and gestured for me to follow her lead. I felt her expectant eyes on me as I took one. I shrugged.

"Well, I guess I'm just good at being organised. We all have different strengths at the end of the day."

I wasn't going to thank her for her compliment, or offer her one in return. Over the last few weeks it had become quite clear that Fran had a problem with my way of working and was affronted by my refusal to adopt her slap-dash approach to supporting our clients.

Fran nodded enthusiastically as she crunched through another mouthful of oily starch.

"Too true, hen. So, is everything else going okay? Are those lot treating you well?"

"If by 'those lot' you are referring to the service users on my caseload, then yes," I bristled. Fran looked up, meeting my gaze full on for the first time that evening. She put her hand over her mouth as she desperately tried to swallow her food before bursting with mirth.

"Yes, Emily, that is what I meant." Regaining her composure, she sat back in her chair and folded her arms in her lap. Her eyes were still sparkling with amusement as they searched my face. "I'm sorry, but you take everything so seriously. In fact, you've seemed a little stressed and, if I'm honest, been a bit snappy for a while now. Are you sure you're okay?"

Her head had dropped to one side, her mocking smile softened to one of concern. I couldn't help but let my icy exterior melt a little. I concentrated on lifting my wine to my lips.

"I'm fine. I just sometimes feel like some people don't think I'm capable of doing this job."

I managed to keep my voice even, but the truth of my words hit me as I spoke them out loud. Fran, my dad, Eric, even my clients... none of them seemed to have any faith in me. Quickly I took another mouthful from my glass. Fran's hand landed softly on my wrist as it returned to the table.

"Em, no one thinks that, honey. It's just…" She paused for a moment, her eyes searching the pub behind me for inspiration. "I just think that sometimes you put a lot of pressure on yourself to do things and figure out how to approach difficult situations on your own rather than asking for help. Not that I'm saying that you don't know what you're doing," she added quickly, raising the hand that had been resting on my arm in defence. "It's just that, at the end of the day, you're very young and very inexperienced in this field, and I worry that you plough your way through things on your own when there are a lot of people around you who are more than willing to give you a hand."

I sat in silence as Fran finished her speech, my gaze resting on my drink. Around me the other patrons of the pub chattered away. Somewhere behind me a man laughed too loudly. Glasses clinked together awkwardly behind the bar as they were shoved back onto the shelves in handfuls.

"Hen?"

I looked up. Fran was watching me, her forearms resting on the sticky dark wood between us. I squeezed my eyes together in an exaggerated blink and looked at her brightly.

"Sorry, Fran, I was in my own little world for a moment then."

She smiled softly.

"You were, weren't you? Anyway, I hope you don't mind me saying that. I want you to be able to come to me if things get a bit tricky, that's all. Okay?"

She raised her eyebrows expectantly. I hesitated.

"Okay. But I do know what I'm doing, and I'm doing things my way."

I impressed myself with the certainty of my voice. I knew that, at the end of the day, I had to do things differently. I was never going to make a difference if I took the same old tack that had failed my clients for so many years.

"Good for you, Emily. In fact it's a philosophy I stick to myself." She raised her glass, already nearly half empty. "Here's to doing things 'Our Way'."

She sang out the last two words in a warbling tenor, her free hand held out to aid her failing Sinatra impersonation. I couldn't help but giggle as I clinked her glass. She grinned back at me.

"That's more like it. I don't like to see my girls looking too serious all the time." She took another swig from her glass before slamming it onto the table and rubbing her hands together theatrically.

"Anyway, enough work talk. Tell me what else is going on with you."

I giggled again despite myself as I sipped my wine. The alcohol was warming me up nicely. In fact, I was starting to feel a bit bad about my attitude towards Fran of late.

"Well?" she pressed as she helped herself to another handful of crisps.

I shrugged. "Oh, nothing much."

It was the truth. I hadn't seen Lorraine in weeks, and my flatmates weren't exactly a sociable bunch. Beatrice had been away for days, and even when she was back in London she was hardly ever home. As for Dad, well, I hadn't spoken to him in over a fortnight.

"Oh, come on. You must have some gossip for me? How are you finding living in London? Been anywhere exciting?"

I pulled a face.

"Oh, you know, the usual. The British Museum, the Tate, St Paul's. Camden Market."

Fran's face matched my own.

"Camden Market? Oh, hen, you can do so much better than that. It's got so commercial and touristy. Try Spitalfields and Brick Lane on a Sunday. Much better."

"Oh okay," I beamed. The truth was I hated Camden Market's hustle and bustle too, but had added it to my list in the hope that Fran would approve.

"The Tate is pretty cool, though. I just love the Turbine Hall, they always have something really interesting there." Fran polished off the last of the crisps with a frown. "What's there at the moment?"

"I dunno. I think they're changing over the exhibition."

The truth was, I hadn't really looked. In fact I'd only stayed in the building for about twenty minutes. Modern art wasn't for me either. The Tate Britain was much more my thing, and much quieter.

"Oh. I'll have to look at *Time Out* and see who's coming up next. Haven't been there in ages." Fran rose her gaze to the heavens and grinned. I smiled back uncertainly. The conversation was getting far too close to exposing the reality of my solitary existence to my colleague – Fran, the cool girl, with all her friends, who everyone loved. Fran, who could do no wrong at work, and was worshipped by all her clients, old and new.

"So…" She was folding the crisp packet into a neat little triangle. "Any nice young men on the scene? Or women, for that matter?" Her lopsided smile reached towards a raised eyebrow. My own face burned.

"Well, certainly no women," I laughed, trying to sound less horrified than I actually was that she had even considered that I might be a lesbian. Fran nodded with self-assurance.

"Fair enough. Just don't like to make assumptions about these things." Her eyes twinkled. "So, what about members of the opposite sex, then?"

I found myself grinning like an idiot once more. The wine had well and truly loosened me up. I was dying to tell someone about the chemistry between me and David, but didn't know how she'd react.

"Ah, so there is someone, is there? Go on, spill the beans. Is it anyone I know?"

I giggled again as I tried to sip my wine. Fran shook her head and slid out from her chair.

"Okay, lady, I'm going to pop to the loo then I'll get us another drink in. The same again?"

I looked at the glass in my hand. It was almost empty. Fran downed the remainder of her pint before looking at me pointedly.

"Well?"

I nodded mutely, my foolish grin still plastered across my face.

"Good girl." Fran winked before disappearing from view. I looked behind me and watched her as she strode across the pub towards the toilets. Several pairs of eyes followed her as she passed through, some with distaste at her unconventional appearance but most with admiration – or desire. As she disappeared through the door I turned back to the table and swallowed the last mouthful in my glass. A guffaw rose from next to the bar. I looked up to see a group of Suits, ties loosened and jackets off, watching me with amusement. I averted my eyes back to the table, my face hot. They must have seen me watching Fran like a lovesick puppy. I felt my eyes burn along with my cheeks and dived into my bag for a prop to distract me – and to make me look like less like a loner. I pulled out my phone and opened up my messages. There were no new ones. The last one I had received from Lorraine was over three weeks ago and my dad had never got into texting. Or texting me, at least. I busied myself scrolling through Lorraine's messages. One- or two-word replies to my ramblings. I considered writing her another. The men at the bar cheered and laughed again. I looked over from behind the curtain of hair that had dropped across my face. Fran was standing next to them, one hand on her hip, the other resting on the bar. Her lips were pressed together in an amused pout, her eyebrows raised. A comment from one of the Suits split open her red mouth as she hollered with laughter.

I looked back down at my phone and rapidly composed a message.

Hi Lorraine, how are you? Im out with fran from work, shes really cool. Fancy meeting up soon? Emily xxx

I pressed send hurriedly and shoved my phone back into my bag as Fran headed back to our table. She spilt some of her beer onto the table as she dumped our drinks in front of me.

"Ah, caught you in the act! Was that him who you were texting? Hope it wasn't anything naughty, young lady?"

She laughed at herself as she plonked back down into her seat. I couldn't help but laugh along with her.

"No, just texting Lorraine. I haven't been in touch with her for a while. I've just been so busy," I lied breezily.

"Oh okay. I believe you, thousands wouldn't." She took a swig of her fresh pint before leaning across the table towards me. "Now tell."

I struggled to meet her intense gaze.

"It's nothing, really." If my laugh betrayed my unease, Fran was too merry to notice.

"Oh, so what then? It's just sex?" Her raised eyebrow punctuated her last word. I nearly choked on my wine.

"No! No, I mean, there's just someone that I've connected with. It's complicated. Nothing's happened."

"Yet!" Fran hooted before collapsing into a fit of laughter. Helplessly I joined in.

"Who is it, then?" Fran asked as soon as she was able to speak again. "Someone at work?"

I shrugged nonchalantly and gulped down another mouthful of wine. Fran's eyes widened.

"I knew it! Is it Jim? I know he really likes you..."

The shaking of my head stopped her dead in her tracks. Grabbing her drink, she frowned.

"Oh. Well, who else do you really talk to at work? Andrew? Gary?"

I shook my head firmly as I giggled. Fran sat back in her seat and folded her arms.

"Who, then?" she pouted.

"You'll never guess."

"Well, if you like your men older, I guess it could be Eric."

I opened my mouth in horror. Fran threw back her head.

"I'm sorry, I couldn't resist," she laughed. I straightened myself in my chair.

"There's older, then there's old," I said primly.

"So they are older..." Fran's eyes roamed around the pub again. Suddenly they snapped onto mine. Her mouth dropped open a little.

"Not David?"

I squeezed my eyes shut and nodded before falling into another fit of merriment. When I opened my eyes I saw that Fran hadn't joined in. That small telltale line between her eyebrows had appeared, although she was smiling. My laughter subsided swiftly.

"Hen, you know he's married, don't you?"

I cleared my throat.

"Yes, but he's really not happy. It's practically over."

Fran's eyebrows shot up again.

"He told you that?"

I raised mine back at her as I took a sip of wine.

"Well, in so many words, yes."

She leant back and let her hands fall to her lap. Blowing out her cheeks she shook her head.

"Well, I have to say I'm surprised. Are you sure?"

I felt that old irritation spike through my inebriation.

"Yes, Fran, I'm sure," I retorted. Fran held up her hands.

"Okay, I believe you. Just… be careful there, Em. That's all."

"Why?"

"Because he's married!" she spluttered. "And he's got kids. No matter what he says, they aren't about to just disappear into thin air. And trust me, when a man says that his marriage is over, that doesn't necessarily mean that it is. Experience has taught me that." She shook her head to herself and she raised her glass to her lips. I watched her in silence.

"The other thing you need to remember is his age," she continued, oblivious to the outrage that was rising inside me. "When a bloke approaches forty, he starts to panic. They realise that their youth is slipping away from them and they grasp onto it any way that they can. Whether that's by going out and getting drunk every night, buying a stupidly inappropriate car or starting an affair with a younger woman." She glanced at me. I stared back, my eyes boring into hers until she looked away.

"I'm sorry, Emily, I just don't think it's a good idea," she said quietly. I nodded dumbly as angry tears sprang to my eyes. She was right, it wasn't an easy situation, but what my colleague had failed to understand was that my feelings were beyond some kind of hot-headed fling. They were deeper than that – and so were David's. Something that for Fran, with her liberal views and carefree approach to relationships, was clearly beyond comprehension. She leant across the table once more and rested her hand on mine. "Hen…"

I pulled it away quickly and blinked up at her. Her frown had deepened.

"Don't 'hen' me," I snapped. "You're just jealous."

Fran's mouth opened wide. "Jealous? Not even close!"

"Just because you don't get on with David doesn't mean that other people can't. Some men are interested in more than some skimpy clothes, a sexy tattoo and red lipstick," I continued. Any trace of humour evaporated from Fran's face. She watched me blankly as I furiously wiped at my eyes.

"Okay, hen. I'm assuming you're just saying that because you're upset. But what I am telling you is purely because I don't want to see you get hurt, or used, or worse." She pulled her rucksack towards her and carefully stood up. "Anyway, I think we've both had more than enough to drink for one night. Let me get you to the tube."

"I don't need your help, Fran," I sniffed, grappling for my bag, my sight impaired by my tears. "I can get home perfectly fine by myself." Unsteadily I pulled myself to my feet and made my way over to the door. Someone tutted as I banged into them, but I didn't care. As I pushed open the heavy door I heard Fran call my name behind me. I let the door swing shut behind me and took a deep breath. A mixture of bus fumes and cigarette smoke hit my lungs and my stomach simultaneously. Blindly, I stumbled towards the tube, grabbing onto anything I could to help me on my way.

I managed to get to the Underground entrance before the cocktail of wine and city air made me sick.

13

"Yeah?"

"Hi, Ian, it's Emily. Your new support worker?"

I didn't catch Ian's muttered response through the crackling intercom, but the door buzzed open. I stepped into the lobby and walked quickly over to the lift. It seemed like an age since I had last been in the block with Fran. Either the stench of urine had got worse and the hallway even dingier, or my memory had been kind. Instinctively I held my breath as the lift approached the fifth floor.

The Indian summer sun illuminated the disrepair and dubious stains along the balcony. Ska music I vaguely recognised blared out from Ian's flat. I knocked firmly on the open door and waited. The hallway was cleaner than I remembered, the piles of unopened post and coating of filth absent from view. Wondering if I'd got the wrong flat, I tentatively knocked again.

"Yeah yeah, come in, will yer?"

The gritty voice eliminated my doubts. I took a deep breath before diving into the flat. Stale smoke tinged the air rather than dominating it. Either that or I was just getting used to working in such an environment. In the living room, Ian was sitting in his armchair. If it wasn't for the absence of grey stubble and the replacement of his grubby T-shirt with a checked shirt, I would have doubted that he had actually moved since I visited with Fran almost three months ago.

Fran. Memories of last night hit me in my stomach, still tender from my purge outside Camden Town station.

"Oh yeah, I remember you."

Ian eyed me warily as I walked over to the sofa. The floor was clear of empty beer cans, the towers of books reduced to a conservative pile of three paperbacks at his feet. I pushed Fran's hurt face out of my mind and smiled brightly at my client.

"Good morning, Ian. How are you today?"

He stared at me blankly for a long moment before allowing a throaty chuckle to escape.

"All the better for seeing you." He nodded his head towards the battered leather sofa. "Go on, sit down."

Obediently I did as I was told before pulling out my notepad and phone. My obligatory call to the office complete, I turned my attention back to Ian. A small smile had cracked across his face.

"Very business like, aren't you?"

"I like to think of it as being professional, Ian."

His caustic laugh made my cheeks burn. I waited as his laughter morphed into a hacking cough, trying to ignore the rattle of phlegm on his chest.

"Now, shall we turn our attention back to you, Ian? After all, that's why we are here, isn't it?"

Ian wiped away the spittle around his mouth with the back of his hand.

"Well, I think I'm a lot less interesting. How old are you, anyway?"

I took a deep breath.

"I'm not sure what that has got to do with anything, Ian. Now, how have you been? I have to say, you're looking better than you did when I first met you."

"Well, there you go. I'm doing better. That's your first question answered." Ian's eyes gleamed beneath his dark grey eyebrows. "Now you answer mine? What are you? Twenty-five?"

"I'm nearly twenty-three," I said, instinctively sitting taller in my seat. Ian's mouth popped open.

"Twenty-two, then? Fucking 'ell."

"So, Fran told me in our handover that you've stopped drinking again? That's really good."

Ian snorted.

"It's really fucking boring, that's what it is." The repeat of the profanity made me wince. He cocked his head to one side. "You don't like swearing, do you?"

I hoped my shrug was as indifferent as I intended.

"Well, I just don't see the need for it. There's so many other words in the English language that we can use that are a lot more expressive."

"I disagree." Ian's eyes bored into mine. "That's right, you're a reader, aren't you? How did you get on with that book I leant you? You know, *The Girl with the Dragon Tattoo*?"

My face burned as I remembered Ian's gift when I had first met him. The truth was I had thrown the tatty paperback into the recycling bin as soon as I had got home. It wasn't that I didn't want to read it, but the stench of tobacco emanating from its pages had been too much for me to bear. I had bought a new copy from the Waterstones across the road from the office as soon as I had heard that Ian was coming onto my caseload, but my third reading of *Jane Eyre* had prevented me from even turning over the front cover. I had intended to start it last night, but my trip to the pub with Fran had put that plan to rest.

"Oh, it was okay. Not my usual cup of tea, but very interesting all the same."

Ian nodded slowly.

"Interesting, you say? What did you make of the heroine? What was her name?"

I puffed out my cheeks and let my eyes wander across the room.

"Oh, gee, I can't remember. I liked her though."

"Identified with her, did you?"

Ian's cool gaze was starting to make me feel uncomfortable. I hesitated for a moment.

"Yes. Yes, I think I did."

The smile that crept across my client's haggard face did nothing to reduce my unease.

"Really?"

I shrugged.

"Well, yes. Why, did you?"

"Well, I wouldn't go that far. But she certainly had something going for her. I'd fuck her any day of the week. Not sure I'd say the same about the mouse in front of me."

Ian's expression remained static as I stared back at him. Desperately I searched through the training manual I had memorised from the course David had made me do only weeks before for an appropriate challenge.

"What's the matter, Little Miss Professionalism? Cat got your tongue?"

I snapped shut my gaping mouth and swallowed.

"I'm not sure that is an appropriate thing to say, Ian."

The words were strangled by my dry throat.

"No shit. Well, let me tell you something. Our girl with the dragon tattoo wouldn't stand for that kind of behaviour either. In fact, if she was sat where you are now, she would probably have chopped my balls off by now. But then I guess if you'd read the book you'd know that yourself."

I looked down at the open page of my notebook, as blank as my mind. The hot blood pulsing through my head was starting to make me feel faint.

"Anyway, shall we move on?"

I heard Ian's seat creak and looked up quickly. The smile on his face as he pulled a crumpled pack of tobacco from his pocket and began to roll a cigarette made my skin prickle cold. His roll-up between his lips, he glanced up at me before flicking open his lighter.

"So we've established that I've stopped drinking, am bored shitless, and have an unhealthy interest in shagging fictitious Swedes. And that you're barely out of nappies, are really bad at lying and shock way too easily." He craned his neck to take a look at my notebook. "So what's next on the agenda?"

I followed his gaze, silently cursing myself for having not prepared for my visit a little better. Of course I had intended to print off the support plan that Fran had completed with him in preparation for her handover but, in my hurry to follow my colleague to the pub yesterday, had forgotten. The anger that seeped through me whenever Fran interfered with my professional – and now private – life returned with a vengeance. Images of her and Ian laughing together as they discussed my ineptitude flashed through my mind like a silent movie.

"Well?"

I looked up to see Ian inspecting his yellowing fingernails, his sickening smile still firmly in place. I took a deep, jarring breath. I was not going to let these two get the better of me.

"Well, Ian, I think I am going to terminate this visit." The look of surprise on his face strengthened my resolve. "I am not willing to continue this interview if you are going to speak to me in such a disrespectful manner."

With shaking hands I pushed my notebook and phone back into my satchel. As I stood up Ian broke his silence with yet another cackle. I looked at him with as much disdain as I could muster.

"Is something funny, Ian?"

Ian stopped laughing almost as suddenly as he started, but his leer remained firmly in place.

"Yes, something is funny. I guess I got you wrong after all."

"Maybe you did, Ian. I shall write to you with another appointment for next week. Let's just hope that by then you've had time to think about your behaviour today and can conduct yourself more properly."

I lifted my bag onto my shoulder and walked stiffly towards the door.

"Yeah, I got you wrong alright. I think I'd fuck you after all."

I hesitated in the doorway, willing a witty retort to materialise in the midst of my confusion. Ian started to choke on his own mirth before fitting words would come into my mind. Burning with rage, I hurried through the hallway and out onto the balcony. Seeing that the lift was occupied I ran down the stairs, only slowing down once the bus stop that would take me back to the sanctuary of the office was in sight.

14

"Come in."

Slowly I opened the door to Eric's office. David was standing at the corner desk, stooped over the keyboard he was frantically punching with slender fingers. His white shirt hung loose around his hips, the sleeves rolled up to above his elbows, exposing those toned arms, still tanned by the late summer sun. He glanced up at me and grinned before turning back to his work.

"Well, hello there. Take a seat and I'll be with you in one sec." Triumphantly he clicked his mouse and straightened his back with a groan. "Bloody hell. Emily, do yourself a favour and never get old, will you?"

"Oh, you're not old, David." My face coloured instantly at my clumsy comment. David laughed loudly as I carefully sat at the table.

"Thank you very much, but we'll have to agree to disagree on that one. Having such a bright-eyed and bushy-tailed team of support workers doesn't help with my sense of antiquity, mind. I'm going to have to start recruiting old age pensioners to get the balance right."

I looked up from my notebook, my eyes wide. He smiled at me warmly for a long moment before turning back to the monitor.

"Okay, so enough about me being an old codger. Let me just grab your last supervision's notes from the printer then we'll get down to business, okay?"

He smiled at me again as he strode out of the room. As the vibrations of his footsteps across the office pulsed through me I wondered if he knew what effect those dimples had on women – on me – when he smiled like that.

"Okay, we're good to go." He slammed the door shut and sat on the chair next to me in one swift movement. I glanced at the small space between us before turning my attention back to the printout David had placed in front of me. He was so close I could smell his citrusy aftershave.

"So, was there anything you wanted to add to the agenda before we start?"

I hesitated.

"Well, I've been having a bit of trouble with one of my clients. And I wondered if we could talk about some team issues too. If that's okay?" My visit to Ian's flat the week before was still playing on my mind – along with what seemed to have become an ongoing conflict with Fran. I was still ridiculously angry with her and had avoided her as much as I could get away with since our night in the pub.

David shrugged, his eyebrows slightly raised, as he noted my request. "Sure. Well, can we discuss your difficult client when we go through your cases and address the other thing at the end?"

I nodded silently, my lips pressed together. David finished scribbling on his page and looked up at me. I met his gaze with difficulty.

"So how have things been? How you doing generally?"

It was my turn to shrug.

"Okay, I think."

David nodded enthusiastically.

"Good. Is there anything specific stopping it from being more than okay for you?"

I shifted in my seat.

"Well, other than the things I've asked you to add to the agenda, I don't think so. I'm just struggling with a couple of things, that's all."

David smiled, his dimples returning.

"Okay then. Well, from where I'm sitting, you seem to be doing very well. Your case management skills are excellent and you look to be really on top of everything when it comes to dealing with any difficulties that crop up."

"Thanks," I said quietly, carefully keeping my pleasure at his words in check. David dropped his head and peered at my face, his eyebrows raised in obvious amusement.

"I mean it, Emily. You're doing really well. Learn to accept a compliment, okay?"

I giggled despite myself and stole a look through the slats of the blind out into the corridor. The office was almost deserted.

"Okay. So, no issues with leave or sickness, right?" David frowned at the papers in front of him. "I don't think you've taken a day off since you started."

I sat up straight in my seat and nodded. The lines across his forehead deepened. "Well, make sure you get to use all your leave entitlement before the end of the year. They don't really let you carry it over anymore, you know."

"Oh, that's okay. I don't think I'll need to use it all anyway."

David's pen paused mid-sentence before he dropped it. He sat up in his chair and stared at me, his mouth open.

"Sorry, what? You don't want to use all your leave?"

I giggled again. "Well, I don't have any holidays or anything planned yet. I don't feel like I need it."

David puffed out his cheeks and shook his head slowly.

"Well, if you don't want it, or need it, I'll take it." He shook his head again, his eyes wide, before cracking into another grin. "Seriously though, make sure you do take regular breaks, okay? This work can be really challenging and I don't want you burning out." He held up his hand as I started to protest. "I'm not saying that I think you will or anything, just... look after yourself, okay? Take a couple of long weekends and go see your dad or friends or something. Deal?"

Deciding better than to argue I smiled and nodded again. The concern on David's face smoothed into another of his smiles.

"Good. Now, shall we move on to your caseload? Who do you want to start with?" He glanced at his notes. "Stacey? How is she doing?"

I pulled a face.

"Okay, I think. She's been a bit stressed lately with her benefits and stuff but seems to have got over it."

"Good stuff. So her money's sorted now?"

"Yes."

"And she's got through it without a lapse?"

I hesitated as Stacey's round face loomed into my mind. At her request, I hadn't recorded her alcohol-fuelled night in her risk assessment.

"I think so, yes. No signs of one anyway."

David's eyebrows disappeared under the mop of hair that had fallen over his forehead. I wondered how he would react if I was to brush it aside for him as he noted down my lie.

"That's fantastic. Real progress. A year ago she would have gone on a real bender in that situation and probably ended up in hospital." He looked up at me, his hair still dangling in front of his eyes, and smiled. "Well done."

I grinned back before quickly averting my eyes down to my own notebook. I scribbled down a pointless record of his observation myself.

"So, what is happening about her getting back into work? She wanted to go back to college or something, didn't she?"

I took a sip from my bottle of water as I tried to remember. Being alone in David's company was proving to be very distracting.

"Yes, she did. I think that all the benefits stuff has got in the way of it a bit, to be honest."

He sat up in his chair and rolled his shoulders back into a stretch. I averted my eyes from his chest as it pressed against his shirt.

"Fair enough. But now it's all sorted, maybe that's something you can pick up on again? From what Fran has said before she's a smart girl and needs something meaningful in her life. Other than her daughter, of course," he added, holding up his hands again. I giggled but avoided looking up at his face. "So, is that cool?"

"Sure. I've already started researching opportunities for her." Another lie. The reality was I couldn't wait to get rid of her and that child from my caseload. My visits just seemed like a waste of time.

"Excellent. But make sure you don't do all the donkey work for her. She needs to feel confident to look into these things for herself at the end of the day." My perma-smile faded slightly. I dared to look up at David's face. He was beaming back at me. "Don't look so worried, Em. You're doing fine. Honest."

He held my gaze for a moment longer before turning back to his notes.

"So, shall we move on? Ian. He's just come onto your caseload, hasn't he? How's he getting on?"

I took a deep breath.

"Well, he seems to be doing a lot better than he was when I first met him. His flat is cleaner and tidier, and he's stopped drinking."

David shook his head as he noted my observations.

"Wow. Another success story in the making. So what is he doing to keep himself dry? AA? Meditation? Flower arranging?"

"Well, he reads a lot," I offered.

"Mmm, he always has been a reader has our Ian." David leant back in his seat and folded his arms. "He was one of my clients when I started working here, you know. Really quite an interesting guy. Very smart. I guess the challenge is how do we keep him distracted from the drink in the long term?"

I chewed my lip as David studied the exposed brickwork of the office wall. I took a deep breath.

"When you worked with Ian, was he ever... rude to you?"

David's eyes sped back to mine.

"Ian? Rude?" His mouth twitched with amusement. "You could say that, yes. I'm afraid it comes with the territory with people who've been dealt the hand that he has, Emily."

My face flushed instantly.

"I know that. But what I mean is, has he ever been inappropriate before?"

Confusion clouded David's features.

"Well, some of the things he called me in the early days were less than flattering. Why? What has he been up to?"

I hesitated as I tried to find the right words.

"When I visited him last week he started making comments about my age. Then he... he started to make comments about wanting to sleep with me." I swallowed, hoping the action would keep the tears that threatened my eyes – and the blood rising to my face – at bay.

"You're kidding me, right?"

I dared to glance up at David. All trace of humour had left his face as he gazed at mine. I quickly looked back down at my notebook again. David took a deep breath.

"Well, that certainly does fall into the category of inappropriate, doesn't it?" he said softly. "What had you been talking about before?"

I shrugged.

"Well, books."

"And he appeared sober at the time?"

"Yes."

David must have picked up the tremor in my voice. As I discreetly wiped my eye his hand rested on my shoulder.

"I'm sorry, Emily. That was bang out of order of him. How did you leave it?"

His hand was still there, its warmth radiating through the thin cotton of my T-shirt.

"I told him that I was terminating the visit and would write to him with another appointment."

"And have you arranged the appointment?"

"Yes. It's on Friday."

David took another deep breath. He gently squeezed my shoulder before removing his hand. When I dared to look at him again he was slowly running his fingers through his hair.

"Okay. That gives us a few days. Let me have a word with Fran to see if she has had any similar experiences with him. Maybe I should re-allocate him back to her."

"No!"

David looked at me, the usual humour back in his eyes.

"No?"

I took a steadying breath and closed my eyes.

"I can handle it, David. I just need a bit of... reassurance, that's all."

I kept my eyes shut as he silently registered my comment, willing his hand to return to me.

"Okay."

I opened my eyes slowly. David was rubbing the side of his face as he watched me, his eyebrows drawn together.

"I still think we need to talk to Fran about this…" He raised his eyebrows as I opened my mouth to protest and carried on. "Just because we need to know if this, or anything similar or worse even, has happened before. To help us risk assess if nothing else. Okay?"

I clamped my mouth shut, silenced by the resolve in his voice. His eyes were wide, his jaw visibly tense. I looked down at my hands, limp in my lap.

"Emily?"

I nodded dumbly.

"It's got nothing to do with your performance or anything. I just need to know what we are dealing with here. Fran has worked with Ian for quite a while and knows him pretty well. She will probably be able to shed some light on where this has come from."

"I know, it's just…" My hands became obscured by a veil of tears. "It's just, I don't want Fran to think that I can't work with Ian. That's all." I brushed the back of my hand across my cheek, angry at myself for getting so upset, angry at Ian for putting me in this position, angry at Fran for getting involved in one of my cases again, willingly or not.

"Emily. Look at me."

I glanced up at him from behind my beaded eyelashes. David was smiling down at me again, his head slightly to one side.

"Fran has no reason to believe that you can't deal with this situation, or any other for that matter. She's been working with you for, what, three or four months now and knows as well as I do that you are more than competent at your job."

I held his gaze for a moment longer before returning it to my hands.

"I don't know that she does, actually."

I had intended to raise my concerns about Fran during our meeting but I had hoped that they would have come out in a less adolescent manner. I pulled my shoulders back and rested my eyes on the table in front of me, hoping that my change in posture would return a level of professionalism to my demeanour. David's laugh had the dryness of my father's.

"What makes you say that? I hope she hasn't been rude as well. I don't think I can cope with two cases of inappropriate behaviour."

When I failed to respond, I heard David suck in a deep breath.

"Sorry. That wasn't very funny."

I shrugged.

"It's okay."

He sighed.

"No, it isn't. You're having a hard time and I'm being an arsehole. Give me a second chance?"

As soon as I looked at him he was forgiven. His deep blue eyes and mop of dishevelled hair was enough to melt even the steeliest of resolves. Besides, it wasn't David who was the problem. He was doing his best to help me.

To protect me.

I grinned back at him.

"That's my girl." He smiled back. "So, what's going on with Fran? Has she hen-pecked you into oblivion already?"

My girly giggle returned.

"No. It's just that... she seems to criticise everything that I do. Questions everything that I say. At first I thought she was just trying to be helpful but..." I bit my lip. David raised his eyebrows.

"But?"

I twisted my mouth in concentration.

"But it hasn't stopped. If anything it has got worse, even though I think I've explained to her time and time again why I do things my way and not hers."

David's smile widened.

"You mean you're not doing everything our old Scottish battle-axe tells you to do and she doesn't like it?"

Relief flushed my face. He understood. I nodded, my grin firmly in place.

"I see. You want me to have a word?"

I hesitated. I wanted to say yes, just to get her off my back and to make her realise that David appreciated my approach to support work even if she didn't. "I don't know," I sighed. "I don't want her to think I've been running to you and slagging her off."

David appeared to accept my blasé tone.

"Understood – although, as your manager, it is my job to help you with these things," he added firmly. "How about if I promise to do it subtly?"

I acted out further consideration.

"Okay," I said finally, and smiled at him appreciatively. "Thank you."

"You're welcome." He smiled back, all previous tension now released from his beautiful face. "And thank you for telling me what's been going on. It mustn't have been easy. I know you like to solve your own problems, but it's really important to let me know when things get tricky, even if you have a plan on how to deal with it."

I lowered my gaze to my notebook again, overwhelmed by the tenderness in his words.

"Thanks, David," I murmured.

"Like I said, you're welcome. Now, I think we've spent more than enough time on Ian, and Fran, for that matter. Let's move on, shall we?"

I nodded my consent, despite my disappointment. I didn't want the intensity of our conversation to fade. I was excited by the new level of intimacy we had reached in such a short period of time and, as I watched David talk over my next client, I could see in his eyes that he felt the same. I nodded along as he shared with me his insight and tried my best to concentrate. We had a job to do, and he was my manager, and I needed to focus on that. For the moment, anyway.

15

I stared at the conveyor belt as it carried brightly coloured dishes of alien food around the restaurant. Excited chatter distorted the electronic music playing. As I waited for Lorraine I sipped at my complimentary sparkling water, topping it up from the personal water fountain at my table every couple of minutes. She was late again, and I'd already had to ward off three groups from our table, assuring them as well as myself that the rest of my party was on its way. My thoughts of David kept my anxiety at bay, the memory of his smile keeping me company in my solitude.

"Hi, Em."

Lorraine had slipped onto the padded bench opposite me. Reluctantly I returned to the present.

"Hi, Lorraine. How are you?" I chirped, sitting up in my seat and beaming at my old friend. I had resolved to show her a front of self-assurance similar to that she had developed herself whilst living in London. Before leaving work I had carefully re-applied my mascara, which had left a trail of black dandruff on the dark circles under my eyes after my emotional meeting with David, added a sweep of eyeliner along my lower lashes and a dab of red lipstick on my lips. The face that had stared back at me in the badly lit mirror had been mine alright, but the added definition to my features made me look harsh, unnatural. I had dismissed my reservations as a natural reaction against my new look and, after brushing my lank hair and smoothing the clothes covering my skinny frame, strode out of the ladies and down to the high street with my head held high.

Lorraine, content with her own appearance, snapped shut the compact in her hand and popped it into a sleek monochrome handbag. She looked at me wearily.

"Yeah, I'm okay. Bloody knackered though." She looked around the restaurant impatiently. "Where's the bloody waiter? I need a drink."

Within seconds a waitress appeared at our table. In her expensive-looking suit and designer frames, Lorraine seemed to have no problem getting attention. I watched her as she ordered her beer. Her red lipstick seemed to add luminosity to her skin rather than muddying it like my own did. Her blonde hair, whilst poker straight, still managed to have the bounce that my own locks lacked. She looked at me sharply as the waitress left.

"What?"

I looked back at the sushi as it wandered past our table and shrugged.

"Nothing. Was just thinking you looked nice, that's all."

Lorraine's laugh was lower than it used to be.

"I should hope so too. I got my hair done at the weekend. Best part of two hundred quid."

I looked back at her, my mouth hanging open.

"Really?"

"Really." Her gaze met mine for the first time that evening. She smirked before turning her attention to her iPhone. "By the way, you have a blob of mascara or something under your eye."

I rubbed away the faux pas as discreetly as I could as she tapped a quick message.

"So, shall we eat? I'm bloody starving," she muttered, snapping up the menu and scanning it swiftly. Flipping it over, she sucked at her teeth. "Don't they have the calories listed on this thing?"

"Well, it's sushi, so it can't be that bad." I hoped that I sounded knowledgeable. Eighteen months ago Lorraine wouldn't have given such trivialities a thought. When we were students Lorraine didn't carry designer handbags and would have balked at the thought of spending more than forty pounds at the hairdressers. Discarding the menu, she snorted.

"You'd think. But it's amazing how these chains add unnecessary carbs to their food. You can get much better sushi in Soho, you know."

I decided against confirming my ignorance on the matter. The only sushi I'd eaten before was from Tesco and, as far as I could tell, the stuff in Yo! Sushi looked exactly the same.

"Well, there's twenty percent off everything today so at least it will save us some money. You know, for hair and clothes," I added.

"True." Lorraine had helped herself to one of the dishes and was inspecting it carefully through its plastic lid. She glanced at me as she placed it in front of her and selected a packet of chopsticks. "So, are you going to do some shopping now you're a fully fledged working girl? You know, update your wardrobe a bit?"

"I've been picking up a few bits here and there. Like this top," I added, carefully retrieving a dish from the cheaper price bracket. Lorraine laughed again.

"Have you thought about shopping somewhere else? I don't know, somewhere a bit more... interesting?"

Even though I wasn't looking at her, I knew that she was eyeing my outfit with distaste. Deliberately I sprinkled some soya sauce onto the lump of rice stuffed with unidentified flesh in front of me.

"I dunno. I'm just trying to look professional, that's all." My voice was tight in my throat.

"Fair enough. But you know you can look professional and attractive, Em. I mean, you're never going to get a boyfriend looking like a rejected nun."

I watched Lorraine in silence as she delicately nibbled at her food. She glanced up at me and raised an eyebrow. I awkwardly swallowed a sliver of raw fish.

"Some people like the understated look," I whispered. Lorraine hooted.

"Like who?"

"Well, someone made a pass at me at work last week. And a colleague of mine is really into me."

For a moment, Lorraine's poise slipped.

"What? Really? Who?" she spluttered, her eyes almost as wide as the frames around them. Coolly I took another sip of my water.

"One of my clients basically told me he wanted to sleep with me. And..."

Lorraine's laughter was crueller than ever.

"You mean one of your addicts? Jesus Christ."

"And my manager is so into me it's embarrassing," I added, ignoring her mirth. Quickly, her laughter subsided. I looked at her as I popped the remainder of my dish in my mouth. Her mouth, a perfect "O", slowly dropped closed as she raised her eyebrows at me.

"Your manager? Wow, you don't waste any time, do you?"

"Nothing's happened. Yet. But the feeling's mutual," I added, smugly selecting another dish from the conveyor belt.

"So there are feelings involved?"

I looked up at Lorraine and frowned.

"Of course. Why?"

"Well, in my experience there is only one reason to sleep with your boss. And it hasn't got anything to do with feelings." Lorraine looked at me pointedly over the top of her glasses. It was my turn to look shocked.

"Oh no, it's nothing like that. We've just clicked, that's all."

Lorraine nodded to herself as she simultaneously ate and played with her phone.

"What's wrong with him, then?"

"Nothing!"

Lorraine slammed her phone on the table and rolled her eyes.

"Then why hasn't anything happened yet?"

I looked around the restaurant desperately, suddenly self-conscious about my disclosure – and my friend's apparent irritation at it. The other patrons carried on with their meals, oblivious to our conversation.

"He's professional, like me. We need to be discreet about it, Lorraine," I said, my voice low.

"If he was that into you it wouldn't make the slightest bit of difference," she continued in the same loud voice. She looked up at me from her food, a smile playing at the corner of her mouth. "It didn't matter to me and Josh, anyway."

"Who?" I didn't bother to hide the disapproval in my voice. I'd lost count of the amount of men Lorraine had slept with since working in PR, something that would have been completely out of character for the girl I had known at uni.

"Josh," she said airily. "He's one of the seniors. He's been really helping me with some of my accounts at work. And he's been showing me how I can land some more impressive ones, too."

"Well, David's been helping me too. In fact, he helps me a lot more than he needs to. We enjoy each other's company."

Lorraine shrugged as she picked up her phone again.

"Okay then. Well, let me know if it actually develops into anything noteworthy."

I glared at her phone, once again getting the attention I had worked hard to secure for an evening for so long.

"It will do. He just needs to let his wife down gently."

Lorraine's gaze snapped up.

"His wife?"

With difficulty I kept my triumphant smile hidden behind my cool façade. "Yes. It's been over for a while, but they've been staying together for the sake of the kids."

Lorraine's eyes widened further. "Kids?"

I nodded through my mouthful. "Yes. It's really sad. I know David feels really bad about it, but she's just cut him out emotionally since they were born."

Lorraine's dark blue eyes didn't flicker as she took a swig at her beer. "And you're sure he's that into you?"

I snorted. "Yes, Lorraine, I'm sure."

"Wow." She hesitated. "Just be careful. It sounds like he has some serious baggage. And, if it all goes wrong, you still have to work with him."

"I know," I nodded. "But when it's serious those things don't matter, right?"

The smile at the corner of Lorraine's mouth flickered as she lifted her drink to her cherry lips.

"Right."

16

The scream jolted me from my book. As it dissolved into a peal of laughter I relaxed back onto my pillow. Rebecca had friends over and their conversation had been growing steadily louder over the last three hours, along with the Latino music booming from her room across the landing. The scented candle burning on my bedside cabinet had done little to disguise the smell of exotic spices that had wafted up the stairs since my flatmate and her cronies had arrived home. The stench had been successful in suppressing my own appetite and had saved me from having to venture downstairs to the kitchen whilst the gaggle of girls made a start on what sounded like several bottles of wine. When they had finally disappeared into Rebecca's lair I had crept downstairs and made myself a couple of slices of toast, noting with amazement that, even when she was entertaining, Rebecca had managed to leave the kitchen spotless. Rebelliously I had left my butter knife in the sink before retreating back to the haven of my room.

I looked at the digital alarm clock next to me. It was almost ten o'clock and the party showed no signs of winding up. With a sigh I sat up to rearrange the nest of pillows I had built at the corner of my bed. Satisfied with my handiwork, I took a sip of my orange juice before settling back with my book. I had finally made a start on *The Girl with the Dragon Tattoo* and, despite having spent the entire evening ploughing through its pages, I was struggling to warm to the bleak storyline and the stark style of its author. I had barely read another line when a scratching at my door offered a welcome distraction. Matt must be home and looking for backup on his way into battle with our less than considerate flatmate. I slid off my bed and pulled my towelling dressing gown over my pyjamas before pulling open the door. Beatrice's cat snaked her way through the gap and around my legs, mewing softly. I looked out into the hallway. It was deserted. With a sigh I closed the door and picked up my feline friend, nuzzling the fur at the back of her neck. Beatrice was away again and Felix had become quite attached to me when she was absent. He crawled onto my lap as soon as I sat him down on the knitted throw next to me and purred loudly as I scratched his chin. Absently I looked around my room. My life stared back at me: the bookshelf heaving with Penguin Classics, the collection of scruffy cuddly toys stuffed among them, the degree certificate blu-tacked to the wall. A framed photo of my mum and dad on their wedding day, blissfully unaware that their marriage would be cut short by their unborn daughter, sat on my utilitarian computer desk. My mobile phone, sitting expectantly on my bedside cabinet, was silent. It had been over a week since I had met Lorraine for dinner and she hadn't replied to any of my texts. Facebook showed her out and about at various locations across the capital, the much older Josh permanently at her side, his white teeth almost as sparkling as the champagne they seemed to be constantly drinking. My dad hadn't called in much longer. In fact, I wasn't sure that my dad had actually called me once since I had moved here.

Felix mewed impatiently as I reached over to my phone, momentarily disturbing his bed. I resumed his massage as I selected my dad's number and pressed call. It rang several times before he picked up.

"Hello?" His voice sounded gruff, like he had been drinking, or sleeping. I hesitated for a moment.

"Hi, Dad, it's me."

"Emily? Are you alright? What time is it?"

I looked at my digital clock again.

"It's five to ten, Dad. Sorry, did I wake you up?"

My dad took a jagged intake of breath and groaned. I could see him now, slumped in his ancient brown armchair, Scotch in one hand, suppressing a yawn as he blinked at the flat screen telly in front of him. A scene I had witnessed practically every night for the first eighteen years of my life – and many more since.

"No, I was just watching the television."

"Anything good?"

My dad snorted. "Doubtful. Anyway, what's up?"

Pointlessly I shrugged.

"Nothing much. I was just thinking about you. I haven't heard from you in a while."

There was momentary silence on the other end of the phone. I bit my lip, regretting already the petulant tone in my voice.

"Well, your father does have his own life, and it's keeping him pretty busy, believe it or not. Besides, I assumed my daughter would be busy getting on with her new life in London?"

I closed my eyes against his irritation.

"Sorry, Dad. I just miss you. That's all."

137

"Emily, we didn't live together for three years whilst you were at university and it never seemed to bother you then. What's brought this on?"

His question caught me off guard. Why did I miss him now? It was true, when I was at uni we hardly spoke. But I was a student then. My dad's life had seemed so distant, so remote – and mine to him.

"I guess it's work, Dad," I concluded. "You know, now we work in similar fields."

"Why? What's wrong with work? Has something happened?" Any concern was disguised by his bark.

"No. Well, I've had a tricky couple of weeks but it's fine, Dad."

My dad suppressed another yawn.

"Well, I did warn you, Emily. I still think you've bitten off more than you can chew."

My heart sank with each word.

"No I haven't, Dad."

"Really."

I thought back over the last couple of weeks. Okay, so maybe I could have handled Ian a bit better, but since my visit with David last week, he had been good as gold. Even Fran, who had tagged along to his appointment this week, had found no reason to complain. In fact, she hadn't criticised me – or said much else to me for that matter – since our night out over two weeks ago.

"Actually, Dad, I think I'm doing really well. I've got one really tricky client but I think we've got a mutual respect for each other now. He used to be a really heavy heroin user and now he's thinking about going back to work and everything." Talking to Ian about getting a voluntary job in the Oxfam bookshop had been David's idea, but I wasn't about to tell my dad that.

"Well, don't hold your breath, Emily. Actions speak louder than words."

"Another of my clients is going back to college this month, too. I'm so proud of her," I gushed, interrupting my dad's cynicism before it could penetrate my confidence.

"Good for her." There was a pause whilst my dad took a sip of his drink. "So how's Lorraine? I haven't seen her in ages."

The truth was my dad had only met Lorraine twice, once when she came home with me during our first year and again when we had graduated. I'd invited her back to Lincolnshire several times since her first visit but she always found some excuse not to go. She'd had the decency not to say why, but even I, who had grown up with my dad, was aware that the atmosphere was less than welcoming.

"She's okay. Really busy with work, and she's got a boyfriend. She looks different too," I added pointlessly.

"Good for her. I had a feeling she'd do well for herself."

Felix leapt out from my lap and padded to the door. Reluctantly I got up to let him out.

"Well, I worry about her. She's lost weight. And she seems so... uptight and impatient all the time."

My dad sighed.

"Give her a break, Emily. She's probably under a lot of pressure, that's all. So, what about that other friend of yours? You know, the one from work?"

It was my turn to sigh. I was beginning to regret calling my dad at all.

"She's okay, Dad. I've not seen much of her lately either."

"Oh." My dad paused, for effect, I was sure. "You know, you're going to have to go out and make an effort to meet some new people down there, Emily. You won't find them moping about at home."

I considered pointing out that I had three flatmates right under my roof but decided against it. Apart from Beatrice, who was never home anyway, the word "mates" could only be loosely applied at best.

"I've got a boyfriend, Dad."

The words were out before the revelation had time to fully register in my head. There was another pause.

"Really?"

I took a deep breath.

"Yes. His name's David. I met him at work."

"So how long has this been going on?"

"Well, we've liked each other pretty much since I started. But we've only just admitted it to each other."

"I see." The line buzzed quietly as my dad digested the news. "Well, be careful. It could get awkward at work if things don't work out."

I smiled smugly to myself.

"Don't worry, Dad, I will. What about you?"

"What about me?"

I'd never asked my dad about his private life before, but then we'd never really spoken about mine either.

"Well, have you met anyone?"

His laughter caught me off guard.

"Me? Oh I don't think so, Emily. I think I'm a bit beyond meeting anyone now."

"It's never too late…"

"It is for me."

The fleeting hint of intimacy in his voice was gone, the usual sharpness back in its place. Desperately I tried to think of something else to say. My dad beat me to it.

"It's getting late. I need to take the dog for a walk before bed."

"Okay, Dad," I almost whispered. I heard him take another sip from his drink.

"I promise to call you. Okay?"

"Okay."

The line clicked dead before I could say goodbye. I let my phone drop onto my bed next to me. Slowly I lifted my legs towards my chest and curled up on top of my duvet as another howl of hilarity pierced the air. Exhaustion was consuming my body, making my eyes droop against the disturbance. I reached over to set my alarm and switch off my lamp before pulling my throw over my body and giving in to the overwhelming desire to sleep.

17

As soon as I walked into the pub, I knew I had got it all wrong. Gathered by the bar my colleagues chattered amongst themselves, modelling office party chic with ease. Day-to-day blouses had been replaced with tops adorned with sequins, 40-denier-clad legs with limbs shimmering in glitter. Even the men had made just the right amount of effort, from Jim in his figure-hugging white shirt to Eric in his red jumper and reindeer antlers.

"Emily! Where've you been?" Fran bounded up to me, her rosy red cheeks matching her trademark mini skirt and the Santa hat perched on top of her dreads. She grinned at me idiotically.

"Wow, you've certainly made an effort, haven't you? Now, let's get you a drink."

She grabbed my free hand and pulled me towards the bar, narrowly missing a bar stool or three in her haste. Dressed in the charcoal shift dress and matching heels I had worn for my cousin's winter wedding two years ago, I teetered after her. As we approached the bar the jovial banter was replaced by hushed tones. I lowered my head, desperate not to meet the gaze of any member of my jury.

"So, what will it be? The usual red?"

I lifted my head only as much as needed to nod my reply. My hand still in hers, Fran squeezed it before letting it go to gesture wildly at the overwhelmed eighteen-year-old at the other end of the bar.

"Anthony! Large glass of Merlot when you're ready, lad."

Anthony acknowledged her order with a nod before returning to the pint he was pulling with shaky hands. His acne-ridden jaw cracked into a smile as he laughed at an unheard joke. David was standing on the other side of the brass pumps, his elbow resting on the sticky wood of the bar. Despite the late hour, he was clean-shaven, his usual shirt replaced with a long-sleeved black V-neck. As I watched he leant away from the bar and threw his head back, his eyes shining and his dimples deepening with his laugh.

"Hen?"

I looked at Fran blankly. Her face morphed from one of concern to one of amusement.

"I said what are you doing for Christmas?"

I ignored the burning in my cheeks and waved my hand vaguely.

"Oh, you know, the usual. Going home to see my dad, catching up with friends. Eating and drinking too much too, I expect." I rolled my eyes. "What about you? You going back home?"

Fran snorted into her pint.

"You're kidding, right? And spend Christmas listening to my folks go on about Jesus and the Virgin and all that shite before being forced to go to Mass only to be lectured about hell and damnation?" She winked. "No thanks. I'll be volunteering at a refuge out near Redbridge."

My mouth fell open involuntarily.

"Really? I can't imagine that being very merry."

Fran smiled sweetly at Anthony and handed over a tenner as he placed my glass of wine on the bar in front of us. She turned back to me as she waited for her change, her face suddenly serious.

"Maybe not in a conventional sense. But delivering presents to the kids and giving their mums chance to unwind for a bit whilst we play games and sing carols is so humbling – it makes me so grateful for, well, everything." She shrugged and smiled. "Plus I get loads of cuddles back from the little ones, so it isn't completely selfless."

I took a sip of my wine and smiled back as I considered my own fruitless plans. In truth, I didn't really want to spend Christmas at my dad's, but I didn't really have much choice. Staying in London on my own would just be admitting to my flatmates that I had no life – an opinion that hadn't been helped by Lorraine. She had cancelled our last two dinner dates, both of which I had proudly announced to Matt before being blown out at the last minute and returning home on my own a little after 6.30.

"Do you think I could come along?" I blurted.

Fran looked at me, her eyes wide.

"You'd really want to, Em?"

"Why wouldn't I?"

Fran shrugged, acknowledging my point whilst ignoring my defensiveness.

"You just didn't sound keen when I first told you what I was doing, that's all. But I'm afraid you have to apply months in advance. They actually get loads of applications – not as many as the shelters, mind, but more than they need. But with your experience, I'm sure you'd get a place. I'll tell you when they're recruiting for next year, if you want?"

"Recruiting for what? I hope you're not leaving us already, Emily?"

It was David, suddenly at my side, his hand on my elbow. His touch sent a fresh wave of heat to my face. His eyes twinkled mischievously as they met mine.

"Oh no, of course not. Fran was just telling me about her voluntary job over Christmas, that's all."

David's eyebrows rose as he gulped down a couple of mouthfuls of Guinness.

"Volunteering again, are you, Fran?"

Fran smiled triumphantly.

"Yes I am, David. And your fine self? Are you doing anything charitable this year?"

"Well, the amount I've spent on the kids so far, I'm looking for a bit of charity myself." He turned to me, his hand still on my arm. "You know how much my last credit card bill was? Eight hundred and sixty pounds. Sterling. And I haven't even got started on the wife yet."

I stifled a giggle as he took another sip of Guinness. Fran sucked at her teeth.

"You know, at their age, I doubt the kids will even be that fussed about their presents. As long as they get a couple of parcels under the tree, get to play some games and eat a few chocolates they'll be content."

"Oh here we go," David interrupted. "The anti-Capitalist brigade has arrived. She's not trying to recruit you onto one of her marches as well, is she?" His eyes wide, David dumped his pint onto the bar and slid closer to me, gripping me with both hands in mock horror. Fran raised a perfectly shaped eyebrow.

"Hey, it's your money, not mine. I'm just saying you don't have to get yourselves into loads of debt to have a good Christmas, that's all."

"Well, you haven't met my kids recently, have you? Demanding doesn't even come close." David dropped his arms, releasing mine, and dug into his jeans pockets. "Anyway, I owe you two a drink. Think of it as your Christmas bonus."

He grinned at me as he pulled out a fistful of change. "So, Emily, what will it be?"

I looked down at my glass, ready to decline. It was almost empty.

"Merlot? Pinot Noir? Chateau Neuf du Pape?"

"Merlot, please," I managed, trying my best to ignore Fran's mocking face behind him. She straightened it as he turned to face her.

"And for you? Star? Amstel? San Miguel?"

"One of each, please."

David groaned at her, then grinned at me before turning his attention to the barman. Fran leaned into my line of vision and looked at me pointedly. She jerked her head in David's direction and shook her head, her Santa hat slipping precariously. A wave of irritation and excitement, along with the rush of alcohol entering my blood stream, flushed my face further. Behind her, David took a steadying step back as he counted his money. Under the influence of alcohol, his guard was down and his affection towards me more obvious than ever. I glanced back at Fran before gazing up to the heavens, smiling smugly to myself as I did so.

"Okay, one glass of red for the lady and one pint of beer for, er, Fran."

I couldn't help but snigger as the generous glass of wine found its way into my hand. I looked up to see David grinning broadly at us both. Before Fran could respond, his eyes widened at a new distraction.

"Oi! Jim! Over here."

Fran caught my eye before following David's gaze. Jim was making his way through the crowd, noticeably calm among his merry co-workers. As he approached our little trio David lurched forward to give him a hug. Staggering under the force of his manager's embrace, Jim laughed nervously.

"Alright there, mate." He patted David on the back with his free hand, expertly avoiding spilling the drink in his other. He smiled at me over David's shoulder.

"Hi, Emily. You're looking lovely."

"Isn't she just?" Fran added, linking her arm through Jim's as soon as he was released. "It's nice to see a little bit of class in this place, don't you think?"

Jim's gaze didn't leave my face as Fran made a show of looking me up and down. I looked from him to her then back to where David had been standing seconds earlier. He was gone, no doubt on a mission to greet another of his mates. Unsure whether to be thankful that he was not here to hear my colleagues' jeers or pained that he had deserted me in my hour of need, I looked back at their mocking faces.

"What?" I hissed, my irritation suddenly beyond control.

"Hen, I was just saying how nice you look. Jim agrees, don't you, Jim?" Fran prompted him with a squeeze of his arm, seemingly oblivious to the change in my mood. Jim's smile slipped slowly from his face as I failed to return it.

"Yes, I do. Em, are you okay?" The lines on his freckled forehead deepened as I took a deep drink of wine.

"I'd be a lot better if she stopped taking the mickey out of me."

The words came out a lot louder than I had intended. Somebody nearby shushed their babble noisily.

"No one's taking the mick, Emily, honest. Fran was just paying you a compliment."

"Sure she was," I snapped. The silence that had started to spread around us seemed to jolt Fran from her oblivion.

"Oh, lovey, I was just saying to Jim here how nice you look. You make the rest of us look like a right bunch of ragamuffins." She accented her last word with a swoop of her beer-wielding hand. A wave of the amber liquid sloshed out of the glass and landed on the toe of my shoe. Fran's eyes widened as they watched the stain darken the otherwise spotless suede before returning her gaze to mine. She held it for a few moments before her face cracked again.

"Oh, I'm really sorry, hen, but your face is a picture." She clapped her hand over her mouth and looked up at Jim. He was eyeing me nervously.

"Okay, Fran, I think maybe you've had one too many, but Emily, that was an accident. Fran didn't mean to do that."

His slow deliberate tone did nothing to pacify me. Above Slade's ancient Christmas hit I heard someone whisper, a giggle behind me. Jim's face began to blur behind a barrier of tears and wine.

"Emily, honey, I'm really sorry, I didn't mean to upset you. Hell, I was trying to be nice…"

Fran's voice was thick with alcohol, her hand on my shoulder heavy. When I pushed it away she staggered a little.

"Well, if that is you trying to be nice, don't bother. And don't touch me." The last word left me as a hiccup. Hungrily I gulped down the rest of my drink before staggering to the door, my face as red as the wine I had just swallowed. Around me a sea of faces blurred into one huge mass of quivering flesh. I pushed at the door three times before pulling it open.

*

Outside I could hear laughter from within the pub, no doubt at my expense. The wooden decking was slippery with a coating of winter drizzle. Tentatively I picked my way through the revellers outside, shivering in groups or glued to their phones as they smoked. Spotting an oversized planter by the window, I pushed past a couple immersed in each other's embrace and perched on its edge. Tears were falling freely down my face, but nobody noticed. Nobody cared. A new wave of self-pity deepened my sobs.

"Emily?"

I didn't need to look up to see who it was. And I certainly didn't want him to see how upset I was. As I quickly wiped my face with the back of my hand David sat next to me, wobbling slightly as he balanced on the narrow rim. I glanced at his knees, almost touching mine. His forearm was resting on his lap, a cigarette dangling from his fingers. He lifted it towards me.

"You want a drag? I'd offer you one but I had to skag this one off someone else."

I shook my head vigorously before taking a peek at his face. His earlier joviality had disappeared. His blue eyes searched my own blankly. I dared to stare back at them for a moment before looking back down at the floor, wishing desperately that he was easier to read. I heard the tobacco crackle as he pulled on his cigarette. He was so close to me that I could hear his breath as he exhaled.

"So, are you going to tell me what's wrong or am I going to have to try some amateur psychoanalysis on you?"

My response was half laugh, half sob. As I put my hand over my mouth, I felt David's hand on my shoulder.

"Christ, Em, I know it was a bad joke but I didn't think it was that bad."

I managed a giggle in return and looked at him again. His face had softened, his eyes smiling. I felt a pang of guilt as it hit me how much seeing my tears had upset him.

"Sorry," I stammered. David raised his eyebrows.

"Sorry? What for?"

I pointed at my damp face. His frown was exaggerated, clown-like.

"Hey, don't worry about it. It's a Christmas do. Someone's got to have an emotional meltdown, right?"

I giggled again.

"I was starting to worry that I was going to have to do the honours. I thought it was Fran's turn but even my best attempts to wind her up didn't crack that nut."

His mouth broke into a smile as I laughed some more. He released my shoulder to push his hair out of his face.

"That's better. Now, tell your Uncle Dave what's up."

I shrugged and looked down at my hands, my laughter fading.

"Oh, it's nothing..."

"No, it isn't. Now spit it out." He elbowed me softly as he spoke, his warm smile encouraging me. I took a deep breath.

"Okay, well..." I bit my lip and looked up at him through my eyelashes. He nodded his encouragement. "It's Fran. If she isn't criticising me then she's making fun of me. You should have heard her just then." The words tumbled out of my mouth, almost tripping each other up in their haste. David's eyebrows drew together.

"Really? Why, what was she saying?"

I hesitated for a moment, suddenly unsure whether telling my manager, our manager, was the best way to deal with Fran. But it wasn't just our manager; it was David.

"She was making comments about what I was wearing." Involuntarily I sniffed. "I know I'm not exactly cool or anything, but..."

"Hey, hey, enough of that." This time his arm was around my shoulders, squeezing me. "No more tears, okay? And, you know what? There's nothing wrong with how you dress. I mean, just because Fran chooses to dress like a skinhead stuck in the seventies doesn't mean that you have to."

I covered my face with my hand as I snorted another laugh.

"Okay?" He squeezed me again. I looked at his eyes. They were so close to mine, my face so close to his. I felt my stomach lurch with excitement.

"Okay," I whispered, my gaze not leaving his, willing him to kiss me. He stared back for what felt like an eternity before his eyes flickered away. His arm fell away from me, taking with it the heat of his body. I followed his gaze as it scanned the scene in front of us. A handful of hardcore smokers were still gathered by the door, huddled together like penguins. Suddenly I was all too aware of the bitterness in the air around me. David put his hands on his knees and pushed himself to his feet.

"Good, that's settled then," he said, turning to face me as he dug his hands into his pockets. His smile was bright but void of the intimacy I had just felt. I stared at him dumbly.

"Bloody hell it's cold. I'm going back in. You coming?" He shivered dramatically as he nodded towards the door, his hands still firmly in his pockets. I looked behind me through the window of the pub. The party was in full swing, my colleagues getting louder by the minute as alcohol melted away their inhibitions. But not completely. Even in his inebriated state, David wasn't about to admit his feelings for me here, not with the entire service looking on. I turned to him. He grinned back before striding over to the door. He swung it open and waved his hand through grandly.

"Ladies first." He nodded his head in a small bow as he spoke. I stood up and gingerly walked towards him, unsteadied by heels and wine. As I approached him I glanced up at his face. Meeting my gaze his smile intensified, deepening his dimples. I smiled back before walking into the pub, my head bowed, not with embarrassment, but to hide the joy that was illuminating my face.

18

The last of the dishes put away, I closed the cupboard doors carefully and hung the threadbare tea towel over the back of one of the chairs neatly tucked around the kitchen table. I looked around the room, my heart sinking as it became apparent that there was nothing else that needed tidying away, wiping down or washing up. In the living room next door I could hear Dad's new telly blaring out another re-run of some eighties sitcom Christmas Special. The canned laughter depressed me. It was likely to be the only merriment I would hear over the holidays. My half-hearted attempts to contact my old school mates to arrange a catch up had been either ignored or rebuffed with a thousand excuses. It was just me, Dad and Barney, right up until I went back to work on 28 December. By the back door Barney sat with his tongue hanging out, staring at me idiotically as I moved around the kitchen. I chose to ignore his pleading eyes and wandered into the living room, lit only by the widescreen in front of the window. Dad's face, illuminated by its glow, didn't move as I stood by his armchair. I followed his grim gaze.

"*Only Fools and Horses?*" I offered. He grunted.

"Yes. But not one of the better ones. They should have left it alone after Granddad died."

Pointlessly I nodded and looked back at my dad. In the semi-darkness he looked grey, his complexion almost the same shade as his stone eyes. His hair was definitely more salt and less pepper these days, his unshaven chin speckled with white. He glanced up at me before turning back to the screen.

"Can I get you anything, Dad?" I said quickly, taking from him the opportunity to comment on my lingering presence. "Tea? Mulled wine? Mince pie?"

"A whisky, please. With ice." His lips hardly moved as he spoke.

"Okay, Dad." I hesitated for a moment, wondering if I should offer him a mince pie again but scurried away as an impatient sigh hissed through his nose. Back in the kitchen, I slowly prepared his drink, taking deliberate care to make sure that the crystal tumbler was spotless and free from chips, the ice cubes not so small that they melted too quickly as he nursed his drink, that the measure of whisky was generous enough to ensure that he did not send me back for more but not as generous as he would pour himself. The unopened box of mince pies eyed me mournfully on the far corner of the cream worktop, my festive offering pushed aside by my dad as he had prepared our dinner. Decisively I pulled the box towards me and popped one on a plate before tiptoeing back to my dad's side. His hand rose automatically as I approached. Awkwardly I placed the tumbler in his fingers.

"Thanks."

"I brought you a pie too. You know, in case you fancy it."

He grunted as I placed it by his feet. As I straightened up, I looked at the telly again. Rodney and Del were running through the streets of Peckham, their superhero outfits the cause of much hilarity to an invisible audience. My dad's face didn't crack.

"Well, I'm going to heat up some of that mulled wine I brought back with me. Then do you fancy a game of cards?"

My dad turned his face towards me, a look of surprise on his face. My face burned under the intensity of his sudden attention. I looked at my feet, alien looking in my toe socks, before looking up at him again. His expression was suddenly pained, the lines on his face deeper.

"Sorry, love, I don't really feel like it," he said softly. I looked down again, the unusual affection making me uncomfortable. When I looked up again, his eyes were once more glued to the telly, the whisky at his thin line of a mouth.

"Make sure you have some pudding, Emily. You're looking too thin," he added in his more familiar monotone as I walked out of the room. Obediently, I pulled the plastic tray of pies out of the box and shoved the pastry into my mouth, hoping its dryness would soak the tears that threatened my tired eyes. Grabbing the bottle of mulled wine, I unscrewed the cap and took a swig before pouring the rest into a saucepan and lighting the hob. Cold, it tasted sickly sweet, but I felt better instantly. I watched the red liquid as it slowly began to simmer. It had been my Secret Santa present, handed to me by Jim last Friday as he had distributed the gifts from an old pillowcase. His deep ho ho hos, which had caused much hilarity among my colleagues, had diminished a little as he approached my desk, his "Merry Christmas" a little less hearty, his smile less broad. I had smiled my thanks, but I knew that the damage was done. My behaviour in the pub hadn't exactly boosted my popularity, and even he seemed to have been put off by my alcohol-induced outburst, which my Secret Santa was obviously referencing with the bottle now in my hand. It was official: everyone in the office hated me.

Everyone but David.

The thought of his kind eyes, those strong, long fingers as they ran through his hair, his dimples deepening as he laughed at one of my goofy jokes softened me as I poured a generous helping of warmed wine into my mug. Throwing Barney one of the pies, I took another for myself and settled at the kitchen table, my back to the rest of the house. I pulled my laptop out of the rucksack propped against the wall next to me and fired it up. I hadn't had chance to unpack since my epic journey home, and was quite happily putting it off. Since my departure to London almost six months ago, my dad had already re-decorated my room, storing any books, clothes and knick-knacks I hadn't taken with me in boxes up in the loft, and swapped the girly pink with white and green. He had even replaced my old childhood furniture, never upgraded during my adolescence, with shiny new pine, my posters of seals and otters with framed art prints. Nothing of me remained, all trace carefully erased, like I'd never lived there. Or even existed.

The mouthful of wine placated me as I clicked on Google Chrome. As it loaded I nibbled at my pie. I was still hungry, even after my dad's half-hearted attempt at mushroom stroganoff. I had hardly eaten all day, breakfast consisting of a solitary crust of toast and lunch a coffee purchased at a petrol station halfway up the snail-paced A1. Hiring a car had seemed like a good idea, especially as a lot of my old school mates lived out in the countryside, but now none of them appeared to be free over the holidays it had become much more hassle than it was worth.

Finally on Facebook, I scrolled quickly through my newsfeed. It didn't take me long to find a post from David – I only had a handful of "friends" and most of them were clearly far too busy having fun to bother with virtual socialising. His profile picture was becoming more than a little familiar

– David dressed in a faded American football T-shirt, paper pint in hand, smile firmly in place. I smiled back at him before reading his post.

The best thing about Christmas Eve? Telling your kids that if they don't go to bed NOW Santa won't be coming to town. I really wish it was Christmas every day...

My smile faded a little, despite his humour. David was at home, with his kids and his wife, and I was here with my dad. My stomach churned uneasily. I knew David liked me and that he was unhappy in his private life, but when would we be together? I took another sip of wine and clicked on his name. His profile popped up instantly, full of photos of David, usually with his kids or some pasty-looking woman with dark curls running wild around her face – Gill, his wife. I stared at her face, so often next to David's. Her eyes were dark and intense, her wide lips rarely smiling and, when they did, lacking the sincerity of her husband's. Quickly I flicked back to my newsfeed, and David's comment. My confidence strengthened by my drink, I clicked "Like" before adding my comment,

Love that song :)

I watched the screen expectantly, waiting for David's response, or a "Like" back. As I downed the rest of my wine, it had still not materialised. Irritably I shut down my computer and stood up, pushing my chair noisily across the terracotta floor as I did so.

"Bloody hell, Emily, watch those tiles, will you?"

My dad's voice was thick with whisky and sleep.

"Sorry, Dad. I'm going to take Barney out. Is that okay?"

I didn't catch his muttered response. I grabbed my fleece from the hook by the back door and slipped Barney's lead over his head. Outside it was drizzling lazily. The grey sky, huge against the low horizon, had an orange tint from the excess of artificial light below. As I walked down my dad's street, laughter and music taunted me from behind windows framed with twinkling fairy lights, the life behind them hidden by dark curtains. A few streets away a chorus of drunk voices attempted a rendition of "Away in a Manger". An inflated snowman swayed as we walked past, a stupid smile on its bulbous face. I looked down at Barney. His sandy fur was bedraggled with moisture, his ears drooping forlornly. Barney had never had a very merry Christmas either, but then Barney was none the wiser – he didn't know that he was supposed to be having a good time. He pulled at his lead, his silent request to urinate. I watched him as he cocked his leg up to wee against a lamppost. His business done, he trotted on, ignorant of the tragedy of his existence – of our existence.

I opened the back door carefully and pushed it closed as quietly as I could. His bladder emptied, Barney padded into the living room, no doubt to bed down on his designated corner of the sofa. I followed him as far as the door. My dad was still in his seat, his head lolling back and his mouth open. The tumbler was lying by his feet. Picking it up, I checked the beige carpet for any spills, but it was dry. I tiptoed across the room to the telly before realising I had no idea how to turn it off. Back in the kitchen I poured myself more tepid wine and switched on my laptop again. Facebook was still eerily quiet – but I had a notification.

It was David.

Didn't realise you were so old school! Merry Christmas :)

My body flushed, warmed by the remote contact. He was thinking of me. I looked again at the notification, then at my watch. It was 12.11, and he had messaged me four minutes ago. On Christmas Day. I started typing a message back, but quickly stopped. He was with his family right now, and I needed to respect that, despite our feelings for each other. Our time would come. My time would come. I just needed to bide it.

Smiling to myself, I kissed my fingertips and pressed them against David's grinning face. I let them linger for a moment before shutting down my laptop once more, grabbing my rucksack and creeping past the lounge and to the room that was no longer mine.

But that didn't matter anymore. Nothing mattered anymore, other than David. And I knew that, this time next year, he would be with me. Things would be different, better, and I would be happy again – or, rather, at last.

19

"Excuse me, please."

My voice sounded like it belonged to someone else. Loud, steady, strong. I squeezed past my fellow commuters who, despite my new-found confidence, had refused to budge, and grabbed onto the handrail above my head as the train lurched out of the station. My feet firmly planted either side of my satchel, I looked at the window in search of my reflection. It was the New Year, and I was a new me. I'd spent those long lonely days between Christmas and New Year trawling the sales for new clothes, new make-up – new anything that would contribute to my transformation. I'd completely replaced my ageing make-up collection with a palette from Boots and treated myself to an evergreen V-neck from Monsoon, along with a handful of more affordable bargains from Marks & Spencer and Top Shop. I looked down at my new trousers and boots as I polished my front teeth with my tongue, suddenly aware that I hadn't checked them after applying a deep red to my lips. The brown wool of the bootlegs wasn't a million miles away from my usual dark shades, but the gold thread of pinstripe gave them the lift that they – that I – so badly needed. And, whilst the heels of my patent leather boots were already making the balls of my feet ache, they made me stand differently, my back straight and my head held high. Besides, Lorraine swore by heels for making her legs look longer and her overall silhouette slimmer.

Lorraine. Whilst I hadn't doubted that she would have some trendy New Year's Eve party to go to with one of her cool new work friends, I couldn't help but feel disappointed that she'd turned down my invitation to meet up over the holidays. Her present was still sitting on my computer desk, carefully wrapped and adorned with a curled bow. I had bought it back in November whilst wandering around Camden Market after work one evening – a jade necklace in the shape of a turtle. I had been so sure when I had bought it that she would love it – when we were students she'd gushed for weeks about the turtles she'd seen on her trip to Greece. But that was back when I felt like I actually knew her. These days, I just didn't know.

A sharp corner in the track jolted me from my thoughts. I looked around me, suddenly aware I had no idea how many stops I'd passed through. The teenager next to me stopped chewing for long enough to suck at her teeth as I tried to look around her to catch a glimpse of the station's name as we rolled alongside the platform. It was Camden Town, packed with passengers huddled together where years of commuting had told them the doors would sweep open. Pushing its way through the uniform blacks and greys I spotted a smudge of red beneath a shock of pink. It was Fran, her newly dyed dreads clashing against her winter coat. I turned quickly, almost toppling off a heel as I did so. I didn't want to deal with her, not here, not yet. She'd texted me a few times since we had said our stilted goodbyes on Christmas Eve, wishing me a Happy Holiday and inviting me to a party in a squat somewhere in East London to bring in the New Year. I'd replied, albeit curtly, but had made my excuses. I didn't want Fran to think I had nothing better to do, and sitting in on my own had been preferable to being rescued by her once more. Even Matt's pitying look as he passed me in the kitchen on his way out had been better than having to admit to her that, once more, I was a social disaster.

But things were about to change. Things had already changed, and not just with my new wardrobe and makeover. I knew that David liked me and it was only a matter of time before he admitted it to himself – and everyone else – that he wanted to be with me. And, right now, that was enough for me.

"Hey, Em!"

I'd got to the bottom of the escalator when she finally caught up with me. Her fake fur coat flapped in the icy wind as it whipped down from the high street above. Shivering, she pulled it around her as she jumped onto the step behind me.

"Brr, it's a bit nesh, isn't it? So, how are you? How was your Christmas?"

Her grin was wide, forced, emphasising the lines at either side of her mouth. Noting the layer of powder covering her skin and the thick black line above her lashes, I wondered who she was out to impress this year.

"It was fine, thanks. How was yours?" I said, checking my watch as I did so.

"Don't worry, it's only eight-fifty," she shrugged, oblivious to my attempt at feigning disinterest in our conversation. "Yeah, it was good, thanks. It was hard, you know, at the refuge, but so worth it. As for New Year?" She threw her head back and hooted. "What a night. I swear I've never partied so hard. Well, not since last New Year, anyway."

I nodded my understanding, hoping that would be the end of it. I didn't really want to have to elaborate on the lies I had already told her, and I didn't really want to hear more about her own debauchery either. As we passed through the barrier and jostled our way through the congested pavement towards the nearest crossing, I thought that maybe she'd taken the hint.

"Anyway, Em, I'm glad I caught you before we got to the office," she said above the roar of traffic, her deeply ringed fingers on my arm. I looked at it, making a conscious effort not to bristle at her touch.

"Look, I know things got a bit weird before Christmas. I'm really sorry if you've ever thought I was taking the piss, or poking my nose into your business, or meddling with your work. I certainly never meant to. I just," she paused as we crossed the road, "I was just trying to be helpful, and to make you feel at home. God knows it's an age since I upped sticks and moved to London and, although I admit I don't remember it wholly, I remember enough to know it was a hard time."

Her pace slowed as we approached the office. Reluctantly, I held back too. Although she had more than irritated me over the last few months, I knew that she was telling the truth. To snub her now would be social suicide – at work, if not beyond. She stepped in front of me before I could reach the door, her hand once more on my arm.

"Emily?"

Her voice was soft. I looked at her face. She was watching me intently, her earlier joviality all but gone. Aware of the attention we were attracting, that Fran with her pink hair was attracting, I shrugged a smile.

"Yeah, sure. I'm sorry too. I guess I just… freaked out or something." My laugh was shrill and almost as artificial as my words. Fran's smile crept back.

"No need to apologise, hen. I know that the last six months or so have been a bit difficult for you. But just remember, your old mate Fran is on your side. Even though she sometimes puts her foot in it and gets the wrong end of the stick. Okay?"

She let go of my arm and extended her own towards me in search of a hug. I hesitated momentarily before leaning in, awkward and gangly in my heels compared to my petite yet larger than life friend. She patted my back firmly before releasing me.

"Ah, that's better," she grinned, pushing her locks behind her shoulder. Stamping her feet she turned to the door and punched in the entry code with gloved fingers. "Okay, shall we see what the New Year has in store for us all here at DAA? Or shall we head to the café and pretend it's lunchtime already?"

I walked past Fran as she gestured me into the warm and I giggled despite myself. The year was getting better by the minute, and it had only just begun.

*

Gain recognition at work
Update my look
Get a boyfriend

I stared at the note I had started typing myself in my Outlook calendar. I debated deleting "a boyfriend" and replacing it with "David" but thought the better of it. It would be embarrassing enough if anyone managed to open the entry as it was, but I needed to keep a record of my plan, even if it was in part coded. I hit save and closed it quickly as I heard footsteps approach from behind. I relaxed as they passed my desk, and began to set myself six-weekly reminders to review my progress. It had just gone eleven and, having followed David's advice to keep my day free to catch up on emails, voicemails and any risk assessment and support plans that may have passed their review date over the Christmas break, I had already run out of things to do. I looked around me. The office was almost deserted. By the back wall sat a couple of girls whose names I had either never known or had simply forgotten. Other than the occasional sneer or guffaw at my expense, they had paid little attention to me since I had started working there almost half a year ago, and I had repaid them in kind. Pacing by her desk across from me, Fran was on the phone to some rehab down in Bournemouth, using all her manipulative powers to convince the manager to give one of her clients a second chance after a relapse on New Year's Day. She had spent most of the morning cursing to herself in between phone calls to what seemed like an endless stream of addicts who just didn't seem able to cope without her. She had now moved on to liaising with a range of agencies to try and clear up what she quite vocally described as "a whole heap of shit". With a near empty inbox and only one voice message from some social worker who had been looking for Jim, I noticed with shame the same old feelings creeping into my consciousness about my colleague. Envy. Resentment. Jealousy. I looked again at my list of cases on the database. Yes, they were all up to date. I'd updated anything that was due a review over the holidays before going on leave, and made appointments to see all my clients over the following three days. There was literally nothing for me to do.

"Oh for fuck's sake!"

I couldn't help but wince as Fran slammed the receiver back into its cradle, almost smashing it in her rage. I looked over to see her clutching at her dreads and she sank back into the office chair.

"Well, a very Happy New Year to you, Fran."

The blood rushed to my face and drained away almost as quickly at the sound of his voice. I didn't trust myself to look at him, not just yet. Fran had dropped her elbows onto her desk, narrowly missing her laptop.

"It would be a lot happier if it wasn't for those fuckwits at St George's," she muttered before pushing herself upright. "David. How are you?"

I dared myself to look in his direction. He was shrugging his rucksack off his shoulder onto his desk. I didn't recognise the high-necked black coat he was wearing. Maybe he'd picked it up in the sale. Or maybe it had been a Christmas present. From her.

"Oh, you know. Hungover, bloated. About half a stone heavier than I was two weeks ago." He held up his hands in a half-hearted shrug and turned in my direction. "So, Emily! I hope I can rely on you for a more appropriate greeting?"

I willed my cheeks to remain a relatively normal colour as I met his gaze. His eyes crinkled with their usual joviality. The spark in his sea blue eyes as they locked with mine was unmistakeable.

"Hi," I sighed. I heard a snigger behind me and quickly faked a sneeze, hoping to disguise my breathlessness as a symptom of a winter cold. "I mean, Happy New Year."

"Happy New Year to you, too. And *Gesundheit*." He winked at me before turning his attention to arranging his coat on the back of his chair. "I hope that isn't flu?"

I shrugged. "I don't think so. Just a bit of dust or something." I looked over at Fran. She was staring glumly at her laptop, her usually straight back crumpled like a discarded paper bag. I glanced back at David, who had now disappeared behind his monitor as he fired up his computer. I looked back at my own. My Outlook note stared back at me.

"Fran, can I do anything to help?" I said to the screen, almost too loudly. Across the office Fran exhaled loudly.

"I don't think so, hun. But thanks for offering."

I hesitated. "Well, do you want to talk about it? You know what they say, two heads are better than one."

Inside I cringed at my choice of proverb, but looked over at Fran with what I hoped was an expression of calm. She looked back at me, her eyebrows raised slightly.

"Thanks, hen. But there's not really anything to discuss. They're refusing to let him back in, end of story. Which means we're back where we were three months ago." She smiled her crooked smile. "Shit happens."

I smiled back, determined to hide my irritation with her for rebuffing my offer of assistance so adamantly.

"Well, can I at least pop over the road and get you a chai latte?" Her sad smile warmed a little.

"You sure can, kid."

I grinned back, and got to my feet. As Fran reached into her coat pocket, I waved a hand at her dismissively.

"Don't worry about it, I'll get it." I looked over at David. He was staring intently at his monitor. "David?"

"Yeah?"

He sounded distant, distracted. Almost deliberately so. Immediately, I understood.

"Do you want a coffee? Or a tea? I'm popping out."

His head popped up from behind his computer like a meerkat. I couldn't help but smile as his eyes widened with glee.

"Oh, really? Well, I wouldn't say no to a latte. With an extra shot of espresso, if that's okay?"

"Sure." I looked away before he had a chance to respond. I wanted to keep my cool and wasn't sure how I would react if he was to smile that smile, the one that made his eyes shine and those dimples spring to life. I pulled on my coat and threw my satchel over my shoulder before striding towards the exit. I was almost level with his desk when I misplaced my weight on my heel and stumbled. Grabbing onto the row of lockers against the wall, I just managed to save myself from plummeting to the floor. I held my breath as I clung on to the cold metal, waiting for the howls of laughter to start. When someone sniggered at the back of the office I closed my eyes.

"Yeah, yeah, very funny."

It was David's voice, close to me, but unusually stern. His hand was on my arm, strong and supportive. I opened my eyes and looked up at him. His gaze met mine.

"You alright there?"

I nodded dumbly. A smile played at the corner of his mouth, but his eyes were soft. A grin spread across my face and spilled out into a giggle. When he grinned back I averted my eyes, unsure of how I would react to his beautiful smile in such close proximity. He gave my arm a squeeze before releasing me and wandering back to his desk.

"Just try not to do that when you've got my chai in your hand, alright, hen?"

I looked around to see Fran sat at her desk, her phone cradled between her cheek and her shoulder as her fingers thundered over her keyboard. She glanced up at me and raised an amused eyebrow before returning to her work. I grinned back at her bowed head and shook my head before walking gingerly towards the stairs.

20

It took the last of my strength to push open the heavy front door. I let it slam behind me as I pulled myself up the stairs.

"Rebecca?"

I paused on the stairs as Matt stomped through the kitchen and into the hallway. He opened his mouth to speak but hesitated when he saw my face looking down at him.

"Oh. It's you."

His disappointment was almost enough to push the tears that threatened over the rims of my tired eyes. I held his gaze for a moment before continuing towards the half-hearted haven of my room.

"Bad day?" he offered as I reached the landing. I paused again and looked over my shoulder. He was lingering at the bottom of the stairs, his hair shiny in the light from the bare bulb that hung by the front door. I took a deep breath.

"You could say that."

"Well, you know what they say. Don't let the bastards grind you down."

As I fumbled the key into the lock of my door I snorted a laugh, despite my melancholy state. I felt my flatmate's eyes bore into my back and willed him to go away. Although we weren't exactly friends, he seemed to tolerate my presence and, in the absence of Beatrice, was my only ally against the less amicable Rebecca. Slamming my door in his face was not really an option.

"Listen. Let's have a coffee and talk."

Before I could respond to his instruction he had strode back into the kitchen. Below me the kettle clicked on. I took a deep breath and dumped my bag and coat outside my room before sloping back down the dark stairs.

Matt was humming to himself as he spooned ground coffee into a deeply stained cafetière. I blinked at him under the florescent light as he turned to the fridge next to me and retrieved a pint of full fat milk. As he silently poured a splash into the two mugs in front of him I began to wonder if he knew that I was there, that I had imagined his invite. Finally he glanced at me as he poured the freshly boiled water into the pot.

"So, what is it? Work? Play? Men?"

I watched carefully as he replaced the plastic kettle into its cradle and took a wide step across the kitchen to dump his spoon in the sink, hoping my apparent interest in his task would bide me some time before I had to decide exactly what I was going to tell him, whether he would help me – and if I could trust him.

"Well?"

He turned to face me, one hand on his hip, the other leaning against the fake marble worktop. I hesitated again as I searched for something appropriate to say.

"Oh… it's just work stuff, that's all." I smiled brightly before averting my eyes to the floor.

"Ha. But it's more than just a hard day at the office, right?"

I studied the black and white tiles intently. The truth was, every day was hard, and not necessarily because I was struggling with my cases.

"Some of the people in my office really don't like me."

The words were out before I could acknowledge their significance. It was the first time I had admitted the truth to myself, let alone admit it out loud. Some of my colleagues not only disliked me, but seemed to hold me in contempt, almost hate me. The realisation made my eyes prickle. Only hours earlier had I been subjected to sniggering behind my back every time I opened my mouth, which had erupted into blatant guffawing when I'd admitted to not really understanding the difference between methadone and Subutex, let alone who the Kooples were. Then there were the silences when I walked into the kitchen, the sly looks when I tried to touch up my lipstick in the toilets. In fact, their disdain was so blatant, I was surprised that I hadn't noticed it as much before.

"So what? I fucking hate some of the people I work with. I mean, just because I'm a teacher doesn't mean I have to tolerate everyone." With a flurry Matt plunged the filter down over the coffee infusion and poured the steaming liquid onto the milk. I sighed.

"I just want to fit in, that's all," I said quietly. Matt passed me my cup without looking at my face. I wrapped my fingers around the china, relishing the heat that radiated through, even though it almost burned my skin.

"Never going to happen."

I looked up in surprise. Matt was sipping his drink tentatively. Eventually his cold eyes flicked up to meet mine.

"Not all of us fit in, Emily. What you need is for people to accept you. And in order for that to happen you need to accept yourself."

I watched him as he lowered his gaze and took another sip of his drink.

"I mean, you're never going to be trendy or anything, so why not accept that and just be yourself? Otherwise you just look like you're trying too hard." He pointedly looked over my outfit before glancing at my face again. "You know what I mean?"

I looked down at my clothes. My gold-threaded trousers were having their second outing and had today been paired with an old brown V-neck jumper and a ridiculous fake fur gilet. Maybe he had a point. Somehow, on me, the combination wasn't quite right, didn't quite fit. My heart sank.

"I just want to look nice, that's all," I whispered into my coffee.

"Fair enough. Just make sure you do it your way. And do it with conviction. And don't give those fuckers the satisfaction of seeing that they get to you. Understand?"

I lifted my eyes back to his. He stared back blankly as he pulled a crumpled packet of Marlboro Lights from his back pocket and pinched one between his lips.

"Okay." I watched him, my anxiety rising as he lifted a lighter up to his cigarette. "Rebecca will kill you if you light that in here," I spluttered.

He hesitated, his hand cupped around the flame already burning, his eyes stern.

"Quite frankly, my dear Emily, I don't give a damn."

21

The face in the mirror in front of me stared back forlornly. Despite the make-up painted under my eyes, the shadows were still visible. Paired with the brown eyeshadow, it looked like I had coloured in a dark circle around my green eyes. I parted my lips and checked for lipstick on my teeth. Satisfied they were clear I resigned myself to my general appearance. Dressed in my old black trousers and one of my new jumpers, I had pared down my updated look to one that felt more like me, but was struggling with the self-assurance Matt had preached. I made a final attempt to fluff some life into my lank hair, scooped up my notebook and diary from next to the sink in front of me and walked out of the ladies. As I passed the kitchen I thrust my head high into the air in a bid to demonstrate the defiance I so wanted to possess. I reached Eric's office without incident and firmly knocked on the door. It flew open almost immediately.

"Emily! Blimey. You'd make a good cop with a knock like that."

It was Eric. I tried to hide my disappointment and panic. Where was David? Why was Eric here? Was he going to be doing my supervision? I heard someone tapping at the keyboard behind him and looked around the service manager's bulk. The sight of David, his hair an artful mess and his shirt slightly crumpled from a day of labour, soothed my anxiety almost instantly.

"Don't worry, I'll be getting out of your hair in just one sec. I just needed to catch up with your manager before the service user forum."

I averted my eyes back to the older man with difficulty. His piggy eyes searched my face from above that huge red nose. He smiled at me briefly before turning back to the office. With effort he reached down to pick up a carrier bag stuffed full of papers next to the desk. He groaned as he stood up, his hand on the lumbar of his spine. David shook his head as he stared at the computer's monitor. His long fingers continued to dance over the keyboard.

"Eric, for God's sake, man, go back to the doc's with that back of yours, will you?"

Eric snorted his response and rolled his eyes as he waddled towards me. I jumped out of his way and watched him as he stiffly walked towards the lift.

"That man is as stubborn as an ox. Brilliant, but stubborn."

I looked back at David. He was on his feet, collecting a selection of papers from the chaos spread over Eric's desk. He glanced at me and smiled grimly as he headed over to the table by the door.

"Do me a favour, Emily, and if I ever tell you to go to the doctor's or take the day off sick, listen to me, okay?"

I smiled back at him and nodded, warmed by his concern. He gestured to one of the chairs without looking at me. Quickly I shut the door and obediently took a seat. David cleared his throat as he shuffled his papers into an orderly pile. As I opened my notebook I stole a look at his face. His jawline, speckled with stubble, seemed tense, the lines across his forehead more pronounced than usual.

"Are you okay?" I asked in what I hoped was a soothing tone. David looked up at me, his eyes wide.

"Me? Yeah, yeah, I'm fine. Just the usual day-to-day stresses, you know." He smiled at me all too briefly and coughed again as he turned back to his papers. "So, is there anything particular you wanted to discuss today or are you happy with the standard agenda?"

I sat up straight and shook my head, my hands resting in my lap. David glanced at me and nodded.

"Good. Okay, so let's get started. How are things going for you?"

I shifted my weight in my seat. There was something different about him, and it was more than just a bad day. He was different with me. I thought of Eric, standing in the doorway. "*I just needed to catch up with your manager.*" Why? Had David told him how he felt about me? Had Eric figured it out? Had he warned David off me, reminded him of his obligations as a husband, a father? Or was the warning about his job?

"Oh, okay," I heard myself say. David looked at me, his eyebrows slightly raised, and gestured vaguely with his free hand.

"Go on."

I straightened in my seat even more.

"Well, everything seems to be going quite smoothly. All my admin is up to date and everyone on my caseload seems to be progressing quite well."

David tapped the pencil in his other hand against the plywood desk. His eyes were back on the pile of papers in front of him.

"Okay. And how do you feel you are getting on with other people who work here?"

174

I shrugged.

"Fine. I mean, I'm not friends with the entire service or anything, but I reckon I get on quite well with everyone in our team," I added, with what I hoped was a self-deprecating smile. David nodded before dropping his pencil on the table. He took a deep breath and stretched back in his chair before looking at me again. His beautiful eyes were absent of their usual light – somehow sad, sorrowful.

"What about your spat with Fran at the Christmas do. Do you want to talk about it?"

I smiled, almost laughed out loud. Was that what he was so worried about?

"Oh, that? That was nothing. It's all sorted now."

David raised his eyebrows.

"Really?"

My smile widened of its own accord.

"Really. I just completely mistook something she said to me, that's all." I bit my lip and looked up at him from beneath my lashes. "I think I'd had too much to drink."

David smiled briefly.

"That's good. I have to admit that, even though sometimes we don't see eye to eye, Fran is a good girl. She knows her stuff. And I think she's got a soft spot for you, too."

I smiled back and lowered my eyes. I understood now. He was looking out for me, that was all. The thought made my body flush pleasantly.

"And I heard Jim was involved? All good there, too?"

I let myself giggle girlishly. He was just too sweet.

"Yes, all good there. He's really nice, too. And helpful."

David smiled down at the desk.

"That's good to know."

His face had hardened again, the tension back along his jaw and at his temples. I suddenly realised what I had said. Did he think I liked Jim as more than a friend, a colleague? I felt panic rise from my belly as I frantically tried to think of a way of undoing what I had just said.

"It's just, even though things are fine with those guys, I'm a bit concerned that you might not be settling in so well here."

I stared at him dumbly. He glanced at me from behind the mop of hair that had fallen over his forehead.

"Do you talk much to other people outside of the team?"

I shook my head.

"No. Why? Am I supposed to?"

David took a steadying breath, pulled his shoulders back in another stretch, and looked me in the eye.

"Well, it's not in your job description or anything. But it's good to be fully integrated into the service. To be able to get on with everyone, to be able to go to them if you need help, to learn from them. It helps you grow as a worker and keeps the service strong. Does that make any sense?"

He was tapping his pencil against the table again. His gaze wavered. I looked down at my hands, limp in my lap, as I tried to process what he had just said.

"I'm a weakness in the service?" I whispered. Next to me, David sucked in a sharp breath between his teeth.

"That's not exactly what I said. I think that maybe you need to break out of your comfort zone. Get to know other people a bit more. You never know, you might quite like some of them."

I recognised the slightly jokey tone as he uttered his last sentence, but failed to mirror it in my own.

"That might be the case, but some of them just don't like me, David. You saw how some of them reacted when I tripped over the other day. Are they being told to integrate more, too?"

"Emily." The touch of his hand on the knitted sleeve of my jumper just made me want to cry even more. "Trust me, I spoke to them both after you left, and I've had a word with their line manager about it, too. But it isn't just them, is it? I've spoken to a few managers and they've noticed it. You just need to make a bit of an effort with people, otherwise you just come across as..." David lifted his hand briefly and hesitated. "Well, dismissive. Haughty. Do you understand what I mean?"

My eyes began to overload with familiar salty water.

"You think I'm haughty?"

"No!" He squeezed my arm as he said the word, uttered so immediately that I couldn't doubt that he meant it. This wasn't what he thought. It was what other people thought. People like Eric. "But then I know you. You've had no choice but to talk to me, and for that I pity you." That squeeze again. "But I can understand how other people might interpret your shyness. Just saying hello to people in the morning, asking how someone is when you're grabbing a cuppa in the kitchen, it would be a start. Okay?"

He released my arm and thrust his hand into his pocket, retrieving a handkerchief, fresh from its packaging. In its corner was an embroidered Rudolph.

"From the kids. Apparently they chose it, too."

I glanced up at him as I dabbed my eyes. He was smiling at me warmly. I smiled back before lowering my gaze once more.

"So, shall we move on?"

I nodded quickly, my haste a reflection of my desire to talk about anything but my difficult colleagues.

"Okay, well shall we start looking at your caseload? Do you mind if we start with Alan?"

I hesitated before nodding again, mild panic rising again.

"So, how's it going with him? Have you any concerns?"

Frantically I searched my mind for something positive to say. David had brought him up for a reason, but I couldn't think why.

"Well, he's the same really. He still wants to move so I've been supporting him with that process, and when I last saw him he was still struggling with his budgeting. He wasn't home when I visited him last, though."

David nodded slowly.

"So, what have you been doing with him around the cash flow problem?"

"Well, I've been trying to talk to him about his budgeting skills and offered to help him draw up a plan. But he always wants an instant solution." I sighed and looked up at my manager with what I hoped were knowing eyes. He met my gaze for a moment before turning his attention to his pile of papers. He flicked through them with his long fingers, pausing only a few pages from the top.

"I think there might be something a bit more going on with Alan than just poor life skills. I got an email from one of the council wardens the other day about him." He pulled a paper out of his bundle and handed it to me. "Basically it sounds like he's been begging down in King's Cross over the holidays. Quite aggressively, too."

I scanned the email printout in front of me. The words swam in front of my eyes.

"Is there any indication that he might be using again, Emily? Has he lost weight? And how does his flat look? Is he washing himself?"

I closed my eyes as I tried to remember my last contact with the man. He hadn't been in when I had visited him just before Christmas, despite the note I had left him after his no-show the week before. In fact, the last time I had seen him had been the middle of November. Coming up to two months ago. Panic rose again, but I swallowed it down.

"He didn't seem any worse than before. I mean, he's always been quite skinny and unkempt." I opened my eyes. David's eyes searched mine, his frown lines deep. "I'll do an unannounced visit tomorrow and get onto it," I added, my tone pitched to meet with the apparent gravity of the situation. He flicked me a smile.

"Thanks." He looked back down at his papers. "Just be careful. And, please," he looked up at me again; the concern was still there, almost haunting his face, "just ask if you need help, or someone to do a home visit with you. You know, to get someone else's opinion on how he's doing? Okay?"

I looked back as steadily as I could.

"Of course I will. I promise." I smiled what I hoped was a comforting smile. He returned it, but without the confidence I had hoped for.

22

Pulling the sleeve of my coat over my gloved knuckles, I hammered on the standard issue door again. I took a step back and eyed the letterbox uncertainly. I'd seen Fran hollering through a letterbox many a time, but was not convinced it was my style. A greasy blind covered the window, keeping the state of Alan's kitchen a mystery, despite my attempts to peek through the gaps. I looked at my watch. I'd been there for almost five minutes, and nothing. I turned around and looked over the balcony to the world below me. A Bengali woman was watching me suspiciously as she walked past with her pram and a tottering kid. I smiled at her and waved, but she looked away, hurrying her child out of the council estate.

The lock behind me clicked, making me jump. I turned around to see Alan pull the door open. Through the thick stubble on his chin his mouth was a hard line. His hair stuck· out at all angles from his thin face. He looked older than when I had last seen him. Much older.

"What? What, what's with all the fucking banging on my door? Who the fuck are you, anyway?"

I stared at him in silence for a moment, floored by the stench that emanated from his wiry body.

"I'm Emily. Your support worker, remember? And I need to see you."

Alan's mouth dropped open and his eyes widened as he gripped onto the frame of his door.

"My support worker? Well, you could have fooled me, hammering on my door like that. I thought the fucking pigs were after me."

His laugh, low and rasping, was clearly not meant to reassure me. Its accompanying gaze chilled me even more than the January air.

"Now, if you'll excuse me, I don't believe we have an appointment. And I'm a very busy man. Can you come back tomorrow?"

Alan stepped back and began to close the door.

"Alan, wait." I stepped forward and put my hand firmly on the door. There was no way I was going to let the first chance in weeks to engage with him slip away so easily. I had no doubt that he could have pushed it shut quite easily, but he didn't. I looked up at his face, which was uncomfortably close to mine. His breath was warm and stale.

"Hello, what's this? Does someone think it's okay to force their way into my property? Even if you were a cop, don't you need a warrant for that?" His voice was slick with mirth. I didn't care.

"Look, Alan, I need to talk with you. I've received a report that you've been begging and I'm very concerned for your welfare."

Alan threw back his head as he laughed, saving me from another fetid blast of breath. I looked down at the floor and waited.

"Well, let me tell you, you have absolutely no cause for concern. I'm just tickety-boo, I promise." He put his hand on his chest as he leant closer to peer into my face. "But then, if I wasn't, I'm not sure you'd be able to help me much anyway, would you? I mean, you haven't been able to do anything for me so far. I'm still living in this shithole, I'm still skint, and I'm still a fucking junkie, aren't I?"

His voice grew quieter as he leant closer and closer towards me. His forehead was nearly touching mine, his smell overwhelming. I took a step back, removing my booted foot from the door. Satisfied, he straightened up. I looked down at his bare feet, his toes surprisingly white. I took a deep breath.

"You don't have to be any of those things, Alan. If you work with me I can help you."

He rolled his eyes.

"Well, if past performance is anything to go by, I'd say you can't. Now, if you'll excuse me, I need to go to work."

He started to shut the door. Desperately I searched for something to say, something to stop him shutting that door, today, forever. Something to stop me from failing.

"Look, Alan, there's a walk-in clinic at one of the drug treatment centres in Camden every Thursday. Let's go together, okay? I'll buy you lunch."

Alan hesitated, the door still slightly ajar. I knew I sounded desperate, preposterous, but the mocking laughter didn't come. "If we get you into treatment, Alan, everything else will sort itself out. Once you're stable we can get on top of your money, and your housing. We could argue with the council that you need to move to stay clean, to stay safe. Okay?"

The door opened a touch more. Alan peered at me with blank eyes. I stared back at them.

"Okay," he said after what felt like forever. "But I need some cash to tide me over until then."

I blinked.

"Alan, you know I can't do that…"

I jumped as his fist slammed against the wall of the hallway. I watched, mouth open, as he gripped his hand with the other, his face twisted with anger and pain as he inspected his bleeding knuckles. Eventually he looked up at me, the rage that filled his eyes seconds ago suddenly absent and replaced with something new. Desperation. He closed them before he spoke.

"Please. I promise, I'll never ask again. I'll come along on Thursday and do whatever I need to. But I have no food, no money to wash my clothes, even." He opened his eyes and looked down at his pitiful frame, his grubby green T-shirt and pale jeans, almost grey with grime. He laughed softly before returning his gaze to me. "I just need a bit of help to straighten myself out until then. That's all."

I hesitated for a moment. I knew that I wasn't supposed to, but then I knew that if I said no, that would be it. I'd never see Alan again, never be able to get him off drugs. Never be able to tell David that I'd pulled him back from the brink, saved him from himself, to show Eric what I was made of. Slowly I reached into my satchel.

"Okay, Alan. But this is the last time. And you need to come with me on Thursday."

Alan closed his eyes again and nodded. As the twenty pound note crackled in my hand he opened them again, finally releasing his bleeding hand. His eyes widened as he saw the money.

"I don't have anything smaller," I explained with a small shrug. He nodded.

"Well, I don't have any change, so…?" He looked from the money to my face. His eyes were wide and expectant, like a child's. Decisively, I held out the money. He grabbed it with his injured hand.

"Thank you." The note was in his pocket before the words were out. He smiled grimly, wincing as he pulled his injured hand away. He looked past me and down into the estate, as though suddenly aware of the world beyond his squalid flat. His eyes searched the area expectantly before returning to me. He cleared his throat.

"Well, I better let you go, then. I'll see you on Thursday, yeah?" His hand was on the door already, slowly closing it.

"Yes. I'll be here at ten. Don't forget, okay?"

"Sure. See yer."

I stood and stared at the closed door for a moment as I tried to collect my thoughts. Inside the flat I could hear no movement, nothing. No light had clicked on, no radio was playing, no water was running. I began to wonder if Alan had ever answered the door or if I'd imagined the entire conversation. I looked down at my purse, still in my hand, and peered inside. The cash I had withdrawn that morning had definitely gone. I clipped it shut and shoved it back into my bag. I made sure my head was held high, my stride purposeful as I walked along the balcony to the stairwell, just in case Alan was watching, judging whether he could rely on me, whether I had the strength to help him, to enable him. As I jogged down the stairs I felt my confidence rise, any doubt falling away with every step. As I pushed open the gate to the estate I let myself smile. I had turned things around, and this case was going to be a success. My grin widened as I imagined David's face as I told him that I'd got Alan, impossible Alan, into treatment, clean, stable and safe. The thought warmed me as I bowed my head against the icy air.

23

"Excuse me... excuse me, please?"

My attempt at assertion was, in reality, little more than a whining plea. For the third time I tried to push myself onto the already overflowing train, and for the third time the doors slid shut in front of my face. I let my flushed face hang as the train accelerated out of the station, disappearing into the dark tunnel on its way to North London. I looked at the service display above my head. The next train was not due for another four minutes. Already the platform was filling up with impatient Londoners, all as desperate to get to work as me, but with the additional disregard for others that only comes with long-term exposure to the capital's public transport, groaning under the strain of its impossible task. Above the low hum of rustling papers, irritable mutterings and obscured music escaping from headphones, the speaker crackled with yet another announcement apologising for the inconvenience. My concentration wandered as the disjointed voice went on to list a range of excuses for the delayed service. I looked at my watch. Having arrived at my usual station at the usual time, I had been turned away by a spot-ridden teenager who seemed more than happy to share with the world the fate of the man who had decided to end his life in front of a train that morning. Cursing my luck, I had run to the nearest bus stop and jumped on the first bus that was headed in the direction of another line. That had been almost fifty minutes ago. I was going to be late. My eyes prickled as bolder passengers muscled in front of me, securing their space on the next train and guaranteeing my own on the platform as yet another train came and went.

*

By the time I got out of the tube I was over an hour late. As soon as I was out of the station I broke into a trot. As I approached the imposing tower of concrete that was Alan's estate I slowed to a fast walk before reducing my pace further. I felt my throat tighten as I pressed the trade button and pushed open the heavy gate. He hadn't been in on Thursday, so I'd left him a note telling him I'd be back the following day at 9.30. It was 10.35 already. Even if he had waited for me, he'd probably have left by now, or, even worse, had been working himself into a frenzy over my tardiness for the last sixty-five minutes. I pulled out my mobile phone as I reached the top of the urine-soaked stairs. I had missed two calls since emerging from the Underground, three voice messages and a text. It was Fran.

U okay? Know there r delays on the tube but call as soon as u can. Stay safe x

I shoved my phone back into my pocket as I walked along the balcony, my irritation rising as I approached the all-too familiar door. Even after all these months Fran still seemed to have no

186

faith in my ability to do my job, or to look after myself. I shook my head to myself as I knocked. Instinctively I took a step back. If Alan answered, I doubted that his mood would be at its best. I looked at the window. The greasy blind was slightly rolled up, leaving a few inches of insight into Alan's world. I stepped towards it and bent down to take a look. My heart sank as I took in the chair on its side, the upended table with a missing leg, the fridge door ajar, the eclectic collection of dirty pots and pans strewn over the grimy worktop and scattered over the floor. I stood up quickly, almost banging my head on the narrow windowsill in my haste to escape from the stark reality represented by what I had just seen. I banged on the door again before crouching down to peer through the letterbox. The disarray had spread into the hallway. Takeaway menus littered the floor. The bookshelf that usually hugged the wall was leaning across the narrow space, blocking the only escape route. I stood up slowly as I processed what I had seen. Alan had been back to his flat since I had visited yesterday, that was for sure, and something had happened. Something bad. I swallowed back my rising panic as I hurried away from the door. I almost jumped when my mobile started to ring. It was the office.

"Hen, are you okay?"

Fran.

"Yes, yes, I'm fine. Sorry, was just about to call. I was delayed this morning and my 9.30 isn't in."

"It was Alan, wasn't it?"

"Yes, it was Alan, Fran."

I knew when there was a moment's hesitation on the other end of the line that she had picked up on my annoyance.

"Okay, Em. So are you going to head to your eleven o'clock now?"

I looked at my watch. It was nearly quarter to. As Alan had been a no-show, I could just about get there on time. I let myself relax a little as my planned schedule slid back into place.

"Yes, I will. I'll see you later."

I hung up before Fran could question me any further. I took a deep breath to calm myself as I exited the estate and hurried in the direction of my next appointment, pausing only briefly at the bus stop before dismissing the unappealing thought of public transport so soon after my earlier ordeal.

24

"Emily?"

I blinked as I looked up from my laptop. It was Jim, frowning despite the smile spread across his freckled face.

"Yes?"

My tone did little to hide my irritation at the interruption. Jim looked away and laughed, his eyes shining. He pulled his hands out of his pockets and held them out in front of him.

"Sorry to disturb you, I just wondered if you wanted a cup of tea or something? You haven't left your desk since you got into the office."

I felt myself blush, partly at his mirth but also at the knowledge that he had been observing me so closely. Fran was forever teasing that, despite my aloofness, he still seemed to have an interest in me beyond just being another of his colleagues.

"Um, no it's okay. I'm fine, thanks."

I smiled at him briefly before turning back to my work. I clicked open a case note at random and began to read it in earnest, willing him to go away.

"Are you sure? I have some really nice ginger tea in my locker. It's great for this time of year."

"Oh, that sounds lovely, Jim. I'll have one, mate."

Jim and I looked up at David as he strode to his desk, unwinding a scarf from around his neck as he did so. He grinned at Jim before turning his attention to me. My face reddened further as he winked.

"Actually I wasn't offering you. As I said, it's a really nice tea. Way too good to waste on the likes of some people."

David widened his eyes and gasped as he threw his jacket onto the back of his chair. As he sat down his grin returned.

"Fair enough. In that case I'll have a PG Tips, please. Milk, one sugar. Oh, and be quick about it, will you?"

His dimples deepened as Jim shook his head before turning his attention back to me.

"Just because they become managers, some people think they're all that, don't they?"

I looked at him blankly before turning back to David. He was still smiling, his eyes already glued to his monitor. Unsure what to say, I shrugged.

"Now, Jim, stop trying to rile up the troops. It'll never work, especially with sensible people like Emily around."

Jim pouted at our manager before throwing me another smile.

"Oh well, it was worth a try. Now are you sure you don't want a cuppa?"

I nodded dumbly at my laptop. Jim hovered at my side for a few seconds before finally walking off in the direction of the kitchen. Even his walk was full of confidence, his yellow T-shirt unashamedly loud for the grey afternoon. As he disappeared from view I glanced over at David. He was watching me, a lopsided smile on his face. I dived back behind my computer, my face burning. Had he seen me looking at Jim? My mind raced as I realised what it must have looked like. I dropped my head into my hands. Why did Jim insist on talking to me all the time? Things were difficult enough as it was without David thinking I might be interested in someone else.

My mobile sprang to life next to me. With a sigh I picked it up.

"Is this Emily?"

"Yes," I almost whispered. I suddenly felt ridiculously tired and, whatever the phone call was about, I wasn't sure I had the energy to match the urgency of the voice at the other end of the line.

"Hi there, this is Stephanie. You left me a message about our good friend Alan."

I sat up straight in my seat and looked around me. The office was almost empty, and no one was sitting nearby.

"Oh, yes. Thanks for calling back," I gushed.

"Not a problem. I have to say, I'm amazed we haven't spoken before. You've got a real handful on your hands there, my dear. I know he used to give Fran the right run around." Her laugh was throaty, loud, and brief. "So, what's going on?"

I looked around again. David was almost entirely hidden behind his computer screen, clearly absorbed by whatever it was disclosing.

"Oh, nothing much. I just haven't seen him in a while and wondered if you had any concerns about him."

"So you mean he's relapsed." That grating laugh scratched at my ear again. "Well, I can't say I'm surprised, honey. If I had a pound for every time that man fell off the wagon, well, I might not be a millionaire yet but I'd be a lot better off than I am now."

"Have you seen him?" I persisted over the other woman's laughter. I was really starting to regret having called the housing officer in the first place. Fran had suggested it when I had returned to the office after my visit the other day, her face earnest in her eagerness to get her claws into my cases yet again.

"No, my dear, I haven't seen him. But what I can see plain and simple is that he is in rent arrears again. It looks like his housing benefit is okay at the minute, but he hasn't paid his contribution in over two months." She sucked at her teeth. "Oh, and we've had complaints about noise from his flat."

"So he's still at the property, then?"

"Oh yeah, he's still there. Him and every other crack addict in the city by the sounds of it." She clicked her tongue again. "You know, I've sent him so many warning letters about this. I think it's about time this guy is served notice on his flat."

When I finally hung up I was exhausted. Although I had established that Alan was still staying at his flat, it seemed that things had deteriorated even more since I had last seen him, not even a week ago. I took a deep breath and looked out of the office window. The high street below was as busy as ever, teeming with tourists and locals alike despite the cold weather. I watched them as they bobbed along, searched for inspiration among the woolly hats, the shopping trolleys, the odd skateboard. Alan was in real trouble, and I had no idea what to do about it. All I did know was that I had to do something, and fast, to save him – and show David that I could do it without Fran's help, or anyone else's.

"Emily?"

I let my head flop back at the sound of her voice.

"Yes?" I said, louder than necessary.

"Don't you have another visit booked for three o'clock?"

"Yes," I repeated, in the same sing-song voice.

"Well, hen, I hate to break it to you but it's already ten-to. You'd better get your skinny butt out of here."

I sat bolt upright and looked at my watch. Shit, she was right. I sprang out of my seat and threw my coat over my shoulders, catching Fran's eye a couple of desks back from mine. She smiled at me, but that telltale line between her brows was clear and present.

"Thanks." I smiled at her, and rolled my eyes. Her smile widened a touch before she turned back to her work.

"No worries, hen. Always here to help."

I smiled again, but she was not looking at me. I hesitated for a moment before grabbing my satchel and scurrying towards the exit.

*

"Hello, Stacey?"

Releasing the flap of the letterbox, I straightened up. I was just about to walk away from yet another closed door when I heard movement on the other side of the heavy wood. I smoothed my coat with my mittened hands and took a deep breath. So far my day had not been going so well, but I was confident that, with Stacey, I could regain at least a little bit of control.

As soon as the door opened, I knew something wasn't right. It wasn't just my client's face, drawn and tired, that alerted me, but her top. Whilst most mothers of young children probably wouldn't worry about their clothes being a bit grubby, I knew that the stains scattered across her chest and discoloured neckline were not Stacey's style.

"Hello, Emily."

Her eyes didn't meet mine before she turned to lead me into her home. The front room was dark, the curtains closed. She flicked on the freestanding lamp in the corner of the room before collapsing onto the nearest sofa. I looked around the room for somewhere to sit. My usual perch on the sofa opposite her was strewn with laundry, the two chairs next to the foldaway dining table stacked with letters, toys, empty cans of lager.

My heart sank.

"Stacey. What happened?" I whispered. She glanced at me, her eyes not reaching higher than my thighs, and reached for the packet of cigarettes on the coffee table.

"Well, I guess you could say I've had a bit of a rocky start to the New Year." She sighed a soulless laugh as she placed a cigarette between her lips. Finally she looked me in the eye. Tentatively she held out the packet in her hands. "You want one?"

I shook my head quickly, and looked around the room as she lit up. Along with the surface clutter, the flat looked to be in need of an early spring clean. Suddenly I realised what was missing.

"Where's your baby?"

She looked at me again, her eyes suddenly wide.

"She's with my neighbour. Why?"

I shrugged and looked around again. "So how long has this been going on, Stacey?"

I knew my tone was all wrong. I should have been supportive and understanding, but my voice was full of the anger and disappointment I felt towards the woman in front of me, my one client who was supposed to be moving on with her life. I ignored the shake in her breath as she exhaled.

"Oh, I don't know. A few weeks, I guess? Not to this level, though," she added quickly, suddenly making the effort to sit up in her seat. "I just had a particularly heavy session last night."

"So I see." I nodded at the empty cans to emphasise my point. "And exactly how long has your child been with your neighbour?"

Stacey snorted.

"And exactly what business of yours is that?"

I looked at her face. Her usually smooth face was lined with worry, the usually rounded cheeks slightly sunken. Behind her anger, I could see her fear. I took a deep breath.

"Well, Stacey, I'm concerned for your welfare right now, and for that of your child. I know you would never mean to harm her," I raised my hand as she opened her mouth in protest, "but you and I know that when you've had a drink you are less able to look after her."

"And that is exactly why she is with my neighbour," she stammered, her wide eyes searching the room for support. Eventually they met my own. I held her gaze for a few seconds before looking at the floor and shaking my head.

"I understand that, Stacey. But she can't stay with her forever. And... look at you."

I gestured at her with an open hand. She stared at it for a moment, before looking at the cigarette she was nursing in her own and the front of her un-ironed grey sweater. Her eyes wandered to the floor as she gulped down a lungful of smoke.

"You're right. I'm a mess." She exhaled, her voice wobbling precariously. She looked up at me again suddenly, expectantly, her free hand clutching at the arm of her sofa. "But you can help me. With you, I can pull this back, Emily. I've done it before, and I can do it again. Please."

I gave her what I hoped was my most sympathetic smile and clasped my hands in front of me.

"Of course I will, Stacey. I can get you on to a detox programme by the end of the week, no problem. And I'll give you a list of support groups and help you draw up a plan for your recovery before I leave." I saw the anguish on her face melt as I talked. She gazed at me in awe as I recited my well-rehearsed spiel into how I was going to get her back on the straight and narrow. It was almost verbatim for what I had said in my interview when asked how I would react in this very situation. I was almost grateful to the pathetic creature in front of me for giving me the opportunity to finally put the words into practice.

"Oh, thank you so much, Emily, I really appreciate it," she sniffed, her eyes bulging with unshed tears. She scrambled out of her seat and pulled at her sweater in a vain attempt to straighten out the creases. "Look, can I get you a cup of tea? I'm really sorry, I didn't think to offer you one when you came in." She giggled nervously, still tugging at her clothes. I held up my hand and smiled graciously.

"No, it's okay, Stacey. Let's just get you sorted, shall we?"

She giggled again as she sat down on the edge of her sofa, her knees and feet together. She reached for her pack of cigarettes again and winced.

"Do you mind?"

I smiled again.

"In the circumstances, I'll let it go."

She smiled back as she pulled out another cigarette and lit it, her shoulders hunched around her ears. I took a deep breath before the room filled with smoke again.

"Of course, the only other thing we need to discuss is your child." She froze. "I know you won't like it, Stacey, but I am going to have to notify Social Services about this. I doubt very much they will do anything about it, but I have a duty as a professional, because of your history, to advise them of what has happened. They may even be able to offer you help, too."

I fully expected my client to start wailing at me, to beg me not to tell them, possibly for her to become hysterical and scream at me to get out. Instead, she looked at me steadily and shook her head.

"No, Emily. There is no need, I promise you." She pushed the strands of hair that had come away from her tight ponytail out of her face and sat up even straighter. "All I need is this. The talking to you have just given me, and support you have offered me." She pressed her hand to her chest. "I am done, I swear. This was just a stupid, stupid thing I let happen and I won't let it happen again. My baby and our future together are more important to me than anything."

"Stacey..."

"Look, if you feel that you need to, well, then you have to. But I am telling you now that you will be wasting yours and their time. You said it yourself, they won't do anything about it, and the chances of them offering me any support that I haven't already got is, quite honestly, a bit of a joke. All they'll do is come and ask me lots of questions, make lots of notes then close my case." She shrugged, her gaze steadily holding mine. I looked at her carefully. Despite her dishevelled appearance, the lines no longer hidden in the plumpness of her face, the previously unnoticed greys poking through her abundance of dark hair, I had never seen her looking so certain, so confident about anything since I had met her. My confidence suddenly wavering, I looked down at my bag and busied myself finding my notebook and a folder full of yet unused leaflets and printouts of local AA meetings.

"Okay then, Stacey," I said finally. "But if things haven't changed by the end of the week I will have to call them. Do you understand?"

"Yes, I understand. And I promise you, you won't have to call them, ever. Not because of me, anyway."

I glanced up from the papers I was flicking through. She was still looking at me steadily. I nodded before looking down again, still unsure of the bargain I had just made.

25

"Cheers!"

I lifted my glass automatically to clink it against the others suspended above the table. I wasn't sure what we were toasting. We'd been in the pub for over an hour and I was already on my second glass of wine. Jim had insisted on buying me another after I practically downed my first. My anxiety levels had been steadily creeping up since we had arrived, not only because I was all too aware of the spectacle I had made of myself last time I had socialised with my colleagues, but also due to David's absence. When we had left the office he had assured us that he would be joining us in the next ten minutes, but he still hadn't shown up.

"Penny for your thoughts?"

Fran's friendly elbow nearly made me spill my drink. Sitting right next to me, she was leaning towards me unnecessarily. Her red lips were grinning stupidly. Like me, she was also on her second drink, and didn't look like she needed a third.

"Oh, they aren't very interesting." I shrugged and took another sip of my wine. Fran laughed loudly.

"I doubt that, hen." Suddenly her face was serious, her dark eyebrows knitted together. "Are you okay, though? You've been really quiet all night."

I felt myself blush.

"Oh I'm fine, just tired, that's all."

"Well, I'm not surprised. You seem to be the first in and the last to leave these days, young lady." The sudden presence of Eric's booming voice almost made me jump. I looked up at him. His little eyes were on me, studying my face as it steadily became hotter.

"Well, she's a hard worker, this one," Fran said, putting her arm around my shoulders. With effort I managed to resist pulling away from her. "I reckon she'll be after your job before long, boss."

Eric roared with laughter. "I tell you what, she's more than welcome to it." He looked at me again as he took a sip of his orange juice. "So, what do you reckon? Fancy doing a job swap?"

"Listen, can people stop trying to poach members of my team when I'm not around, please?"

David's voice came from behind me, a soothing influence amongst so many stressors. I glanced over my shoulder to check that it was really him, that he was really here. He was shrugging off his coat, his hair, damp from the rain, clinging to his forehead. He caught my eye and gave me a wink. I smiled back before averting my eyes back to the table.

"Well, I was offering my fine self in return, but I know when I'm not wanted."

"Aw, stop it with the guilt trip, old man. Now what can I get everyone to drink?"

As the table erupted with shouted orders, I slipped out of my seat. I looked shyly up at David. "I'll help you."

He looked at me, his eyes wide, and smiled back. "Thanks, Emily." He looked back at the table. "Right, so an Amstel, an orange juice and lemonade, a vodka-cranberry and a Guinness?" he said, ticking off the orders on his long fingers. Satisfied, he gave me a nod and strode over to the bar. I followed him obediently.

"I almost forgot, what can I get your fine self?" he asked as he leant his hands on the sticky wood. I watched him as he caught the attention of the pretty blonde behind the bar.

"Um, a glass of red wine, please," I murmured as I enviously watched her perfectly curvaceous body slink towards us. David smiled at her widely before rattling off his order. His task complete, he popped his elbow onto the bar and turned to look at me.

"So, how are you today, Emily?"

Faltering under the intensity of his gaze I looked down at the beer-stained carpet.

"Okay. A bit tired, but okay."

"Well, I'm not surprised. You have been working quite late the last couple of weeks. Is anything up?"

I glanced up at him. His beautiful eyes were full of concern. I looked away again and smiled.

"Not really, everything's fine. Just a bit busy."

The truth was I'd been staying later as it was the best opportunity to see him. After five, most people had already gone home, but David was often there until after 6.30.

"Well, make sure you take some time off in lieu when it calms down. I don't like to see my team looking wiped out." Suddenly he put his hand on my shoulder. I looked up at his wide eyes. "Not that I'm saying you're not looking lovely, you understand." He grinned, his dimples deepening. I giggled back, my face glowing. He gave my shoulder a squeeze before releasing it and resting his hand back on the bar. I looked at it with longing.

"So, how are you, though? You were a little late getting to the pub. Is everything okay?"

He shrugged, his eyes following the progress of our order.

"Yeah, fine thanks. Just had to finish off a couple of reports for the old man," he jerked his head in the direction of our table behind us, "and touch base with the missus."

I felt myself stiffen at the mention of his wife. "Is Gill okay?" I asked, desperately trying to stop my unease showing in my voice. A smile flickered across David's face.

"Well, she's still giving me a hard time at every given opportunity so I think we can assume she's well." His eyes rested on his hands. I hesitated for a moment.

"Do you want to talk about it?" I almost whispered. David looked at me again, his eyebrows raised. I struggled to meet his gaze. He smiled softly, but his eyes lacked their usual joviality.

"No, it's okay. There's not a lot to say, to be honest." He laughed quietly before looking away again.

"Okay, but if you ever need to," I shrugged.

He glanced at me sideways, his smile gently widening. "Thanks."

"That's twenty-three fifty-five, please."

David looked up at the barmaid, his eyes again wide. He let his mouth drop open.

"How much?" he protested loudly before breaking into a grin. The blonde bombshell smiled back at him mildly as she took his debit card. He turned to me and winked as she busied herself at the till. I smiled back before picking up three of the smaller glasses and walking back to our party and away from another delicious moment of intimacy.

*

"Whoa, steady."

Jim grasped my arm tightly as I wobbled precariously. I grabbed hold of the back of his seat with my free hand.

"I'm fine."

My voice was shrill but thankfully not slurred. He let go, holding his hand up in apology, his amusement plastered across his wide face. I looked away without another word and carefully picked my way through the pub to the glass doors at the back of the building. Eric and David had disappeared through them over twenty minutes ago. My third large glass of Merlot had made me brave enough to act on my curiosity – and desire to get David on his own, away from the babble of co-workers. Stepping deliberately over the trip hazard of the doorframe I looked around the decked beer garden, shivering. I heard Eric's voice, almost as large as he was, before I saw the bulk of his back. David was watching his face intently, nodding every now and then. As soon as he saw me walking towards them his expression brightened.

"Well, hello there. Fancied a bit of fresh air?"

Before I could answer he handed me a cigarette. I hesitated before taking it.

"I didn't realise you were a smoker?" Eric enquired as he sucked on his roll-up. "I had you down as a 'my body is a temple' type."

"I'm sure that she is, Eric. But even angels fall from grace once in a while." David grinned at me as he held up his lighter for me. My hand on his, I steadied the flame and inhaled as gently as I could. With effort I managed not to splutter as the smoke curled down my throat.

"Well, you learn something new every day," Eric said, watching me carefully. I stared back at him boldly. I hadn't forgotten Eric's influence on my last supervision with David and was determined to prove his doubts about my abilities to be unfounded. Eric raised his unkempt eyebrows at me before looking back at David. David smiled at him before looking back down at me. His smile quickly turned into a frown.

"Are you cold?"

I stared at him blankly for a moment before noticing that my teeth were chattering. Involuntarily I shivered again.

"A bit," I managed, smiling apologetically. Still frowning, David placed his cigarette between his lips and began to pull off his coat.

"Oh no, I'm okay," I protested, shakily bringing my own cigarette up to my mouth.

"Sorry, but I insist." Carefully David draped the coat over my shoulders. His fingers brushed my ear as he gently pulled my hair free from its itchy woollen collar. I couldn't help but grin up at him, my body warming at his touch as much as from the extra layer.

"Thanks," I whispered, and he smiled back at me, his eyes shining despite the darkness.

"Okay, kids, that's enough of that."

Eric's tone had lost its mirth. We looked at him simultaneously. David spluttered into a laugh.

"What? Can't a manager offer his coat to a member of his team when she's freezing her ass off?"

Eric looked from David to me, then back again. He was holding his roll-up in between a sausage-like finger and thumb as he smoked, the daintiness of the pose made all the more ridiculous by his size.

"You know what I mean, David."

As the two men looked at each other in silence, I realised I had been holding my breath. A sharp inhalation of ice-cold air and smoke made me cough loudly. As I hacked into my hand, David raised his hand and an eyebrow at his boss.

"May I?"

Eric gave a brief nod before shaking his head at the floor. David dropped his smoke and patted me firmly on the back. Eventually my spasms eased. I smiled at him between my final splutters.

"Thanks."

He looked down at me, breaking eye contact with Eric for what had been so long I was beginning to think they'd forgotten I was part of the conversation. His gaze was blank.

"You're welcome."

He spoke so quietly I wondered if I'd imagined it. Eric cleared his throat noisily.

"Right. Can I suggest that now we've all had our nicotine fix we go back inside where the temperature is a little more amicable?"

"Good idea," David said loudly, looking back at his boss and giving my back a final pat before shoving his hands into his pockets. "I need a slash anyway." I started to follow him as he strode back to the door.

"Just a sec, Emily. A quick word, if I may?" As Eric's fingers curled around my arm, I knew that I couldn't escape – pretending I didn't hear him would be one thing, but pulling away from his grip, however unwelcome, wasn't really an option. I took a deep breath and turned towards him.

"Yes?"

I couldn't keep my contempt from my voice. I knew he was the service manager and that I should show him due respect, but I couldn't help but be repulsed by his touch and annoyed at his interference. He took a breath then hesitated, scrutinising me again with those tiny eyes. Eventually he exhaled loudly.

"Look, Emily, I'm not saying this to be deliberately difficult, or trying to patronise you, but I've seen the way you are around David and I can only conclude that you've developed an interest in him beyond his position as your manager."

My mouth dropped open. I couldn't believe what the ruddy, bulbous man in front of me was saying. Thankfully the cold prevented my blush from developing.

"I-I'm not sure that's any of your business," I stammered, lifting my chin defiantly. Eric shrugged.

"Well, I think that it is. At the end of the day, you and David work for a service I manage and I am your boss. And experience tells me that any emotional entanglement will just make things messy for everyone involved. Besides," he continued, "I'm very fond of David and don't want to see him getting into bother, at work or at home."

I looked down at my feet and clasped my hands in front of me. Anger and embarrassment pulsed through me. I looked over at the door with longing before returning my gaze to my lecturer.

"Is that all?" I enquired, desperate to keep any emotion out of my voice.

"Not quite." Eric met my gaze easily. "Emily, David is a wonderful man, and young enough to still be very attractive." His chuckle made me want to scream. "But he's also quite insecure at the moment, and the attentions of a young lady like yourself are no doubt incredibly flattering and doing his bruised ego the world of good. But he's married, Emily. And a father."

Eric's grip on my arm tightened as he uttered the two words I really didn't want to hear. I looked down at his hand, resentful of its part in reminding me of the stark reality of my situation. Our situation.

"Despite the difficulties he's facing with these facts right now, I know that he loves his wife and his children dearly and nothing, or no one, is going to change that." Eric's free hand grasped my other arm. I looked at his round face, too fat to show the telltale lines of his age, and felt nothing more than hate. "Emily, do you understand?"

I clamped my teeth together and looked down at the slippery decking. There was no point arguing with this idiot of a man. He was wrong, so wrong, but too full of his own self-importance to be able to ever admit it. I nodded.

"Good. Now, I'm sorry if I've been harsh with you, but, well, I've been young too, believe it or not, and know how much these situations can screw with you if you let them. And I wouldn't wish that on anyone. Okay?"

When I looked up at him he was smiling, his jowls wobbling with the effort. I forced a smile in return. He exhaled loudly through his nose as he released my arm.

"Good. Now, shall we go back inside so I can buy you a drink? Maybe a lemonade or something to sober you up a bit?" He chuckled again. My expression remained fixed on my face, my smile frozen. I didn't trust myself to respond. Instead, I let him lead the way back into the pub and to the table of inebriated support workers.

When Jim told me David had gone home, I swallowed down my disappointment with a mouthful of the sticky Coke Eric smugly handed me.

26

"Hello?"

"Hi, Dad. It's me."

I could almost feel his irritation crackling down the phone.

"Hello, Emily. What is it?"

I hesitated.

"Nothing, Dad. I just thought I'd call you for a chat." Propped up against my pillows on my bed, I rested my phone between my shoulder and cheek and pulled my legs up to my chest as my father digested the concept.

"A chat. Okay, what do you want to chat about?"

On the other end of the phone I could hear the familiar tinkle of ice against glass. In my mind I could see my dad now, popping the cubes from the ice tray into his favourite tumbler before reaching for the nearest bottle of Scotch.

"How are you?" I blurted. My dad snorted.

"Me? Same as ever. Working, sleeping, eating..."

"Drinking," I added, unable to stop myself. I knew my dad wasn't an alcoholic or anything, but it did bother me that, these days, whenever I saw him or spoke to him, he had a whisky on the go. I bit my lip as I waited for his angry response. His laughter surprised me so much I let my phone slip from its clamped position next to my ear.

"Oh bloody hell, Emily. I know I like a drink after a hard day at the office but I would have thought that, bearing in mind your professional experience, you'd be able to see that I'm not exactly a raving alcoholic."

He was right, of course. Compared to the drinkers on my caseload, my dad's alcohol consumption was negligible. But it still bothered me.

"I know, Dad, but... I worry you drink because you're not happy?" I wrapped my cardigan tightly around myself. Whilst it helped against the chill in my room, the cool tone of his voice was harder to avoid.

"Not happy? Why wouldn't I be happy, Emily? I mean, my life is just peachy, isn't it?"

I shut my eyes.

"Dad, I didn't mean to upset you. I just worry about you, that's all."

He laughed again, but the hint of amusement that had been present before had gone.

"Well, you really shouldn't, Emily. No one's ever worried about me before and I've got along just fine, so there's no need for you to suddenly start. You've never been that concerned about me before."

"Dad..."

"Just drop it, will you?" he snapped. I didn't blame him. My voice had become whiney and clingy, desperate for his assurance. A sure-fire way to irritate him.

"Sorry," I whispered. I heard the clink of ice again as he took a sip of his drink followed by a sigh.

"No, I'm sorry, Emily. I was being really unfair." I squeezed my eyes together even tighter against the tears that threatened. I didn't dare speak. "So, tell me, how's work?"

My dad ummed and grunted in all the appropriate places as I stumbled through a monologue about my work, my clients, my achievements. I deliberately avoided talking about the cases that weren't going as well. I didn't want to worry him, and I certainly didn't want him to think that I wasn't coping.

"And your colleagues? You're still getting on okay with them?"

"Yes, fine," I automatically enthused. There was no way I wanted him to know about the conflict I seemed to have developed with Eric. As for David, well, it was too soon to tell him much about my relationship with my manager. He would only stress about it.

"Good, good." Silence swallowed up the conversation only minutes after it had started. Eventually my dad cleared his throat. "Well, Emily, I better go. I think my dinner's about ready, and the dog's looking a bit hungry too."

I knew it was an excuse but laughed anyway. I didn't want to start another argument. In fact, the chance of ending a conversation with my dad on a high, even if it was artificial, was one I couldn't resist.

"Okay, Dad. Well, enjoy your dinner and say hi to Barney for me."

"I will do, Emily. Bye."

The line clicked as he hung up. I caught my phone as it dropped from my ear and let myself slide into the foetal position. I imagined my dad pottering about in his kitchen getting his home-cooked meal out of the oven, Barney yapping happily at his feet. Even though I knew the jolly scene was a fantasy, I kept it running in my mind until I fell asleep.

27

The beep from my personal mobile phone wasn't the kind of distraction I was used to. I let my eyes wander from the blur of my computer screen and blinked at it. I so rarely got a text message it took me a couple of seconds to figure out what had just happened – the only noise my phone usually made was to alert me that the battery, after days of inactivity, was about to run dry. I looked around, hoping that someone would be around to witness the rare moment of social contact. A couple of the bitchy girls were gossiping at the back of the office, too engrossed in their own little lives to notice anything happening in anyone else's. At the front of the room, in his usual spot by the window, sat David, his headphones firmly stuck in his ears. I grabbed my phone and opened the message. It was Lorraine.

Hey Em, hope ur good? U about for an early evening drink? Will be in Camden in 15.

I stared blankly at the message. Lorraine never messaged me these days, and certainly not to invite me out for a drink. I looked at my watch. 4.56. The two girls yapping behind me would be out the door as soon as the duty line closed at five, leaving me and David alone. It was a rare treat, and one I really didn't want to sacrifice. I bit my lip as I tapped a reply.

Sorry Lorraine, I can't get away until 6. Really busy. Can you meet me then?

The reply was almost instant. My old friend was clearly an accomplished texter, even if I was so rarely the recipient.

No, meeting a client. Can't u pop out for a coffee even? Need to see a friendly face :(

Automatically I hid my phone in my lap under the desk as the two carbon copy blondes swished past me. I glanced at my watch again. 4.58. I looked over at David, but he was too engrossed in whatever he was working on to notice their tardiness.

"Bye, David," one of the girls sang, offering him a coy wave as they sashayed past his desk. David looked up instantly and pulled out one his earplugs.

"What? Oh yeah, see you." He watched them as they disappeared from view, seemingly mesmerised by the casual contact. I couldn't help but feel jealous of his interest in these two flakes. On cue, one of them sniggered. I looked down the corridor to see them both watching me as they pulled on their almost identical faux fur coats. My face burning, I turned back to my phone.

Sorry, I can't. Maybe at the weekend? Xxx

The kisses were an afterthought. Okay, so something was clearly bothering Lorraine, but she had rarely bothered to make time for me in her busy schedule of champagne, parties and men in the whole six months that we had both been in London. I took a sharp breath. Six months. I had been living and working in the capital for almost half a year. And so much had changed.

"You alright there?"

David's voice in such close proximity caught me completely off guard. He started to laugh.

"Sorry, didn't mean to startle you. Everything okay? You sounded like you were about to start hyperventilating."

He smiled down at me, his hands in his pockets. As normal, the end of the working day brought with it the crumpled shirt, not yet pulled free from his belt, the artfully dishevelled hair and so-aptly named five o'clock shadow. Despite the signs of a long day, he still managed to be beautiful. As his smile deepened, I turned away from him, my face suddenly hot. I feigned interest in my phone. Lorraine hadn't replied.

"Oh, no, I'm fine. I just got a message from my friend and she just reminded me how long I've been here."

He threw back his head and laughed loudly. "Well, you've no doubt worked your contracted hours for the week already so, if you feel that way, maybe you should go home?"

My blush deepened at his merriment. "Oh no, I didn't mean that. I mean, I can't believe I've already lived in London for a whole six months. And worked here for that long too."

"Don't worry, Emily, I know what you meant." His eyes glimmered mischievously. "You know what they say, though. Time flies…"

"When you're having fun!" I couldn't help myself but finish off his joke for him before giggling nervously. David joined in.

"Well, we have plenty of that here at Drug and Alcohol Action. Along with lots of tea. A cup of which I'm about to make. Would you like one?"

His smile was so inviting, I couldn't resist the offer, despite my lack of interest in having a hot drink. I nodded up at him, a grin plastered across my face. His dimples deepened in response.

"Good. Milk? Sugar?"

He started to walk in the direction of the kitchen before I could answer, his hands still in his pockets. I jumped out of my seat, anxious not to let our interaction come to an end.

"I'll come with you," I called after him, my voice all too loud. He stopped and looked back at me, an eyebrow raised. "I need a break from my computer," I shrugged, willing the colour of my face to return to normal. He shrugged back and smiled.

"Okay."

*

I lingered by the kitchen door as David busied himself searching through the cupboards for a pair of clean mugs, whistling tunelessly to himself as he did so. He looked at me as he fished out a battered box of teabags.

"Did you say you wanted sugar?"

I shook my head and looked at the floor, even though I knew that, deep down, we should be beyond these awkward moments. Without the aid of alcohol I still struggled to play it cool when we were left alone. I heard the fridge door open and close and dared myself to look at him. He glanced back as he carefully poured milk into our drinks and grinned.

"So, Emily, tell me why you're still here after five rather than out and about enjoying the razzle-dazzle of your new hometown?"

I grinned back at him. He was teasing me. He knew full well why I was there.

"Well, someone needs to make sure that you remember to leave the office, David," I flirted back.

He laughed as he handed me my drink.

"Oh, don't you worry about that. Trust me, if I'm not through the front door by seven, my life isn't worth living." My smile faded at the reference to his family. "Seriously though, is everything okay? Is your workload manageable? Are you struggling with anything specific?"

The sudden switch back to manager-mode momentarily confused me.

"Yes, I, I think so," I stuttered. "I've just been taking a slightly longer lunch break the last few weeks. You know, on the internet and stuff," I added, hoping my explanation would be enough to smooth away his deepening frown. He screwed up his face.

"The internet? Really? Now, I know I'm a bit of an old fart and don't really understand all this social media stuff, but surely going out and seeing your mates face to face is a much better use of your time? Trust me, you'll regret it if you don't. It gets a lot harder when they all start getting married off and having kids."

I saw the regret in his eyes straight away. I wanted to comfort him, tell him things were going to be better, but I didn't want to say too much, to push him when he wasn't ready.

"Well, just because you have kids doesn't mean you can't still see your friends, surely? Maybe she just needs to cut you some slack and let you do what you want to do once in a while."

David's eyebrows shot up. I held my breath as he digested my comment, silently chastising my lack of poise when it came to his wife. To my relief, eventually he laughed.

"Well, to be fair, she does let me go out, Emily. My wife isn't a complete tyrant. It's just sometimes a little bit tricky balancing everything. Besides, I like being with my family," he added, apparently unaware of my burning face. I stared down at my tea.

"I'm sorry, I didn't mean anything. I just... hope she appreciates what she has, that's all."

When David didn't respond, I dared myself to look up at him. He was watching me. The smile that touched the corners of his mouth, combined with the deepening frown across his forehead and blank eyes confused me even further.

"It's okay, Emily, I know what you meant. It's just a bit more complicated than that. One day, you'll see."

He winked at me before taking a sip of his drink and looking at his watch. His eyes widened.

"Bloody hell, I better get on with it. I need to finish typing up these notes before I leave." He ran his hand across his face and frowned. "And I need to start shaving in the mornings again. Sadly when you get to my age any attempt at designer stubble tends to turn out more like Stig of the Dump." He laughed without any real conviction and wandered out of the kitchen.

"I think it suits you," I all but whispered to his back. He paused and looked back at me.

"What?"

"The stubble. It suits you. You should leave it."

He stared at me for a few seconds before his frown broke into a wide grin.

"Really?"

I grinned back. He laughed before nodding thoughtfully to himself.

"Thanks. Maybe I will."

Hugging my mug in my hands, I watched him as he sauntered around the corner back to his desk, still nodding to himself.

28

The creak of the door jolted me back to reality. I looked anxiously past my own reflection in the mirror. My unease crawled up into my throat and settled uncomfortably as one of the office bitches coolly met my gaze. She all but smirked as she swept into one of the cubicles, tossing her poker straight blonde hair majestically as she did so. As the door slammed shut, I turned my attention back to my face. My reflection stared blankly back. I pulled back my shoulders, released my hair from behind my ears and tried a smile. The result was disappointing. I didn't have any make-up other than a lipstick with me and was feeling less than prepared for the supervision David had invited me to only this morning. But then I knew that he was interested in more than just a pretty face. He liked me for who I was, which is more than some of my colleagues would ever be able to say. As the toilet flushed behind me, I smiled again, this time without effort, picked up my satchel and strode out of the ladies before the cow had the opportunity to make me question my new-found confidence.

My pace slowed as I reached the familiar office door. I took a deep breath, shook my hair behind my shoulders and knocked gently. David's voice beckoned me in. He was sitting in Eric's elaborate swivel chair, a phone plastered to his ear. He glanced up at me and nodded to the chair next to the desk before turning his body away from me. I sat down slowly and pulled my notebook and pen out of my bag. David had dropped his head to his free hand, his eyes closed against the torrent I could clearly make out from the other end of the line.

"Yes, yes, I know. Yeah, I understand."

As he nodded along, I looked around the room. Something wasn't right. We normally sat at the round table in the corner, informally, friendly, not at Eric's desk like two strangers. I looked at David again. His eyes were open again, but fixed on the plywood surface his elbow was leaning so heavily on.

He didn't look at me until he had finally got off the phone a good three minutes later. When he did, I knew something was different between us, wrong. His blue eyes, usually so calm and kind, appeared devoid of emotion, his jaw tense. He looked older, tired, the scattering of greys at his temple suddenly more prominent. I swallowed as my mind frantically searched for some explanation for his cold demeanour.

"What's wrong?" I asked quietly when he didn't speak. Slowly he sat up in his chair and took a deep breath.

"That was Social Services on the phone. Apparently Stacey was found by her neighbour unconscious in her flat. Her baby had been wailing for an age and Stacey wasn't answering the door. Her neighbour was worried and got her boyfriend to force it open."

My pen fell to the floor as I covered my mouth with my hand. David's eyes silently searched my face.

"Oh no, that's terrible. W-what happened?" I stuttered under the weight of his scrutiny. David screwed up his face and shrugged.

"She'd had too much to drink, basically. According to the neighbour she's been back on it for weeks. It was only a matter of time."

I nodded down at my lap, suddenly aware that her relapse was probably news to everyone but me. I hadn't told David and, as I'd promised my client, I'd kept Social Services in the dark too. The discomfort I had felt minutes earlier in the ladies returned with a vengeance. I cleared my throat.

"What did Social Services say?"

"Well, they were notified by the ambulance crew who attended. The neighbour offered to look after the kid and Social Services agreed. Apparently she's helped out Stacey a lot in the past and is known to them."

I nodded again. Suddenly I realised that I should probably be making some notes. I bent down to retrieve my pen, opened my notebook and looked up.

"So when did this happen?"

David steadily met my gaze. When he didn't answer straight away, my face began to burn.

"It happened late last night, or rather early this morning. The problem is though, Emily, that the neighbour told Social Services that you were working with Stacey and supporting her to get dry again. But the duty manager can't find any record of you notifying them."

Unable to bear his cold stare anymore, I looked down at my notebook. His anger was torture.

"She'd only had a couple of lapses. We put a support plan in place to stop it happening again, and she was sticking to it. There was no need to call Social Services..."

"But there was." I looked up at David as he spoke, stunned by his slightly raised voice, his harsh tone. He looked down at his hands, clasped together tightly on his knees. "You see, Emily, Stacey might have only told you about two relapses, but her history would suggest that once she's back on it, it isn't just for a one-off. It will be most nights. And with her track record, a call to the social worker was absolutely necessary in this situation. Do you understand?"

I nodded dumbly. Although his voice was soft again, his disappointment simmered audibly under the surface. My eyes burned with sudden tears, desperate to be let out.

"And, Emily, even if you weren't sure about calling Social Services, why didn't you speak to me?"

A tear landed noisily on my notepad, making the paper swell, the printed line fuzz at the edges. David inhaled deeply again.

"Emily, please don't be upset. I just can't understand why you didn't tell me about this."

I didn't dare look at him. I knew I had let him down, got him into trouble even. I took a steadying breath and wiped another tear from under my eye before it could escape any further.

"I was dealing with it. We had a plan and it was working. There was no need. I didn't want to worry you unnecessarily..."

"Emily, with this client group, we expect people to relapse. It happens all the time. We can't stop people from choosing between sobriety and one final hit, another binge. But what we can do is try to minimise the harm it causes if they do make that decision. To themselves and others."

I nodded quickly and sniffed back my emotion.

"I know. I'm sorry. I just... I wanted to show you that I can manage these situations by myself."

David's sigh betrayed his irritation.

"Yes, but sometimes it is better to admit that you are out of your depth and get it right. These are people's lives, Emily."

I dared myself to look up at him. He looked pale, drawn. His gaze refused to meet my own. It was then that I understood. He was angry because I had not confided in him, trusted him. He wanted to be there for me, and I had shunned him. But he couldn't tell me that. Not now anyway.

"I understand, David," I said as steadily as I could. Briefly his eyes locked with mine before darting back down to his hands. Hands that I so wanted to reach out and reassure.

"Good." He straightened up in his chair again but kept his hands locked together, his gaze low. "Although I should warn you, Eric knows about all this. The duty social worker went straight to him when they realised something was amiss, and he isn't happy."

In my mind I saw the service manager's face, his jowls wobbling and his face crimson with rage, ranting at David as he puffed away on one of his roll-ups. Although I couldn't quite understand why, I knew David looked up to Eric and wouldn't want to see him displeased. I bit my lip.

"I'm really sorry," I whispered.

David looked up at me. I held his gaze for as long as I could, relieved to finally have that contact but disturbed by the anguish that my manager so clearly felt.

"I know you are. But, like I say, Eric really isn't happy. At the end of the day, it was negligent for us not to tell Social Services, which means it was negligent of me as your manager not to ensure that it was picked up on. And, it was negligent of you."

My mouth dropped open. Desperately I sought for something to say, something to redeem myself yet reassure David that the blame would not lie on his shoulders.

"I'll tell Eric it was my fault. I should have told you about it. You, you've always told me to come to you if I need to. Always. He can't hold it against you..."

My words faltered as David began to shake his head. He looked down at his hands again.

"Emily, don't worry about me. Okay, so I've had my ear chewed off about it, but I'll get over it." His jaw tensed momentarily as his frown deepened. "What you need to understand, though, is that you are still on your probationary period. Essentially, Eric could give you a week's notice here and now. But," he held out his hand defensively as I inhaled a jagged breath, "but, I've spoken with him and he isn't going to do that. What it does mean, though, is that he's insisted that we extend your probationary period by another three months."

I stared at him dumbly as I digested what he had said. Eric had wanted to fire me. He wanted me out. But David had saved my skin.

"I know you'll be disappointed about this but, in the circumstances, I think he's being more than fair. We really need people here who will follow certain procedures when it comes to Child Protection. At the end of the day, it's probably the thing we are most scrutinised for, and we need to get it right."

He pushed his hair out of his face and turned his chair back to the desk. I watched him as he arranged the usual disarray of paper in front of him into an orderly pile. He glanced at me as he did so.

"If you want to take a bit of time out now, Emily, that's fine. I'll schedule another supervision for next week so we can start looking at how we can address this."

I watched him as he placed his already dog-eared diary on top of the papers and stood up. Hesitantly I looked up at his face. The eyes that looked back were full of regret.

"I'm sorry, Emily."

He offered me half a smile before striding to the door and walking out of Eric's office. As the door slammed behind me my eyes welled up once more. I had let my stupid pride not only jeopardise my job but hurt David at the same time. I wanted to go after him to apologise again and explain that I had done what I did to make him proud, make him see that he could trust me and rely on me. Yes, it had backfired, but if he could see what my intentions had been, he would at least understand.

Laughter from the corridor outside made me sit up in my seat. As it passed by in the direction of the kitchen, I tried to work out if it had been directed at me. I looked around the room, at the white walls, the black carpet, the chair that David had sat in only seconds ago. I felt my face begin to burn again as anger and humiliation rose from my gut. How Eric could blame me for this I didn't know. What would Social Services have done anyway? It was me who was helping her, not anyone else. It was clear that he wanted me out, was threatened by my relationship with David, if not that then my determination to support my clients through their difficulties rather than falter at the first hurdle and run to him for help. I wiped my face with shaking hands and stood up. I wasn't going to let him or anyone else persuade me that I wasn't competent. I took a deep breath, picked up my belongings and walked steadily out of the room and back to my desk. Ignoring the stares, I sat down and switched on my laptop. I wasn't about to let the head of Drug and Alcohol Action bully me out of my job and away from David. I would show him what I was made of – and everyone else who refused to take me seriously, too.

29

I sipped my wine and glanced around. The pub was dimly lit, the shabby chandeliers hanging from the ceiling offering little more light than the fireplace next to me, all but hiding me in my little corner. I'd never been there before but Fran had always raved about it and, when Lorraine had texted me yet again asking to meet, I had decided that it would be on my terms, at a location I had chosen. As I took another sip I spotted her as she pushed her way through the heavy oak door and almost stumble into a group of hipsters drinking artisan beers by the bar. I couldn't help but feel some satisfaction to see her discomfort as she scanned the room for me, her bleached blonde hair and red city coat in sharp contrast to the grungy clientele. I gave her a wave as she looked in my direction. Her face, thinner than I remembered, lit up with recognition before she gestured if I wanted a drink. I pointed at my glass and shook my head but she had already turned to the bearded barman.

A bottle of red in one hand and a glass in the other, I watched her as she weaved her way through the tables, taking care not to brush against any of the patrons who eyed her with interest. Arriving at my table, she dumped her cargo and sat down heavily on the chair opposite me, her cheeks puffed out.

"Well, you really have dragged me to the arse-end of nowhere for this drink, haven't you? It took me half an hour to find this place."

I kept my smile in check as I watched her pour herself a generous glass of wine. She gulped down a mouthful before shrugging off her coat. Her crisp white shirt and scarlet tank top did little to detract the attention she had already received. With her high cheekbones, sharper than ever, and red lips, she really was striking, even if not necessarily beautiful. Her glasses hid the dark circles under her eyes to a degree but, even with a full face of make-up, I could see that she was tired. She looked at me suddenly, catching my scrutiny. I looked away from her face at the bar behind her and shrugged.

"Well, I like it here. It's cosy."

Lorraine snorted.

"Well, that's one way of looking at it. Dark and dingy is another. And full of people who think they're above wearing clean clothes and shaving once in a while."

"Maybe they are just comfortable in their own skin? I mean, not everyone feels the need to keep up appearances all the time." As soon as the words were out, I knew that Lorraine would take them personally. I took another sip of my wine and feigned ignorance at my gaffe as I looked around the room. "I feel comfortable here, anyway."

I was lying, of course. I didn't fit in with the trendy crowd any more than Lorraine and had felt like a fraud as soon as I walked in. But I wasn't about to let my friend know that. I appeared to have the upper hand and fully intended to keep hold of it.

"Well, whatever floats your boat. Anyway, how are you?"

"I'm good, thanks," I said all too chirpily. "How are you?"

"Shite," she drawled as she topped up her glass. She glanced at mine. "Are you on the Shiraz?"

I nodded quickly despite my ignorance of what I was drinking and watched her as she topped it up.

"So what's wrong?"

She shook her head as she drank.

"Well, where do I start? You know that guy from work, Josh?" I nodded away my doubt. "Well, he's pretty much dumped me. You know he was helping me? Well, it appears that his ego can't cope with the fact that I don't need that help anymore. In fact, I've been gaining better clients than he has the last month or so, and rumour has it I'm up for a promotion."

"That's great!" I squeaked. Lorraine looked at me blankly.

"Well, it's long overdue if you ask me. But that's not the point. The point is he's lost interest. And apparently he's been telling everyone that I've been shagging my way to the top."

I watched Lorraine as she took another mouthful of wine. I knew she'd slept with a few people through her connections at work and wasn't wholly surprised by the slur. I chewed on my lip as I pondered what to say. Lorraine looked at me sharply.

"What? Do you think he has a point or something? Because, if you do, please tell me now and I'll…"

"No, no, I don't," I said hurriedly, looking around nervously. A couple sitting at a table nearby were staring at us, no doubt attracted by Lorraine's loud voice. I turned back to her. "I just don't know what to say. That's horrible."

Lorraine forced down more wine. She placed the glass back on the chipped table and stared at it with wide eyes.

"Well, I could cope with the bitching. Let's face it, people will always try to drag you down when they see you getting ahead. But from him?"

Her jaw clenched visibly as she shook her head. I watched her as she drained the contents of her glass.

"I'm sorry," I whispered. Lorraine glanced up at me and gave me a brief smile. Although I hated to see her so upset, I couldn't help but feel some satisfaction to see her back to her old, doubting self, even if it was only fleetingly. The old Lorraine had wanted me in her life, needed me even, and if it meant that I would keep my friend I was happy to see her vulnerable side again. She sniffed as she poured herself another glass.

"Anyway, enough about me. What's going on with you and that manager?"

I looked at her over the top of my wine as I sipped the heavy red. She stared back expectantly. Carefully placing the glass back on the table I sighed.

"It's difficult, Lorraine. I think other people in the service have cottoned on to what is happening between us and they aren't happy about it. In fact, they're deliberately making life difficult for the both of us."

Lorraine snorted. "Sounds familiar. At the end of the day, as long as you're both getting on with your job, it's none of their business."

"Well, Eric seems hell-bent on trying to tell David that I can't do mine. He's really got it in for me."

Lorraine pulled a face.

"Eric? Who's he?"

"The service manager. He had a word with us about our relationship in the pub the other week, you know, trying to warn us off each other. Obviously it didn't work so now he's determined to get David to fail my probationary period. Bastard."

Lorraine watched me closely as I drank.

"So he's trying to get you fired?"

I nodded violently.

"Yep."

Lorraine folded her arms as she leant back in her chair.

"Well, I don't see how he can just because you're having an affair with your boss."

Affair. What an ugly word. I felt my face flush.

"Well, he's been making up excuses. And it isn't an affair."

Lorraine's unfaltering scrutiny increased my discomfort.

"Like what?"

I shrugged again.

"Well, he's basically accused me of not reporting something to Social Services that he reckons I should have."

"What?" Lorraine fired back. I rolled my eyes.

"One of my clients relapsed and she has a little girl. It's no big deal," I added as her eyes widened again. "I mean, we had a plan in place to get her sorted. Eric just freaked out about it, that's all."

Lorraine's eyes searched my face as I took another sip of my wine. My glass was almost empty, and, with my friend's constant top-ups, I knew I had probably exceeded my safe limit.

"Well, I don't know anything about your job, but that sounds pretty serious to me." I glared at her as she filled her glass once more before tipping the remainder of the bottle into mine. "And, you might not like to admit it, Em, but unless he's all of a sudden left his wife for you, it is an affair. So you better get used to it."

Her triumphant smile made my eyes burn.

"Has he left his wife?"

"No," I murmured.

Lorraine clapped her hands together.

"Well, there you have it," she laughed as she shook her head, her ponytail whipping from side to side. "Welcome to the club."

"It isn't an affair because we haven't done anything." My voice was loud and emotional in the cool calm of the pub. This time it was Lorraine's turn to look around, a pink glow around the base of her neck betraying her embarrassment.

"Okay, Emily. Jeez, you don't have to get upset about it."
She wriggled down in her seat, her shoulders hunched. We sat in silence for a long moment, both of us staring at the gnarled table between us. Eventually, Lorraine cleared her throat.

"So, if nothing's happened and he's still with his wife, how do you know he really likes you?"

I looked up at her, surprised. She pouted back at me.

"Well?"

Laughter spluttered out of me. Lorraine sighed impatiently and glanced around the pub again as I struggled to regain my composure. I steadied myself with a sip of wine and grinned at her.

"Lorraine, you don't need to sleep with someone to know how they feel about you. You just know."

She raised an eyebrow.

"Gee, well, thanks for the tip. But has he ever said anything?"

"Yes. Loads of things," I smiled back, my head high and haughty. Lorraine's other eyebrow crept up to meet the other.

"Explicit things? Like he loves you and is going to give up his livelihood for you?"

My smile wavered under the interrogation.

"No. But he doesn't need to. I know how he feels, and I feel the same way. That's all there is to it."

I met Lorraine's gaze defiantly. My triumph was short-lived when she finally broke it.

"Emily, are you sure? I mean, I'm not being funny, but do you think there's a chance that you might have just got the wrong end of the stick?"

"No, I don't think I've got it wrong at all. I think that David is just being subtle, for both our sakes. It's complicated. He's being sensitive to the needs of his family, as well as mine."

Lorraine had picked up her handbag to search its cavernous inside. She eyed me as she pulled out a packet of Marlboros.

"Well, I've got to say, I'm not convinced. Anyway, I'm nipping out for a fag. Back in a min."

I watched her as she strode out of the pub, a little less steadily than when she had entered it. As the door slammed shut behind her, I picked up my glass and downed the last of my wine. Slamming it back down on the table, I glared at Lorraine's coat, still elegantly draped on the back of her chair. She was jealous. Jealous because someone loved me when she had been rejected. Jealous because, unlike Josh and all the other men she had been messing around with, David was treating me with dignity and respect. Things that my friend was denied by the men she slept with and her own self.

"Well, I'd suggest getting another drink, but you look like you've had enough."

I refocused on the room around me, on Lorraine as she slid back onto her seat, that superior smile still playing on her lips.

"Yes, I think you're right. I've had enough of your snide comments about David and I anyway."

Lorraine gaped at me before falling into another fit of laughter.

"Snide? No, Emily, not snide, just based on reality. Something you seem to have lost your grip on these days."

"You know, jealousy really doesn't suit you, Lorraine. That shade of green clashes with your lipstick." I was on my feet, clumsily pushing my arms into the sleeves of my coat. Lorraine's laughter surrounded me.

"Jealous? Of you? Give me a break, Emily." She eyed me coolly as I tried to untangle the strap of my bag from the back of my seat. "I mean, think about it. You're on the verge of losing your job, and you've developed a crush on your boss so bad that you've managed to convince yourself that you're in some kind of 'relationship' with him." She drew the quotation marks in the air with perfectly manicured nails. "So no, I'm not jealous at all. And if that hasn't convinced you, take a look in the mirror. Something you clearly haven't done in quite some time."

My satchel finally over my shoulder, I stared at my friend. She was sipping her wine casually as she regarded me. I pulled my hair free from the back of my coat and sniffed.

"I'm not going to listen to this anymore. Goodbye, Lorraine."

"Yeah. See yer," her voice floated after me as I stumbled out of the pub. Outside, the cold air pinched at my face, wet yet again. I wrapped my coat around me and, not bothering to stop to fasten it, walked quickly towards the tube. I grasped the rail of the escalator, wiped my face with my free hand and took a deep breath in a desperate attempt to control my tears along with the nausea rising from my stomach. On the platform I felt my way along to the nearest bench and shakily sat down. Three trains passed before I could trust myself to board one without being sick. As I sat in the swaying carriage, my eyes closed, I thought about Lorraine's cruel words, cutting me like knives. Breathing deeply, I imagined the day when I'd introduce her to David and tell her about yet another promotion at work. In my mind I listened to her gush at how wonderful he was, how well I had done, how beautiful I looked, how she was sorry, begging me to forgive her for her envious words.

By the time I shook my keys into the door of my room, my head was pounding. I collapsed onto my bed and half-heartedly pulled my duvet over me, my clothes still on. Within seconds I was asleep, but a tired smile was spread across my aching face.

30

"Emily?"

I hid the email I was typing as soon as the voice registered and looked up. Fran was looking down at me from the other side of the desk, her dreads pulled away from her pale face with a bright green scarf. I felt my shoulders relax, reassured. I didn't want anyone to see what I was typing, let alone Fran, but from her position I knew I was safe.

"Yes?" I said brightly.

"I asked if you wanted a coffee or anything? I'm nipping out."

I bit my lip and made a show of pondering her question.

"Um, no, I think I'm okay. But thanks for offering."

She watched me for a moment before shrugging and walking away. She'd been looking at me like that a lot since I told her about the extension of my probationary period, as though she was examining my face for cracks in my cheerful countenance. I knew it was just her nurturing nature kicking in but I couldn't help but find it grating. So far my calm and collected exterior had kept her curiosity at bay, but I knew it was only a matter of time before she tried to pin me down for a session of amateur counselling. I watched her as she disappeared from view before looking around the office. It was quite busy, but luckily the desks around me were deserted. David hadn't been in all day. Some kind of emergency that his wife was unable to deal with had kept him at home. In fact I'd hardly seen him since our meeting about Stacey's relapse. I knew he was in a difficult position, but I couldn't help but feel that he was avoiding me. Whilst I understood, I didn't want Eric's overreaction to the situation to get in the way of our relationship. Which was why I'd decided to email him.

Satisfied that I wasn't being observed, I opened the message again.

Dear David,

I hope you're okay and whatever has happened at home isn't too bad :)

I just wanted to tell you I'm sorry about my mistake with Stacey. I know now I should have spoken to you about it, and if I'd realised how much it was going to affect us I would never have kept it from you.

I hope you understand and can forgive me? I guess it makes sense that we have some distance between us whilst this whole thing blows over, but I hope things go back to how they were soon. I miss our evening chats after everyone else has gone home, and long for the day when we can have them away from the office too, just the two of us.

All my love,
Emily
Xxx

I read through it three times, debating changes here and there. Was it too casual? Should I say more about how I felt? Beg for forgiveness? I didn't want to appear needy, but I didn't want him to think that the whole episode had changed the way I felt about him either, or that I blamed him for the threat to my future at Drug and Alcohol Action. I let the cursor hover over the send button as I considered the tone, the use of a smiley, the kisses at the end. I'd titled it "Supervision", hoping that the title would catch his interest without alerting prying eyes. There were certainly enough of them around.

"I decided to treat you anyway. One chai latte and a blueberry muffin. Should keep you going until you can drag yourself away from this place."

I clicked send and smiled up at Fran as she dumped the unwanted delivery on my desk. She smiled back but that telltale line between her brows betrayed her worry.

"Thanks, Fran. Yummy."

She pointlessly nodded and stuck her hands in the back pockets of her dungarees.

"So, can I help you with anything? I feel bad knocking off at five every day knowing that you're still beavering away."

I frowned at my computer screen. The truth was I didn't have anything to do – all my casework was up to date and, other than materialising Alan from the backwaters of his chaotic lifestyle, there was very little help Fran could give me – and certainly nothing I would ask for her assistance with. Even though David wasn't around, I didn't want to change my routine and make anyone suspicious, or, even worse, think that I'd let my recent problems get in the way of my work ethic. I looked back at Fran, who was staring at me expectantly.

"No, I don't think so. I just need to send a few chasing emails then I think I'll head off myself."

Out of the corner of my eye I saw an email from David ping into my inbox. My stomach lurched.

"Okay, hen. Just make sure you get that muffin down you. I swear you're even skinnier than normal and you're looking very pale all of a sudden."

"Yes, Mum," I called after my colleague as she wandered back to her desk. She looked at me over her shoulder and stuck out her pierced tongue before sinking into her seat. I smiled to myself as I turned back to my computer. My insides flipped again as I looked at his email. With a shaking hand I clicked on it.

Thank you for your message. I'm currently out of the office and will reply to your email on my return. If your enquiry is urgent please call the office on 020 7659 8282.

I slumped back in my seat, disappointment snatching away my remaining energy. With effort I reached for my tea and sucked noisily at the hole in the plastic lid, ignoring the pain of the hot liquid as it scalded the inside of my mouth. Of course he wouldn't reply straight away. Even if he'd picked up my message on his Blackberry, he couldn't really reply when She was about. He'd wait until he had a quiet moment, perhaps when his wife had gone to bed, or on the train in tomorrow. Assuming he was back in tomorrow. Absently I pulled my muffin out of its paper bag and took a bite.

"That's my girl."

I glanced up to see Fran wink at me above her monitor. I gave her a crumby grin back, rubbing my tummy as I did so. A smile spread over her face as she shook her head. I filled my mouth with another chunk of the cloying bun and turned back to David's out of office reply. Clicking delete, I took another swig of hot tea. I had no choice but to be patient. There was a chance that he may still be angry with me over the whole Stacey thing and need time to get over that before he could admit to me how he really felt. But that was okay. I would just have to wait until he was ready.

31

Dear Dad,

I know you're really busy so thought I'd send you an email rather than call you for a catch-up. Hope that's okay?

So, how are you? Is Barney looking after you? I miss you both loads. Work is really busy (hence why I'm emailing you from the office – I won't get home until late) but going well. I'm getting a reputation for being a bit of a workaholic – apparently I take after you after all :)

I've had some difficult cases to deal with but think I am doing well to manage them. My manager is really supportive. I think you'd really like him. His name is David and I get on really well with him. Maybe when things have calmed down a bit you can come down to London and I can introduce you to him?

Anyway I've got to finish off a few things before I go home. I hope your work is going well and a little bit less hectic.

Lots of love,
Emily
X

*

Emily,

Glad everything is going well. Barney and I are fine thanks. I'll let you know about coming down to London – work is busy here too and your old dad needs the weekend to recuperate. Maybe I'll manage it in the summer.

Stop working so late – workaholism will do you no favours. Trust me.

Dad.

32

"Morning, all."

I froze at the sound of his voice. It had been two days since I sent him my email and I hadn't heard back from him. Okay, so he'd been off work, but I found it hard to believe he hadn't checked his emails even once. I dared myself to look over in his direction. He was simultaneously slurping at a Starbucks and pulling off his coat. I smiled affectionately at his aura of chaos. Catching my eye he grinned back.

"David. Good to see you back. Crisis averted?"

Eric was bobbing by his desk, his face as ruddy as ever. David looked over at his boss, a frown clouding his perfect face.

"Well, it's more a case of damage limitation, but things are better, thanks."

Eric nodded gravely.

"Okay, Dave. Pop into my office later if you want to talk about it." He had lowered his voice, but my anxiety to know what was going on inside my manager's mind had made sure that I strained to hear every word.

"Thanks, mate."

David lowered his gaze to his desk as he threw his coat on the back of his chair. Clearing his throat, he sat down, his forehead still lined. Behind me, a colleague laughed. I quickly averted my eyes back to my work, my face burning. I looked at my near-empty inbox. No new messages, not from David, not from anyone. I leant back in my chair, crossed my arms over my chest and took a deep breath before exhaling slowly through my nose. Well, he had smiled at me, which was a good sign, but something was clearly wrong. My mind raced. Had he read my email or not? And why had he been off anyway? Had he told his wife that it was over and had spent the last two days dealing with the fallout, or moving out, even? That would explain his smile for me, as well as his sober exchange with Eric. Of course he wouldn't tell Eric why he had left her, not yet. We had to be subtle, show sensitivity to the situation. I looked over at his desk again. He had gone. Panicked, I looked around to see him disappearing into Eric's office. My heart raced as I pictured David sitting wearily next to his old friend's desk, telling him that his marriage was over, Eric gruffly offering his condolences as he patted the younger man on the shoulder. I sighed again in frustration at my ignorance and let my gaze trail back to my laptop. An alert was flashing on its screen. I had a home visit with Ian in fourteen minutes. Quietly I cursed under my breath, more at the inconvenience of the visit than the fact that I was going to be late. I pulled on my jacket and stalked out of the office. As I passed Eric's office I slowed my pace to take a peek at the wide window and listened carefully to see if I could pick up any clues of the conversation, but the blinds were tightly closed and the room too well soundproofed to offer me more than a low rumble of male voices. I wrapped my jacket around me as I jogged down the stairs and walked quickly in the direction of Kentish Town. I was going to be late even if I jumped on the bus and badly needed to clear my head before I could face my client. Lowering my head against an assault of gabbling tourists I barged past, their protestations lost amongst my all-consuming thoughts of David.

*

"Er, hello? Little Miss Support Worker? Are you with me?"

I looked up from my phone and shoved it into my pocket. Ian was glaring at me from his seat. The smoke from the roll-up clamped between his lips was curling towards the open window, adding a new depth to the air thick with rotting food and body odour. I took a shallow breath against the stench.

"Sorry, Ian. I thought I heard my phone beep. What were you saying?"

Ian hacked out a laugh.

"I was telling you that I was snowballing yesterday and ended up in A&E after ODing. The only reason they let me out was because I said that you were visiting me today. As soon as I mentioned your name, they relaxed. I mean, if anyone can save me from Brown it's you. Although perhaps not today."

I stared at Ian blankly. He stared back as he stubbed his cigarette on the hardback next to him. I winced.

"Don't panic, girl. I'm not about to burn the flat down. But don't waste your time on the *Game of Thrones* series. Seriously shit."

I nodded dumbly. Ian rolled his eyes and pushed himself out of his chair with skinny arms.

"Anyway, if you're all done here I'm going to go out to buy some tobacco."

I stood up too, knocking my notebook onto the greying carpet.

"Sorry, Ian. You were doing what yesterday?"

Ian glanced at me as he stalked over to the hallway. His dark eyes glistened dangerously.

"Nothing. I was doing nothing yesterday. The point was I really wanted to do something, but you're too wrapped up in your own fucking life and that fucking phone to give a shit."

I bent down to pick up my notebook. Ian was shrugging his faded denim jacket on over his rounded shoulders.

"Ian, I'm sorry. Can we start again?"

He glared at me from the doorway.

"No, we can't start again. I've given you enough second chances, girlie. I need a support worker who actually gives a fuck and knows what the hell she's doing. Not one who doesn't even know what fucking snowballing is and seems to need a carer herself."

I let my head hang, partly to show my morose, partly to hide the shame that pinched at my cheeks.

"Ian, please. I've just had a bit of a hard day. Let's try again." I flicked open my notebook and scribbled the date at the top of the first page. "Tell me, how long have you felt like using again?"

I looked up expectantly. Ian had gone. I looked around the living room, hoping to see him back in his chair, surrounded by his books and old takeaway packaging, but it was empty. The front door slammed behind me. I ran into the hallway only to see Ian retreat along the balcony through the stained net curtain that covered his front door.

I had lost him.

*

I held my breath as I walked into the office. It was fairly busy, with a concentrate of workers chatting into their phones and to each other by the duty desks at the end of the room. I dared myself to glance over at his desk. He was there, his phone cradled between his cheek and his shoulder, his fingers typing furiously. His head was a mass of unkempt waves, his face unusually pale. I looked away quickly, not wanting to draw attention to us at this critical time. Whatever had happened between him and his wife had clearly taken its toll on him, and the last thing he needed was to be the subject of office gossip.

Carefully I set my bag of lunch on my desk and sat down, shrugging my jacket onto the back of my chair. I pulled my hummus and vegetable wrap from its packet and took a bite as I resuscitated my computer back to life. With a shaking hand I selected my inbox and scanned it eagerly. Five emails had dropped in since I had been out of the office, but not one of them had been from David. There were two from Fran, a generic one to the entire service from Eric and a couple of circulars. Irritably I deleted them all apart from the ones from Fran. The first one was an invite to lunch, the second a forwarded email from Shelter about up and coming training. I accepted the invite and deleted the latter as I chomped on my sandwich. I looked at the time. 12.33. David had been in for the best part of two hours. He must have seen my email by now. I clicked on my sent items folder and scrolled down. Yes, it was there, delivered over two days ago. So why hadn't he replied? I cracked open my can and took a swig of organic fizz as I opened my case notes. Selecting Ian's file, I felt my face burn again. What was I supposed to write? That I had ignored him when he had tried to tell me that he was scared of relapsing? That he had walked out of his own flat to avoid working with me? That I had messed up again? No matter how I put it, it didn't look good for the assessment at the end of my extended probationary period. I opened up a new case note and hesitated.

Client not in.

I clicked save and closed it quickly, hoping that the haste could somehow make up for my dishonesty, if not my failure.

*

I saw her out of the corner of my eye as she approached my desk. Quickly I opened up a random case and began scanning my latest risk assessment with unseeing eyes.

"You okay, hen?"

I looked up and gave Fran what I hoped was a convincingly surprised smile.

"Oh, hi, Fran. I'm okay. How are you?"

She smiled a lopsided smile back.

"Not bad, ta. I'm off now. Meeting an old friend for a pint over in Hackney, you know, to reminisce about the old days. Are you sure you're okay, though?"

I laughed lightly.

"Of course! Why wouldn't I be?"

She shrugged and dug her hands into her jeans pockets.

"No reason. You've just seemed a bit... restless this afternoon."

I threw my head back and laughed again. Fran's eyebrows shot up in surprise before she looked around the office. I had embarrassed her. The realisation made me laugh even more.

"Oh, Fran, you worry too much. I've just had too much caffeine, that's all."

She didn't look convinced.

"Are you sure?"

I rolled my eyes.

"Yes, I'm sure. Now you go and have fun with your old friends, okay?"

Fran's frown was back.

"Okay. We'll talk over lunch tomorrow, yeah?"

"Sure thing."

She hesitated before wandering back to her desk, her hands still in her pockets. I watched her as she threw on her coat and slung her bag over her shoulder. She looked over again before walking out of the office. I smiled and gave her a little wave.

"Don't do anything I wouldn't do."

She offered a half smile in return before striding towards the door, her head down. I waited for her to disappear from view before slumping back in my chair. The truth was, I was exhausted. Fran was right. I was on edge, and every time an email popped onto my screen my heart leapt to my mouth. David had disappeared from the office at about three and had yet to return. I'd checked his online calendar and he had no meetings or anything booked in for the afternoon. And he hadn't emailed me all day. I looked at the time. It was 5.17, and the office was beginning to empty. I opened up my inbox again. Nothing. With a sigh I opened my sent items and quickly selected the email I had sent David three days ago. I clicked on reply to all and hesitated before I started to type.

Hi David,

Not sure what's going on but hope you're okay? I hope my email didn't make things more complicated for you. I just wanted to acknowledge how we feel about each other – so far it has been unsaid. I'm here for you if you need to talk about whatever is going on at home. I hope we can talk about us too soon, but understand it might be difficult at the moment.

All my love,
Emily
Xxx

Someone approached my desk as I sent my message. Hurriedly I returned to my inbox and began composing a random email to Social Services.

"Hi, Em. How you doing?"

It was Jim, all freckles and smiles. I offered him a half-hearted smile back before turning my attention back to a bogus emergency.

"Hi, Jim."

I carried on typing. He hovered next to me.

"I have to say, Emily, I admire your energy. You always seem to be busy doing something."

I shrugged as I randomly made enquiries into the next Child In Need meeting for a fictional client's daughter.

"Well, there's no rest for the wicked."

He laughed softly.

"Well, I wouldn't call you that just yet. So why don't you finish off what you're doing and we can go to the pub?"

Inwardly I cringed. Why wouldn't he just take the hint that I wasn't interested? The only person I wanted to go out for a drink with was David, and he was so stressed right now he couldn't even talk to me. I swallowed back a pang of sadness.

"Sorry, Jim. I've got plans. Have a great evening, though."

I glanced up and smiled apologetically before scrambling for my notebook to look for a vital bit of information that didn't exist.

"Okay. Will do. Hope you have a good one, too. Glad to hear you've got something on. I'd hate to think you didn't play as hard as you worked."

I smiled briefly at him again as I flicked though my notes. As he walked away, I threw it back onto my desk and looked at my inbox again. Still no reply from David. Irritably I closed my laptop down and gathered up my belongings. Dumping my work stuff in my locker, I hurried out of the office without pausing to put on my jacket. If I couldn't be with David I didn't want to be with anyone, not Jim, not my colleagues, nobody. My skin prickled as the cool air hit my body but I didn't care. I just wanted to get home and shut the door behind me, to be alone with my thoughts of David, knowing that, wherever he was, he was thinking of me too.

33

A click of fingers in front of my face snapped me back into the room.

"Emily! Are you with me?"

I blinked at Fran, sitting across the table from me. Her usual expression of concern had deepened into a scowl of irritability.

"Sorry," I muttered, half-heartedly picking up my untouched falafel pitta and nibbling a corner of dry bread. She sat back in her seat and puffed out her cheeks, her arms slack by her sides.

"Hen, you don't need to apologise. I was just rabbiting on as usual. I just…" She took a deep breath. "I'm really worried about you."

I took a slurp at my mixed juice and bit into my lunch again.

"I told you, I'm fine," I mumbled through my mouthful.

Fran folded her arms. Her face had hardened with determination.

"Sorry, but I'm not going to let you fob me off this time. You're not okay, Emily. I can see it, even if you can't."

"Oh, really? So what exactly can you see?" I snapped back before shoving more food into my face. She hesitated.

"Well... you look exhausted, you're restless, you seem to struggle to concentrate on any kind of human interaction, and since you had your probationary period extended, you've been working ridiculously hard."

I shrugged.

"Okay, so maybe I'm a bit stressed. Surely it's understandable under the circumstances?"

She sighed again.

"Of course it is. I would be pretty strung out in your position too. But..." She looked me in the eye. "I worry if it's gone beyond that. I mean, your symptoms are classic of anxiety, even depression."

I stared at her blankly. She stared back, her eyes clear and focused. Even with her pink dreadlocks, powdered face and bright red lipstick, she was really quite beautiful. She was popular, and cool, and she cared about me. I felt my eyes well up with gratitude. Her harsh expression melted as she reached across the table and took my hand in hers.

"Oh, honey, I'm sorry. I didn't mean to make you cry. Here." She let go of my hand and delved into her hessian bag. I accepted a tissue from the packet she pulled out and dabbed under my eyes.

"Thanks," I whispered. She smiled at me, her hands clasped in front of her on the table.

"No problem." Fran sat back as the waitress cleared away her empty plate. She watched her as she walked out of earshot before turning her attention back to me. "So, what do you think?"

I took another sip of my drink. Suddenly I felt tired, really tired.

"About what?"

"Well, do you think maybe you need to take a step back? I don't know, maybe take some time off, go and see your dad or something? Or perhaps go to the doctor's and ask for some professional help to get you through?"

I pretended to mull over her suggestions as I bit into my lunch again. The thought of taking time off work, let alone leave London at this crucial time, wasn't an option. As for seeing a doctor, I didn't see what they could do. But she was right, I needed to pull myself together and take control of the situation. I nodded as I swallowed.

"Okay, I'll think about it. But I'm not going back to my dad's. One of my friends is going through a really hard time and I don't want to leave her here on her own."

Fran's shoulders relaxed.

"Alright. Well, that will do me. You could even try a bit of meditation or aromatherapy, that might help. Just make sure you look after yourself, or you'll be no good for your friend, or anyone else for that matter. Now finish your lunch. You're not eating enough these days and it's starting to show." She nodded pointedly at my plate, her eyebrow raised. "I want to see that empty when I get back from the ladies, okay?"

I saluted her as she stood up. She smiled back tenderly before weaving her way to the back of the café. As she disappeared into the toilets I turned my attention back to my lunch. Half the pitta and my side salad were still sitting on my plate. I forced down another mouthful from the piece in my hand before wrapping the other half in my napkin and shoving it in my bag. When Fran returned I was picking at my salad.

"That's more like it. Now, can I interest you in a piece of cake for the road? The brownies in here are divine."

I gawped at her and patted my belly. It felt swollen and uncomfortable, even after such a measly meal, and there was no way I was about to force anything else into it.

"Hey, I ate my falafel, didn't I? What more do you want from me?"

She laughed as she slipped back into her seat.

"Well, as you've just given me a glimpse of your old humorous self, I'll leave it this time. But next time I might insist." She grinned at me before catching our waitress's eye and signalling for the bill. Diving back into her bag she pulled out her battered purse.

"So, have you any more thoughts about what I said? You know, about getting help?" she asked as she counted out a fistful of change.

"Well, I know I need to get on top of my stress levels. I'm just not sure how at the moment, but I promise I will."

Fran handed her cash to the waitress with a warm smile and turned back to me.

"As long as you do something, hen." She looked at her watch and groaned. "Shit, I've got to go. Got my supervision with David in ten and I've done nothing to prepare." I stiffened at the mention of his name. Oblivious to my reaction, she stood up and wriggled into her coat. Job done, she looked at me with that lop-sided smile of hers.

"So, are you coming with me or are you playing hookie for the rest of the day?"

I blinked at her dumbly as her words registered. I hurried out of my seat, nearly knocking it over in my haste, and threw on my jacket. Out on the high street Fran caught up with me and put her hand on my arm.

"Hey, slow down, won't you? I was only kidding about you skiving off. And I don't want to get back to the office that quickly." I felt her eyes still on my face as I slowed my pace. "So... why don't you knock off early today? I mean, if you haven't got any visits planned. You could have a nice walk along the canal or something and give yourself some space?"

I glanced at her as I made a show of looking for traffic. She was still looking at me intently.

"Well, I'm waiting on a few emails, but I'll think about it."
She shrugged and followed my gaze.

"Okay. But whatever it is, I'm sure it can wait until tomorrow."

I hesitated before following her across the road. It was true, a lot of what I was working on could wait. But as long as David was in the office and hadn't replied to my message, I wasn't going anywhere.

*

"Wish me luck!"

I gave Fran a smile and waved as she wandered over to Eric's office, her notebook under her arm. I watched her as she knocked on the door before opening it, a wide grin on her face. As I heard the door slam behind her, my mind began to race. What was that grin about? Had David told her? Were they having a good old joke about me in there? Or worse, was she going to try and seduce him herself? I closed my eyes to try and squeeze the images formulating in my mind before unlocking my computer and opening my inbox. My stomach flipped. He had replied. My hands shaking uncontrollably, I opened the email.

*

Re: Supervision

Hi Emily,

Thanks for your messages. Yes, things have been pretty manic the last week or so, but slowly they are going back to normal.

No need to apologise about the situation with Stacey. We all make mistakes, the important thing is that we learn from them – which I admit is easier said than done – but hopefully with a bit of support and relevant training you'll be fine :)

I really value you as part of the team and as a mate, Emily. I might have misinterpreted your emails (and if I have, my apologies – I've never been very good at reading between the lines!) but I just wanted to let you know that and, whilst I enjoy your company, I love my family to bits. Although I admit I moan about them a lot, I wouldn't be without them. I'm really sorry if I've ever given the impression otherwise – I know I can be a terrible flirt when I've had a drink...

Catch up soon :)
David

*

I read his message over and over until the words no longer made any sense, the letters meaningless shapes on the screen in front of me. I looked at the clock on the wall ahead of me – it was only 2.16. I closed his email and turned my attention to the other messages in my inbox. I read them and re-read them without any one of them sinking into my numb brain. I knew he didn't mean what he said. He was just saying what he thought he should say, what was expected of him. He clearly hadn't left his wife, and wasn't ready to, but that didn't mean he didn't love me. I felt myself relax as I slowly understood what he was trying to say. Despite his feelings, he was trying to do the right thing, and I loved him all the more for that. I just knew that he was making a mistake.

I looked at the clock again. 2.21. Fran was right. I needed space to think, and I needed it now. Quickly I shut down my computer and thrust my belongings into my bag. I pushed my arms into the sleeves of my jacket and trotted up to the duty desk. Jim looked up at me, his pale blue eyes expectant.

"Hey, Em. Everything okay?"

"Yeah. I just need to run over to Social Services for an emergency meeting. I probably won't be back, so if anyone asks…"

"Sure, no problem, I'll let everyone know. Anything I can help with?"

"No. It's something I need to sort out for myself," I mumbled as I walked back to my desk. I grabbed my bag and jogged over to my locker to dump my laptop, pausing as I passed Eric's office to listen. The blinds were closed again, the room silent. Swallowing down my anxiety I ran out of the office.

34

Refilling my glass, I cursed to myself as the Salsa music from Rebecca's room became suddenly louder. She didn't sound to have the usual gaggle of girls over, but seemed hell-bent on disturbing me yet again. I debated banging on her door and telling her to turn her incessant racket down, but couldn't really face the inevitable confrontation if I did so, even after half a bottle of wine. Six months ago I wouldn't have dreamt of drinking on my own, but six months ago I wasn't in love. I gulped down the comforting alcohol and pulled my frayed dressing gown around me. When I had got in after a desperate attempt to walk out my restlessness along the South Bank, I'd had a bath to try to again pacify my frantic mind. Matt's tireless knocking on the door had cut it short, leaving me with no other option than to open the bottle of Californian red I had bought when I first moved to London, assuming that I would be entertaining throngs of friends in my new home within days. I pushed the reminder of my social inadequacies out of my mind and returned them to David. David, the one person in the world who truly cared for me, but whose situation prevented him from being with me. Fran was right. I needed to take control of the situation by making him realise that he was making a mistake, but I didn't know how. I took another swig at my wine and wiggled down under my duvet. I felt exhausted, but knew that there was no way I could sleep until I had a plan. I reached down the side of my bed and pulled my notebook and pen out of my bag. Flicking through to the first blank page, I pulled the lid off my pen with my teeth and wrote down his name and began to write. Email. A letter. Supervision. The pub. Well, I had already tried emailing him, and a letter was just a slightly more formal version of this. Supervision. If I tried to talk to him about our relationship in supervision, I would be compromising his professional position, and mine. The pub. The only time we went to the pub together, we were with half the office, and, even though we would be out of work hours, people would talk if I pulled him away from the crowd, which would not only make us both the subject of office gossip but could taint our professional reputations, too. No, I needed to get him alone, away from the office, away from our colleagues, just the two of us, so that we could talk freely, openly. I picked up my drink. It was already empty. I reached for the bottle from my bedside cabinet and emptied its contents into my glass. I knew what I needed to do. I just needed to find the opportunity to do it. Draining the last of my wine, I flicked off my lamp and snuggled further into my bed, my dressing gown still on. Eventually I drifted off to sleep, my unconsciousness swaying awkwardly under the influence of wine and music.

35

I took a deep breath and held it as I stepped into the lift. I found the smell hard to bear at the best of times and, after a bottle of wine the night before, found it even more repulsive than ever. I exhaled and inhaled quickly as soon as I walked out of it, relishing the slightly sweeter Kentish Town air. Alan's flat came into view along the balcony. My relative calm melted away again as I saw the police officer standing outside it. I considered turning and walking away, but his eyes were already on me.

"Can I help, Miss?"

I stopped a few feet short of him and glanced over the balcony into the estate, half expecting to see Alan's body on the concrete below.

"Er, has something happened?"

His eyebrows disappeared under the rim of his helmet.

"Well, we don't tend to hang around outside people's home for no good reason, Miss. Do you mind me asking who you are?"

I fumbled my ID out of my pocket and held it out.

"My name's Emily. I'm his support worker. I mean, Alan's. Has he been arrested?"

As soon as the words were out, I realised how stupid they were. His housing officer had confirmed that the court had agreed to a possession order, and the bailiffs would be tasked to turf him out any day now. Even if he hadn't been evicted yet, I couldn't imagine the news would have provoked good behaviour from my client. The officer took my ID card and studied it carefully before handing it back.

"Not yet he hasn't. He's been taken to hospital. The ambulance service received an anonymous call stating that he had OD'd in his flat and requested that we attend."

I gasped.

"Is he okay? I mean, is he alive?"

The officer chuckled.

"Sadly for us, he is. Just. But he's gonna wish he wasn't when he comes round. As soon as we saw the state of his flat we requested a formal warrant and have seized an awful lot of paraphernalia which suggests that your Alan here was dealing class A drugs. Not to mention handling stolen goods."

I felt the blood drain from my flushed face as the enormity of the situation began to sink in.

"Did you find any drugs?"

The officer pulled a face as he shook his head.

"Nope. But I imagine whoever called 999 helped themselves to anything they could find before scarpering."

"PC Wilson?"

The officer straightened at the sound of the booming voice.

"Yes, Serge?"

"I hope you aren't gossiping with members of the public about this incident?"

The officer turned to the doorway as an older policeman strode out, his hands in his pockets.

"No, Serge. This young lady is a support worker from Drug and Alcohol Action. She has been working with the suspect."

The sergeant regarded me with cool blue eyes. I felt the colour return to my cheeks in an instant as he looked me up and down.

"Drug and Alcohol Action, eh? Well, with no disrespect, I think you're too late to take any action with this one. If he survives, I can't see him going anywhere but HMP Pentonville in the near future. And hopefully he'll stay there for a while, too." He glanced at the more junior officer before turning his attention back to me. "Now, if you'll excuse us, we have a criminal investigation to complete and, as much as PC Wilson loves to chat, he has a job to do, too." He turned back to the flat and hesitated. "And, Miss, again with no disrespect, can I suggest you get on with helping people who aren't beyond it?"

He nodded at me curtly before disappearing into the flat. I looked at PC Wilson who shrugged at me before resuming his formal stance by the door. I turned to walk back to the lift, glancing through the kitchen window as I did so. The pile of plates in the sink was still there, the food encrusted on them now unrecognisable. The broken furniture had moved since I was last there, but was still in disarray. An officer was crouched by the far wall, inspecting what looked like a splattering of blood on the greasy paintwork. A wave of nausea hit me again as I scuttled back to the lift and, without pausing to censor the pungent smell of urine, quickly pressed the button to close the doors behind me.

*

"Emily! Are you okay? You look like you've seen a ghost."

Fran was by my side before I could even reach a free desk. I collapsed into the nearest chair, my bag dangling from my shoulder. I stared past her.

"Alan's had an overdose. He's going to be arrested and chucked out of his flat."

"What?" It was David. He looked at me over Fran's shoulder, pushing his hair out of his face and held it back with his elegant fingers. "What happened?"

I shrugged.

"I turned up this morning and there was a police officer outside his flat. The ambulance had received a call that morning and asked for their assistance. Apparently they found loads of stuff in his flat."

David studied my face.

"And they told you he's going to be evicted?"

I glanced at Fran then back to him.

"No. I found that out yesterday. That's why I had to leave early, to go and meet his housing officer," I lied, relaxing into my seat as my alibi took shape. David puffed out his cheeks. He looked me in the eye.

"Shit."

"Shit indeed," Fran echoed as she perched on my desk and put a hand on my shoulder. "Listen, hen, don't worry. This kind of thing happens. Although it has to be said, Alan's timing could have been better."

I looked up at her and smiled warmly. She smiled back and gave my shoulder a squeeze. The telltale line between her brows appeared as her hand enclosed my prominent collarbone. I looked away from her, praying to God she wouldn't chastise me about my weight loss in front of David.

"Fran's right," he added. His face had relaxed. He released his hair and put his hands in his jeans pockets. He glanced at me before looking over at his desk. "I'm afraid I'll need you to fill out an incident form, though. Have you done one before?"

I looked up at him and shook my head, willing him to look back at me. He met my gaze for a delicious second before turning to Fran.

"Would you mind helping Emily with one? And if you could get it to me by lunchtime that would be great."

"I'm sure I can manage it." My voice was urgent, indignant. Fran and David looked at each other. David hesitated.

"Okay, sure, but can Fran give you a few pointers and check it for you before you hand it in?"

I nodded and smiled at him. He smiled briefly back, a frown clouding his face, before returning to his desk. I watched him as he sat down heavily behind his computer.

"Well, shall I make us both a cuppa whilst you get set up?" Fran was on her feet, her hands on her hips as she stared down at me. I nodded and, with a resigned sigh, dumped my bag onto my desk.

*

Fran looked at me over the top of her oversized glasses and smiled.

"It looks fine, hen. I'd just maybe add a short paragraph about his housing situation, just to cover your back, and you're all done."

I took the form off her and smiled tightly before returning to my desk. I knew full well that there was no need to add that to my report. The incident was his drug overdose, not his impending eviction. Fran just couldn't help herself but to make some amendment to my work. I scribbled my signature at the bottom of the form and walked purposely towards David's desk. He had gone out about half an hour ago. When I checked his online calendar it had been blank, so I could only assume he had popped out for lunch or something. As I approached his workstation I found myself smiling affectionately at the disarray that greeted me. A stack of papers threatened his keyboard with an avalanche, and his mouse sat on top of a pile of books, his open diary on top. I looked around to check

I wasn't being observed before flicking through the fine paper bound in a leather jacket. His scrawled handwriting filled every page with one commitment after another – parents' evenings, dinner with friends, birthday parties. A letter slipped out onto the floor as I turned to the front page. Hurriedly I picked it up and looked around to check no one was watching me before scrutinising its contents.

David Simpson
63A Long Avenue
London
E17 5AG

My heart leapt to my throat. His address, right there in front of me. I felt my pulse thunder through my veins and glanced around the office again. No one was paying me any attention, not even Fran who was gassing on the phone obliviously. I folded up the bill and thrust it into my cardigan pocket. When I looked up again Fran's gaze met mine. She grinned.

"Good luck if you're trying to find somewhere in that hovel of a corner to leave that."

She nodded at the paper in my hand. I groaned theatrically and smiled back before resting it on his keypad. My task complete I crept back to my desk and pulled my own diary out of my bag, tucking the letter next to the back page before stowing it away again. I wasn't sure what exactly I was going to do with this new information, but my instinct told me it was a sign. A sign that I was closer to getting David alone, being able to talk to him, to have him to myself. I took a deep breath, sat back in my chair and turned back to my laptop. My inbox was filling up after the events of the morning and, whilst I knew a lot of them probably wouldn't be easy to deal with, I didn't care. I could almost taste my future with David, it was so close. And that was all that mattered.

36

Satisfied that my inbox was under control, I slumped back in my chair. It had been two days since Alan's overdose, and suddenly everyone wanted to contact me – the housing officer, the police, even the hospital – before he was shipped off to the nearest vacant prison cell. To top it off, Stacey's social worker was insisting on calling a Child Protection conference and had asked for a detailed report on the support I had offered my client and her child. I looked at my watch. It was nearly five o'clock, but the office was still full. Behind me, I heard a gaggle of girls laughing, and blushed. Everyone in the office knew about the incident and had no doubt added it to their list of my shortcomings.

"So, hen, are you coming?"

Inwardly I cringed at the sound of her voice. No matter what I was doing or where I was, Fran was there, pecking around me.

"Where?" I asked wearily, looking up at her with an expression which I hoped illustrated my annoyance. She folded her arms over her tiny chest and rolled her eyes with a tut.

"To Jim's leaving do! It's tonight, remember?" She smiled at my confusion. "My God, you are out of sorts, aren't you?"

"Where's he going?"

"Er, Indonesia, to teach English? Don't you read your emails?"

She had me there. Any message I received from Jim was usually deleted in an attempt to shake off his interest, unless the subject line indicated that it was about work. I felt my face flush again as Fran began to laugh.

"Wow, you really have been working too hard, haven't you? Now, why don't you pack up your stuff so we can go get some medicinal alcohol inside you."

She walked away before I could answer. I looked around the office. Jim was standing by the duty desk, smiling shyly, his thumbs hooked over the waistline of his designer jeans as his groupies gushed around him. He caught my eye and waved. I turned away quickly and looked over at David's desk. He was pulling on his jacket as he bent over a last-minute piece of work. Straightening up, he caught my eye for a second before looking past me towards the back of the office.

"Oi, Jim! Are we going for this drink or what?"

Quickly I shut down my computer and gathered up the papers strewn around me. Scooping up the contents of my desk I hurried over to my locker.

"Emily! You're coming with us?"

I glanced at Jim as I shoved my cargo into my locker. His pale eyes watched me expectantly. My skin crawled in revulsion.

"Yeah, why not?" I beamed as I slammed the door shut. "I'll catch you up, okay?"

He nodded and grinned at me stupidly before one of the office flakes dragged him away. I pushed my way through the throng of support workers back to my desk.

"You want me to wait for you, Em?"

Fran was hovering at the rear of the pack. I looked around. David had gone already.

"No, it's okay. I just want to freshen up a bit. I'll see you over there."

"Okay. I'll be waiting for you with a large glass of Merlot," she called over her shoulder.

As the door slammed, I took a deep breath. I looked around the deserted office and exhaled loudly. It was the first time I had been there completely on my own and, for the first time since I had started at Drug and Alcohol Action, I felt relaxed within its bare brick walls. I sat down again and pulled out my make-up bag. Flipping open my compact I stared at my reflection. The constant shadows under my eyes looked darker than ever, my skin almost transparent as it stretched over my bony face. Quickly I covered it with powder before slicking on my lipstick and carefully drawing around my eyes with eyeliner. Fluffing up my lank hair with my free hand, I inspected my appearance again with a frown. The make-up didn't make me look much better, but at least my lips had some colour, my eyes a bit of definition. I shoved my make-up back into my bag and ran over to the exit, straightening my clothes as I did so. I knew David wasn't shallow, but wanted to look my best if I had the chance to speak to him about us, and an evening in the pub might just provide that opportunity. As I jogged down the stairs my mobile phone beeped in my pocket. I pulled it out as I reached the door. It was Lorraine, no doubt texting to ridicule our relationship again. I dropped it into my bag as I stepped out onto the high street and hurried to the pub.

*

"Cheers!"

I lifted my wine and took a large gulp of it whilst my colleagues clinked glasses around me. I shifted on my seat as the girl next to me wriggled closer to Jim, who was laughing loudly at her side. There had already been three people on the padded bench when I arrived, but I was determined to sit at the same table as David. Jim had welcomed my presence whilst the others around him had done little to conceal their dismay. David was sitting at the other end of the table, sandwiched between the wall and Fran, who was engaging him in one of her hippy debates. He had smiled at me, his jaw tense. I had smiled back my understanding before attempting to engage in the conversation around me. Two glasses of wine and almost an hour later, I had given up on feigning any interest in office politics.

"So, another round?"

Jim slammed his pint glass on the table and looked around expectantly. David looked around Fran's nest of dreads, piled high on her head.

"Sounds like a plan. I'll get them. So, orders please, people?"

"No, I'll get them," I said before anyone could respond. The table all but fell silent as my colleagues stared at me. My face flushed in response to their scrutiny and the alcohol which was rapidly spreading through my body.

"Well, in that case, I'll have another San Miguel," Jim chirped.

I nodded quickly. "Okay, anyone else?"

I pulled out a pen from my bag and scribbled everyone's order on the palm of my hand.

"And did you want to order us some chips or something, hen? To soak up some of the alcohol? Might be wise as we all have to work tomorrow."

I nodded my agreement at Fran's suggestion and walked unsteadily to the bar. It was so obvious that her comment had intended to draw my weight loss to everyone's attention. Another sly attempt to embarrass me in front of our colleagues. In front of David.

When I returned with a tray full of jingling glasses, David had gone. Quickly I distributed the drinks around the table.

"Where's David?" I had intended to sound casual, but my voice was tight, high pitched. Someone sniggered.

"He's outside having a fag."

I picked up his pint of Guinness and my large Merlot and headed out to the beer garden.

"Hen, it's raining. He'll be back soon," Fran called after me.

I debated calling back to her, but pretended not to hear. Awkwardly I pushed the door open and looked around the decked smoking area. He was in the far corner, talking intently into his mobile. I took a deep breath and wove my way through the other smokers towards him. When he saw me his eyebrows shot up in surprise. I held up his drink in a salute and smiled back at him. He gave me the thumbs up and tucked his phone between his cheek and shoulder, freeing up a hand to accept my offering. He looked at me again and smiled his thanks, but the lines across his forehead betrayed his anxiety. I perched on the table next to him and took a sip of my wine and he nodded along to the voice at the other end of the line.

"Okay, hun... Yeah, I understand... Look, don't worry about it, okay?"

He glanced at me as he spoke. I smiled back at him and swung my legs playfully. Dropping his cigarette butt on the floor, he pulled a battered packet of Mayfairs out of his back pocket and offered it to me. I took one and watched him as I lit it before handing the pack back to him.

"Honestly, it's not a problem. In fact, I think it's a good idea. Give you a bit of a break, you know?"

He pulled a cigarette out of the packet with his mouth and lit it quickly, avoiding my gaze. He was clearly on the phone to his wife, and whilst I knew that it was probably difficult for him having me there whilst he spoke to her, I wasn't about to give up on this opportunity to speak to him on his own. Besides, my presence might help him put our situation into perspective. Finally he terminated the call.

"Sorry about that," he said, frowning at his phone before jamming it into his pocket. I shrugged, my hands clasping the table at my sides.

"That's okay." I cocked my head to one side. "Was that Gill?"

He stared at me blankly. I couldn't read the expression in his eyes.

"Yes. Yes, it was. She's thinking about going to her folks' for the weekend."

"Oh." I opened my eyes wide. "Is everything okay?"

David glanced at me before turning his attention to his cigarette.

"Of course. She just needs a bit of a break, that's all."

She needed a break. My heart thumped in my chest as his words sang like music in my ears. I took another sip of my wine and pushed myself off the table. I stepped towards him and placed my hand on his arm.

"I'm sorry to hear that, David."

He stared at me again, his eyebrows raised, before taking a step back, letting my arm fall limply by my side. He glanced at the entrance to the pub and laughed nervously.

"Oh, there's nothing to be sorry about. She's just had a hard time recently and needs to get away from it all." He looked down at me again with a frown. "Everything is fine."

I shrugged again and picked up my wine.

"That's good to know. And it's good to know that she trusts you home alone."

David laughed loudly as I gulped my wine. I could tell that he was nervous, uncomfortable even, but they were feelings I knew he had to come to terms with.

"Well, other than having her doubts about my ability to look after our kids for two days, she has absolutely no reason not to trust me. In all the years we've been together I've never given her an excuse not to."

Until now. He left the words unspoken, and so did I. I dropped my cigarette to the floor and stumbled slightly as I stamped it out. I looked up at him from under the curtain of hair that had fallen across my face.

"Can I have another?"

He hesitated before pulling the packet out of his pocket and handing them over. He watched me as I struggled to light my cigarette. He took one for himself and lit it in silence.

"Well, if you need a hand with the kids over the weekend, let me know," I offered as I sucked on my Mayfair. "It might be fun."

A smile, almost a laugh played at the corner of his mouth.

"I'm not sure that's a good idea. Do you?"

I pouted at him.

"Why not?"

He slowly exhaled a lungful of smoke.

"Emily, you need to understand that Gill and I are fine. Even the most solid of relationships have their ups and down, and, despite them, we are dedicated to our children and each other."

I watched him as he spoke. I heard his words, and I understood them, but I also knew what he was really saying. That he was determined to keep his marriage in one piece, even though he was desperately unhappy. His jaw clenched on cue. His speech over, he let his deep blue eyes wander over my face.

"Emily, do you understand?"

I gazed back at him, stubbornly refusing to release his own once I had caught it. Suddenly fearless with alcohol, I stepped towards him again and reached my hand towards his face.

"Yes, I understand, David. I understand you completely."

"Dave! Mate! You coming in or what?"

David batted my hand away and looked towards the pub. It was Jim, his pint in one hand, the other steadying himself against the doorframe. David stepped around me and walked towards him.

"Yeah, sorry, just got caught up with the missus."

Jim looked past him and stared at me, his jovial expression fading. I looked back at him defiantly, my cigarette clamped between my lips.

"So I see," he muttered, glancing at David before returning his attention back to me. I picked up my wine and took a sip before turning away to hide the blush that was beginning to spread across my face. Whilst I didn't care what Jim thought of me, I knew that he looked up to David and I didn't want that to change because of me. The pang of guilt hit me without warning. No wonder David had been denying his feelings towards me. Jim was his friend and, whilst I had little time for him, David's relationship with him would be compromised if ours flourished. Until now Eric had been the only person who had any inkling about how we felt about each other, and he had let his disapproval get the better of his professionalism. God knew how everyone else involved would react. But then, not everyone else had felt as deeply as we did, and whilst David was still fighting his demons, soon those feelings would get the better of him. Tossing my half-smoked cigarette into the darkness, I tipped the rest of my wine into my mouth. The warming alcohol reinforced my resolve, and, my self-doubt dismissed, I wound my way through the beer garden back to the pub.

37

Sitting at my desk, I downed the rest of my Red Bull and grimaced. I hated the taste of it but, after the amount of wine I had consumed the night before on an empty stomach, I needed the hit of caffeine and sugar the blurb on the side of the tin promised. Ignoring the nausea rising from my protesting stomach, I turned back to my inbox. Its contents were doing little to make me feel better. Alan's housing officer had confirmed that a bailiffs' date had been set, and that, as of yet, Alan hadn't approached the court to appeal. He had been charged with handling stolen goods and possession with intent to supply drugs and, even if he wasn't found guilty, his rent arrears were enough for any protest from my client to fall on deaf ears. I sighed as I slammed my glasses on my desk and stiffly stood up. The syrupy drink had done little to quell my desire to vomit and, if anything, had made it stronger. Accepting my fate, I gingerly walked over to the ladies.

"Hi, Emily."

It was Jim, standing in the doorway of the kitchen as he violently shook up a homemade smoothie in a capped plastic cup. I paused and looked at him. His usual smile was a line across his stern face.

"Hi. Did you have a good time last night?" I offered, suddenly remembering what he had seen the night before. He averted his eyes and inspected his drink.

"Yeah, it was okay. Although seeing my mate trying it on with a girl he knows I like was a bit of a downer."

I watched him as he pulled off the lid and downed half of his concoction. I knew I had to say something to put things right, for David's sake.

"Jim... it isn't his fault. David and I just have some kind of connection. He can't help it, and neither can I."

He looked at me as he wiped his mouth with the back of his hand.

"Sure. And he can't help the fact that this 'connection' seemed to come to fruition the day before his wife goes away without him for the first time in ten years either, right?"

I shrugged.

"Jim, that was her decision. Nothing to do with David and I, but just another sign that their relationship is on the rocks anyway."

Jim looked up at the ceiling and laughed.

"Yeah, of course it is." He shook his head and glanced at me before wandering over to the window, his drink in one hand, the other hooked over his belt. "I just hope you two are very happy together." He took another swig from his cup before holding it up to the light. "I just feel for Gill – and those kids. Knowing what they are about to go through makes me sick to my stomach."

On cue, my own contracted. I pushed my way into the ladies just in time. As I wiped my mouth with a piece of toilet tissue I thought about what Jim had said. Okay, so he was upset because I had fallen for someone other than him. Okay, the circumstances weren't ideal, but it was obvious to everyone that David wasn't happy, and hadn't been for a long time. Flushing the toilet I stepped out of the cubicle and rinsed out my mouth. Luckily no one else was in there – in fact, the office was pretty quiet, no doubt due to numerous sickies pulled by hungover colleagues less dedicated to their work. Even David wasn't in, but his numerous emails about Alan's situation showed that he was at least working from home, no doubt trying to placate his wife's anxieties before she went away. I splashed my face with cold water and looked at my face. It looked more sallow than ever. Silently I thanked fate that he wasn't about to see me in my wretched state. As for Jim, I didn't care what he thought. And the same went for anyone else.

38

I looked at my watch. It was nearly quarter past one and, despite her text stating that she had to talk to me urgently, Fran was late. I flopped back in my seat and pulled my phone out of my bag. Nothing. I threw it onto the table and took a sip of my mixed juice. I'd texted Lorraine earlier that day and had been hoping to see something from my old school mate, but it had been my meddling colleague who had been in touch. But, with nothing else in my diary over the weekend, I had agreed to meet her for lunch. It would make a change from the tea and toast I would have had at home, if nothing else.

"Sorry I'm late."

Fran breezed into the tiny café and sat opposite me before the sentence was out. I noticed with disappointment that she was dressed no differently from when she was at work. I had expected her to turn up in some outlandish outfit from one of the dodgier shops in Camden whose clothes glowed in the dark or left little to the imagination. Her ripped jeans and red and black striped jumper were something of a let-down. She caught my eye and frowned.

"You alright, hen?"

I shrugged and smiled, more to myself than at my colleague.

"Yeah I'm fine. Was just admiring your outfit, that's all."

She smiled, but that telltale line between her brows remained stubbornly in place. I wondered if she had even realised I was being sarcastic, or that I could read her like an open book.

"Thanks. So, have you ordered anything? The baba ghanoush here is amazing." She looked around her and waved over a scrawny middle-aged man who looked like he'd just crawled out of a slum. As he wandered over she looked back at me. "You fancy sharing a mixed mezze?"

I shrugged and took another sip of my drink. She studied my face for a moment before turning back to the waiter and placing our order.

"So, what's up?" I asked as she turned back to me. She stared back, her hands limp in her lap.

"Emily, I spoke to Jim yesterday."

I rolled my eyes at the mention of his name.

"And?"

She laughed incredulously and folded her arms across her chest.

"And I was worried about what he had to say." Her frown deepened. "Hen, what's going on?"

I sucked on my straw slowly. I couldn't help but feel smug about the interest my personal life had created for my colleague. For someone who seemed to relish her reputation for being sexually liberated, seeing Fran so outraged about my own situation was more than a little amusing.

"Well, for a start, Jim's just got his knickers in a twist because he fancies me. Secondly, he hasn't got a clue. He doesn't seem to understand that people can't help but fall in

273

love, and certainly can't force themselves to love someone who they have no interest in whatsoever."

Fran's gaze didn't waver, even when our food arrived.

"So, you're having an affair with David, then?"

I pulled a face.

"Affair is such a dirty word. Besides, we haven't done anything. We just know how we feel about each other and know that we need to be together. But obviously it's a bit complicated."

Fran nodded slowly as she loaded a piece of pitta with a spoonful of green slime.

"Okay. So you think he's going to leave Gill and his kids?"

Tentatively I dipped my bread into a mountain of hummus.

"Well, he's not quite ready to do that yet, but yes, I think he will."

Still nodding, Fran popped an olive in her already full mouth.

"And you're okay with that."

I stared at her. Eventually she looked up from her food and met my gaze.

"Well, I know it's not an ideal situation, but we can't help that, Fran."

She held up her hand.

"I know, hen, but have you really thought this through? I mean, it's a lot to live with, knowing you've broken up someone's family, not to mention the fact that a lot of people will probably blame you for it. And then there's the kids. You sure you want to be a stepmum to two children under five at your age?"

I looked down at the food in my hand, my appetite suddenly gone. Of course I had thought about these things, and they didn't sit comfortably in my consciousness. But I loved David and needed him in my life. And that was all that mattered.

"Fran, have you ever been in love?" I asked quietly. She nodded as she chewed.

"Yes, I have. And it made me do crazy things that I wish I hadn't. Like stay with the bastard even when he started to beat me up."

I watched her as she loaded more bread with another unidentifiable substance.

"Then why are you judging David and I?"

She looked up, her eyes wide.

"Hun, I'm not judging you. I just don't want you to walk into this without having fully considered what it really means. You're young and you have so much more life to live. I'd hate for you to end up tied down with an older man and all his baggage only to regret it later."

"So you think I'm too young to really understand what love is, is that what you're saying?"

Her face contorted as she considered her response. Clearly I had verbalised what she was too scared to say to my face.

"It's not that, hen. I just... well, you might love the idea of being with David now, but how will you feel when you have to live with the reality?"

Her face was full of earnest, desperation even. I sat back in my seat as it became clear what Fran was really so concerned about. I had been right all along. She saw herself in the role that she had painted with black, and wanted me out of the picture. Slowly, I began to nod my head.

"Okay, Fran, I understand. But nothing you can say or do will stop me being with him, okay?"

Her eyes widened even further at my tone.

"Emily, I don't want to stop you doing anything. I just want you to be sure you know what you're doing, that's all."

Carefully I put the piece of pitta in my hand on my plate and wiped the corner of my mouth with a napkin.

"Of course you do, and it has nothing at all to do with your own feelings, does it? Hasn't it occurred to you that if anything was ever going to happen between David and yourself it would have done so by now? I mean, how long have you two been working together? Five years?"

She gaped at me, her mouth open, before falling into a fit of hysterics.

"Hen! Trust me, I do not feel that way about David at all. Hell, most the time I don't even like him, let alone lust after him."

"Of course not. That's why you're so determined to stop anyone else getting close to him." I stood up and pulled on my jacket. "Besides, I love David, I don't just lust after him. Some people are interested in men for reasons other than sex."

I grabbed my bag and walked out the café before she could answer. I had been right about what motivated her interest in my work and my private life from the start. She knew I was a threat and would do everything she could to ridicule me in front of our manager, picking holes in everything that I did. Well, despite her protestations, I had her figured out – and I was done with her.

39

I read and re-read the email in front of me again. Despite my determination to have all my cases up to date before my supervision with David, my excitement about seeing him alone for an hour was destroying my ability to concentrate. With a sigh I locked my laptop and walked purposefully to the ladies, my bag tucked under my arm. If I couldn't be fully up to date with my work, the least I could do was make sure that I looked my best. One of the cubicles was occupied, but I didn't care who saw me as I prepared for our meeting. My colleagues could think what they liked, they weren't important to me. Only David was.

I looked up from my reflection as the toilet behind me flushed and the door creaked open. It was Fran, all pink hair and lipstick. I held her gaze for a moment before turning my attention back to my face. I listened as she washed her hands and dried them briskly with a paper towel. She paused as she walked past, her eyes reflecting back at me in the mirror.

"That eyeshadow really suits you, hen."

She looked away and headed back into the office without waiting for a response. I snorted as I finished applying my eyeliner. If she thought I was going to let her back into my life off the back of one measly compliment, she had clearly underestimated me.

Back at my desk, I looked at my watch. I still had over ten minutes. I puffed out my cheeks and exhaled loudly as I clicked on my inbox again. I selected the troublesome email and rested my head in my hands as I tried to make sense of it.

*

"Emily?"

I looked up, startled. David looked back at me, a pile of ragged papers in his hand. He looked at the clock on the wall opposite, an eyebrow raised. I followed his gaze, jumping out of my chair when I realised I was over ten minutes late for our meeting.

"Oh, sorry," I mumbled. "I just got a bit distracted, that's all. Another email from Alan's housing officer." I rolled my eyes and grinned up at him. He frowned back.

"What does it say?"

I shrugged.

"I'm not sure. I can't make sense of it. That woman uses so many acronyms I need an interpreter to figure out what she's saying most of the time," I laughed nervously, suddenly aware that David didn't seem to be taking the matter as lightly as I was. I flushed, acutely aware that my familiar tone was at best inappropriate and at worst embarrassing for the man I loved.

"Well, do you want to print it out so we can have a look at it together? Could well be important."

I nodded dumbly and looked at my hands.

"I'll see you in Eric's office, okay?"

I nodded again, my gaze still low. After a moment's silence I looked up to see him walking away. As he disappeared from view I quickly clicked on print and gathered up my notebook and pen. Picking up the email on my way, I trotted to Eric's office, slipped in through the half-open door and closed it quietly. David was sitting at the desk, his cheek resting on his fist.

"Sorry about that," I said quietly as I sat down, smiling apologetically when he looked up. His lips smiled stiffly back, but the tension around his jaw and the furrows across his forehead betrayed his torment. His sea blue eyes looked blankly back at me. He nodded at the paper in my lap.

"Do you want me to look at that?"

I obediently handed it over, clasping my hands together as he scanned through the text. His frown deepened.

"Well, it looks like they are close to having outright possession already. And that Alan has pleaded guilty which, whilst sensible, gives his landlord even more ammunition." He passed it back. "Not looking good, I'm afraid."

I shook my head as I folded the paper into my notebook.

"Oh dear. Well, I guess we can help him get back on the housing register when he comes out of prison, right?"

David laughed hollowly.

"Well, we can, but it won't do him much good. He won't get another council flat now. The best we can hope for is a hostel. And that might be tricky."

"Of course. That's what I meant," I added, nodding rapidly. I glanced at David, who was watching me, his eyes suddenly full of remorse. My cheeks flushed again.

"Sorry," I murmured, my eyes flitting away from his gaze. I heard David take a deep breath.

"I'm sorry too, Emily, but..." he looked down at the papers in front of him and hesitated. I held my breath as I tried to pre-empt what he was going to say. As he shook his head, I gently placed my hand on his bare forearm. It was warm, the soft dark hairs that covered his skin strangely comforting. He froze under my touch.

"It's okay, you can say it," I murmured, leaning closer to him. He suddenly pulled his arm away from me and folded it with the other across his chest.

"The thing is, Emily, Eric and I have real concerns about your performance. As you know, your probationary period was extended about a month ago, but to be honest, we haven't seen any real progress."

I stared at him blankly. He was looking at his foot, jiggling manically as it rested on his knee.

"What?" I whispered. He glanced at me before shifting in his chair.

"Well, quite frankly, we still don't see you integrating with others in the service and, if anything, you seem to be becoming more isolated. And," he held up his hand as I opened my mouth to protest, "and, we have concerns about your work, too."

"But my casework is always of a high standard. You've said so yourself," I interrupted, wanting to get the words out before they were engulfed with tears.

"Your paperwork and case notes are always thorough and up to date, yes, but there's more to being a support worker for this client group than administration."

I stared at him again. He looked back, his gaze steady, before turning back to his papers.

"Well, first there's the Child Protection issues with Stacey, which you failed to flag up to me or Social Services. Then there's Alan who, by the sounds of it, has been on the path to self-destruction for some time without you bothering to mention the fact to anyone. As for Ian..."

"Ian's doing fine," I interjected through gritted teeth. I knew full well where this had all come from, and it had nothing to do with my performance. David had clearly confided in Eric about the developments in our relationship, and the older man was pulling out all the stops to get rid of me. The issues he was raising now were as much a distortion of the truth as David's denial of our feelings for each other, and as farcical as his marriage. His head dropped as he sighed.

"Yes, Ian is doing fine. But that's irrelevant when he called up the service last week begging for a new support worker." He looked up at me again, his eyes like ice. "He said that he felt like he couldn't rely on you to give him the emotional or practical support that he needs to stay clean." His gaze flickered as it searched my face. "Emily, do you understand?"

I stared back at his face, his features a blur behind a barrier of tears.

"Emily?"

I dabbed under my eyes with the sleeve of my cardigan and swallowed down my outrage.

"I understand, David. Perfectly."

I met his gaze and held it steadily until he looked away, a flush creeping up his neck from under his shirt. His fingers ran through his hair with an unsteady hand, betraying his unease. He cleared his throat before rattling through some policies and procedures that he advised me to familiarise myself with in the event that I was fired. I nodded along quietly but, as he rambled on, the fact that reading up on my staff handbook was going to do little to save my career – and our relationship – slowly dawned on me. He was the only one who could put an end to the witch-hunt which Eric seemed to have released against me and he knew it as well as I did.

"So, any questions?"

I shook my head, bowed against the lies and hate that had been thrown against me. The silence around us screamed with the injustice of the accusations put to me, the frustration and pain that, at that moment in time, our future together was doomed before it had even had a chance to start. I heard David's chair creak as he slowly got to his feet.

"I'll give you a few moments on your own, Emily. Take your time."

I didn't look up as he strode out of the room, his haste confirming his discomfort despite the ease he forced into his gait. As the door clicked gently behind him, the silence around me screamed what had been left unsaid, words that I knew I needed to say before it was too late.

40

My eyes snapped open as the front door slammed. I listened to footsteps as they crossed the hallway to the kitchen before coming to a halt with a loud rustling of carrier bags. It was Matt, no doubt home after his ritual Wednesday evening trip to the supermarket. Cupboards banged below me as he unpacked his cargo, which probably didn't consist of much more than Marmite, crisps and cheap white bread. I rolled onto my side as a faint aroma of cigarette smoke confirmed that, despite his hungover declaration the Saturday before, he had yet to quit. I pulled my dressing gown around me to cover my exposed thigh, just in case he popped up to offer me some tea and toast.

And perhaps wish me a happy birthday.

I picked up my phone lying next to me and checked it again. I had full reception and my battery was charged, but it remained silent. No text from Lorraine, no call from Dad. Even Fran had kept schtum in the office, which had surprised me despite our current animosity. I tapped on Facebook. It was as quiet as ever, with the few friends I had seemingly determined to ignore my twenty-third year on this planet. I scrolled through my newsfeed to see the usual celebrations and gloatings of my associates. I was about to log off when a message notification popped onto my screen. It was from David. I scrambled to a sitting position, my concerns about my modesty instantly forgotten, and opened the message.

Happy Birthday, Em. I hope you're having a great day.

No kisses, no hugs. But a message, all the same. He was reaching out to me, despite the awkwardness of our situation. I lay back against my pillows and cradled my phone as I read his message again and again. Saying so little, he said so much. He was in as much pain as I was, and probably more conflicted than I could fully understand. He had his job, his marriage, his children. He was respected by those around him, and any move he made towards what he really wanted would destroy his friendship with Jim and Eric which, quite possibly, could end his career. Resisting the urge to reply, I tapped onto my contacts. I needed to talk to someone, yet everyone I knew seemed to have distanced themselves from me, moving further and further away in the bubbles of their own lives.

I took a deep breath and selected Lorraine's name. As I held my phone up to my ear I realised my hand had been shaking uncontrollably and steadied it with the other. Relief instantly relaxed my tense body as it began to ring. My heart leapt to my mouth when she answered.

"Lorraine? Hi, it's Emily."

My pointless introduction was met with muffled music, distant laughter and the unmistakeable rustling of the inside of someone's bag. I helplessly shouted my friend's name over and over. When the line went dead, I dropped my phone onto the bed beside me as my head fell into my hands.

"Emily?"

I looked up at the door and pushed my hair out of my face. Doubting my own senses, I crawled off my bed and opened the door a crack. Matt's face peered back at me, his face almost silhouetted against the landing light.

"Are you alright? I heard shouting."

I stared at him dumbly before falling into hysterics. His eyes widened at my amusement.

"Yes, I'm fine. I was just on the phone to my friend and she couldn't hear me very well."

He nodded slowly, deliberately.

"Oh, okay. You alright, though? You sounded a bit upset."

I gulped down uncontrollable laughter and nodded at him. His ears were glowing pink, illuminated by the light. Another burst of giggles escaped me.

"Are you stoned?"

I shook my head as I steadied myself against the doorframe. Finally, I regained my composure.

"No, but I could really do with a drink."

Matt studied my face, his own expressionless. He hesitated.

"Well, I've just bought a couple of bottles of wine. If you really feel the need help yourself. As long as you replace them, of course." He started down the stairs, turning back to me when he was halfway down. "I'd rather you do that than go out. You seem a bit out of it."

I watched him as he descended the stairs, my hand clapped over my mouth. His door slammed behind him and the blare of his television. I looked across the hallway. Rebecca was out, and I hadn't seen Beatrice in weeks. Tying my dressing gown belt tightly around my waist I tiptoed down to the kitchen. Sure enough, a bottle of Sauvignon Blanc was nestled in the fridge door between a pint of full fat milk and two litres of

Coke. Carefully I slipped it out and shut the fridge door as quietly as I could before retreating back to my room.

*

"Hello?"

"Dad? It's me."

The usual intake of breath.

"Emily. Didn't we speak just the other day?"

"Yeah, but, you know, I've had a bit of a shitty day and wanted someone to talk to."

"Are you drunk?"

His tone had shot from bored to critical in a second. I grimaced. Clearly two glasses on an empty stomach had taken its toll.

"No. I've only had one glass of wine with my mates after work, that's all. You know, to celebrate."

My dad laughed half-heartedly.

"What, so you're celebrating having had a shitty day, are you?"

The gentle reminder had gone unnoticed. I debated pointing out to him the significance of the date, but the thought of having to tell my own father it was my birthday was beyond humiliating.

"Okay, so not celebrating as much as commiserating." I poured myself another glass as I spoke. "I had a bit of a run-in with my boss today."

My dad snorted.

"Trust me, you'll have plenty more of them before you hit retirement. It's called life."

Pointlessly, I shrugged.

"I know. But I thought we had a better relationship than that, that's all."

Another deep breath.

"Well, I'm sure he'll get over it, whatever it was. Otherwise he'd have given you your P45 there and then."

I hesitated. It was the perfect time to tell him exactly what had happened, but my father's words made me stop. It was true, he hadn't fired me. Eric hadn't fired me. If I was really that bad at my job, my dad was right, I'd be on the phone to him on my birthday and unemployed. I tipped more wine into my mouth.

"That's true."

"Yes, it is. Honestly, Emily, you need to learn to put things into perspective."

I took another sip. Again, he had a point.

"Yes. You're right."

"Good. That's settled, then. Now, are there any other crises I need to know about or can I get back to the snooker?"

"No. Everything's fine. Thanks, Dad."

He hung up. No goodbye, no I love you, no nothing. But what he had said had given me hope. I hadn't been fired yet. David was just scared of his own feelings. He was trying to put me off, to push me away in an attempt to temper my passion, as well as his own. But even he knew he had gone too far and was already regretting it – his Facebook message said it all. He had opened a line of communication, and I needed to take advantage of it before he closed it down again – but messaging each other over the internet wasn't the way to do it. Downing the rest of my wine I stumbled off my bed, flung off my dressing gown and ran to my wardrobe. I pulled on my graduation dress, tipped my make-up into my handbag, slipped on my heels and headed out of my room, grabbing the almost-empty bottle of wine on my way.

*

As I turned onto Long Avenue, my pace slowed. I consulted Google Maps again. His house was only a block away. I looked around, and, spotting a bus stop across the road, tottered over, ignoring a blasting horn as I did so.

I dragged my fingers through my hair as I sat down. It was in need of a wash, but it was too late to do anything about that now. I needed to see him, to get to the bottom of our dilemma, and I needed to do it whilst I still had the courage, Dutch or otherwise. I pulled out my compact and inspected my reflection as I patted powder onto my shiny nose. The lipstick I had applied on the tube was still in place, as was the eyeliner, if a little wobbly. Satisfied, I stood up and scurried back across the road.

It was a street property, an old Victorian conversion with a curtained bay window illuminated with soft lighting from inside. A tiny bike with stabilisers was lying in the front garden next to a pair of wheelie bins. Weeds were beginning to poke through the cracked paving slabs. I smiled to myself at the thought of David bending over to pull them up as our future children ran around him, screaming with delight as they played tag. I crept towards the heavy-looking front door and listened. A radio was playing far away. Pots were clattering. There was no chatter, no laughter. My resolve tightened. Things would be different with me.

Tossing my hair over my shoulder, I reached for the silver door knocker and banged it firmly three times. The clattering stopped. I held my breath as slippered feet shuffled towards the other side of the door. I took a steadying breath as it opened, suddenly unnerved at the notion that it might be Gill who answered the door, that David might be out.

My face relaxed into a smile and he stood before me. Dressed in some retro-style jogging bottoms and a plain white T-shirt, his mop of hair was more dishevelled than usual. He looked different, homely with a tea towel in his hands, relaxed in his flip-flops. Only his eyes betrayed his unease.

"Emily? What are you doing here?"

"Hi, David. I need to talk to you," I breathed. He looked over his shoulder and up the stairs. The hallway behind him was minimal, a grey rug and set of black and white photos on the wall the only items that broke up the uniform white. He turned back and stepped towards me, shutting the door slightly behind him. My heart thumped at his closeness, his scent.

"Can't it wait until tomorrow? It's a bit late."

"No, David, it can't. It's waited long enough. I've waited long enough. And after our meeting today, it can't wait any longer."

His features softened a little as my face flushed in response to my boldness.

"Emily, I know today was really hard, and I'm sorry about that. But I would really rather talk to you about it tomorrow. Gill's getting the kids ready for bed and I need to go give her a hand."

I hesitated, thrown by his blatant refusal to acknowledge what I was really saying.

"Emily? Is that okay?" He was pushing the door open again, backing away from me. Instinctively I grabbed his arm. He froze, his beautiful eyes wide.

"No, it isn't okay. We need to stop avoiding what is really going on here. You and I both know that what you told me today was down to Eric trying his best to keep us apart. And whilst he likes and admires you, I'm a dispensable pawn."

David's jaw tensed as I spoke. I had hit a nerve. I knew I was challenging him, but he needed to stop lying to himself, lying to his wife, lying to me. He looked down at my hand on his arm. I willed him to take it in his own.

"Emily, I'm not sure what you're talking about. Eric and I have concerns about your performance, nothing else." The frown that had been developing across his forehead suddenly deepened. "And how did you get my address?"

I smiled despite my frustration.

"I found it where you left it for me. On your desk."

"Dave? Are you done down there?"

The wispy voice from the top of the stairs made us both jump. David's gaze didn't leave mine.

"I'll be up in a sec." His voice was suddenly lower, more sombre than I had ever heard it before. My stomach flipped. He was finally listening to me, taking the situation seriously. I reached for his hand and grasped it, my other still resting on his arm. His fingers were warm and slightly damp from his domestic chores. He looked down at his skin touching mine before pulling away, folding his arms across his chest.

"Emily, this is ridiculous. I didn't leave anything of the sort on my desk. Well, certainly not for you to find it and come over to my house." His voice was low and quiet. I looked into his eyes, suddenly expressionless and cold. I held his gaze until he looked away. "Emily, I know you've developed a bit of a crush on me, and I'm sorry if I've given you any encouragement. But you need to stop now."

He was looking down the street as he spoke, anywhere but at me. He couldn't look me in the eye and tell me he didn't want me. His cold, stubborn words hurt, but I knew their true meaning.

"Why are you still denying how you really feel about me, David? I know it's hard, but you can't carry on living a lie." I reached for his hands again, pulled at his arms to release them. He resisted easily before taking hold of my own. I gazed up at him, my skin tingling under his touch. He was going to kiss me, throw caution to the wind, finally admit to himself and the world that we should be together. I closed my eyes and tilted my head towards his own. After what seemed like an eternity, I felt the pressure of his hands soften and disappear. Confused, I opened my eyes. He had stepped back again, was beginning to close the door on me.

"Goodnight, Emily," he said, his eyes not leaving mine. I looked from the door back to him again, my heart beating fast. I couldn't understand why he was behaving like this, so cold, so distant, even when I had been so open and understanding. I stepped forwards and clumsily grabbed at his free arm with one hand and his waist with the other.

"For fuck's sake, Emily."

His voice was louder, harsher. I felt his hand on my shoulder, trying to push me away. I gulped back a sob and held him to me, my face buried awkwardly in his chest.

"Why are you being like this?" My voice was high and emotional, but I didn't care.

"David? What's going on?"

That thin, breathy voice again, footsteps padding down the stairs. I felt David resist me again.

"Just go back upstairs, Gill, I've got it under control." That hard, firm tone again. I lifted my head and gazed up at his face. He was facing the staircase, looking at his wife. The flimsy summer dress she was wearing flapped around her skinny legs. Her wild hair and wide eyes made her look even scrawnier than in the photos I had seen. The confusion flicking across her face made me giggle despite my tears.

"Sorry, Gill, but David's going to be with me now. He'll still be around for the kids and everything, but he doesn't love you anymore. He loves me."

Her eyes grew even rounder, her face paler as I spoke. She clutched the banister and looked from me to David. He was staring at me, his mouth open, his blood rushing up his neck to his face. Suddenly, he twisted his arm free, shoving me hard on the shoulder as he did so. I stumbled back, tripping over the discarded bike as I did so. From inside the house I heard a child wailing.

"Are you fucking crazy?" He stepped forwards and looked down at me from the doorstep as I regained my balance. Finally steady I looked him in the eye.

"No, David, I'm not. I'm just being honest with you and your wife. It's about time you showed the same courtesy."

"David!"

Gill was out of my sight, but her voice had become a screech, almost hysterical. He turned to her, his hand outstretched towards her.

"Gill, don't listen to her, she's talking shit." The infantile crying from upstairs had become a scream. "Look, go sort the kids out, I'll be up in a minute."

David watched as she retreated up the stairs before turning back to me. His eyes locked with mine.

"Go home, Emily. And don't you ever come back here and upset my wife like that again, do you understand?" He started to shut the door.

"David…"

Hesitating, he looked at me. I stared back, tears falling freely down my face. Looking away he shook his head before slamming the door behind him.

41

My head jolted up as I heard the door to the office open in the distance. My shoulders slumped as one of the office bitches sashayed in, smirking at me as she passed my desk. I turned back to my laptop. More emails had popped into my inbox whilst I had been staring out of the window, agonising over what had happened the previous night. David's behaviour had confused me, but I was beginning to understand. Turning up at the family home had been a mistake. He hadn't been ready. I had tried to apologise over Facebook but he had blocked me, and none of the emails I had received so far had been in reply to my begs for forgiveness either. I opened one of the messages that had just come in and tried to concentrate on its contents, but my mind was far from Alan's imminent eviction and prison sentence. The wine I had consumed the night before had contributed to my state, furnishing me with a banging headache that the Nurofen I had taken refused to budge.

I looked at my watch. It was nearly ten, and the office was still quiet. I had been there since eight and had achieved little other than throwing up the mug of sugary tea I had made myself when I arrived. I'd had to rewrite any emails or notes I had attempted to compose a minimum of three times, and was still not happy to send or save a majority of them. I just needed to hear from him, know that he was going to forgive me, then at least I would be able to concentrate on saving my job, if nothing else.

I jumped when I heard the office door slam. As David strode in, my heart and head began to thump and the nausea I had experienced earlier returned with a vengeance. He didn't look at me or anyone else in the office as he threw his bag on his desk and shrugged his coat off, discarding it carelessly on his chair before walking purposely towards me. As he approached my desk the chatter at the back of the office dropped away. I stared at him, my face hot and my hands clammy.

"Emily. A word. Now."

He didn't look at me and walked away as quickly as he had advanced. Confused, I scrambled out of my seat and followed him, running slightly to keep up. Someone sniggered behind me, but it didn't matter. What mattered was what was about to happen. Was he going to finally confess his feelings to me? Or had the damage I had done the previous night been worse than I had thought? He threw open the door to Eric's office and walked towards the window, his hands on his hips. Quietly I closed the door behind me and took a steadying breath. I needed to respond to whatever he said or did carefully, but my mind and body were in chaos. I watched him in silence as he stood with his back to me, staring out of the window. His back was heaving slightly, betraying his agitation. When he didn't speak I looked around the office, wondering if I should sit down or go to him, speak or stay silent. After what felt like an eternity, he turned slightly towards me and raised his hands to his forehead, pressing his temples.

"David, I, I'm sorry. I know what I did was…"

"Sorry? How can you be sorry? You haven't got the faintest idea what exactly you did last night." His voice was soft, the tone calm but forced. I watched him as he squeezed his fingers more tightly over his forehead, his jaw tense. I bit my lip.

"I know. But I was desperate, David. I needed to talk to you away from the office, away from Eric and all this." I gestured limply at the all-too familiar room. David glanced at me as he dropped his hand back to his waist.

"Emily, 'all this', as you refer to it, is a well-respected service that helps hundreds of people every year to battle with their addictions. Eric has worked his way up through this organisation to drive it on through times when funding has been tight, and needs a workforce who are on the ball and working with statutory services, not against them. Quite honestly, I don't think you really get that, and that is why your position here is under scrutiny, nothing more, nothing less."

His words stung me, their pain as real as any physical inflection. I hung my head, partly in remorse, and partly to gain his sympathy. He was being unfair, and knew it as well as I did. But he didn't stop.

"As for last night…" His laughter made me look up. He pulled his hair out of his face as he shook his head slowly. "I really don't know where to start. You're young, naive and lonely, and you've got some kind of schoolgirl crush. I get that. And I admit it, I was flattered and, perhaps at times, encouraged the attention. Hell, at my age, having a twenty-year-old blush whenever you speak to her and giggle at every half-arsed joke you make does wonders for your ego. But turning up at my fucking house…"

He turned to face me as his voice rose. He looked at me, both hands clutching at his head. His eyes were wide, his face and neck red and tense, every tendon bulging with anger. I stared back.

"I'm twenty-three, David."

His head jutted forwards at my response, his eyes even wider.

"Oh, I'm sorry. But, quite honestly, I don't give a shit. I don't care how old you are, what colour your bathroom is or what your first pet was called. What I do care about is my wife and my children, and seeing them distressed because some loon thinks it's okay to come and knock on my door and throw herself at me, well, that really fucking pisses me off."

I watched him as he spoke. I had known before that he wasn't perfect, that nobody was perfect, but with his spiteful words and his red bulging face, this was a side of him that I had never realised existed. And a side that I wished I had never provoked.

"I'm sorry, David, but…"

"But what? But you and your little fantasy world are more important than my family? But it's okay to tell my wife that I don't love her and cause her even more pain than she is already suffering?"

I shrugged.

"David, I know you two have been having problems…"

"You don't know shit!"

I looked at the door behind me. His voice was growing louder and louder and, despite the soundproofing, our colleagues would no doubt be able to hear his shouting. I felt my face flush at the thought of them all giggling at my expense. I looked back at David. He was still staring at me.

"Emily, one thing you clearly don't understand is how difficult it is to bring up a family. It isn't easy, trust me, and will test a relationship to its limits. But Gill and I love each other and, although we don't always agree on things, our relationship is as strong as it ever has been, if not more so."

I laughed. I know it wasn't appropriate, but his blatant self-denial was comical. David's mouth dropped open at my reaction.

"Sorry, did I miss something? I mean, is something fucking funny here?"

I composed myself and crossed my arms across my chest.

"Yes, there is. David, if everything is so wonderful, why did she have to go away the other weekend? If your relationship is so strong and you're able to work through all your differences, why couldn't you work through whatever her problem was then?"

The angry blood that had stained his face slowly drained away. His eyes searched mine for a moment before he turned away. His hands were back on his waist, his hair free to flop over his eyes as he stared at the window. I watched him, my pulse racing. I had hit a nerve. I was right, and he knew I was right. It had taken drastic action to finally get through to him, and it had brought out the worst in both of us to get to this point, the point where he had no choice but to admit what he had been denying for so long. Finally, he took a deep breath and, his fingers back in his hair, shakily released it.

"Because she'd just miscarried, Emily. She was devastated, as was I, and needed some time out. And, because I love her, I wanted her to take it, and I'm glad she did, because it did her the world of good. She was well on the mend. Or at least was until you decided to show up last night."

His voice was soft, his anger replaced with sorrow. I watched him as he stared out at the rooftops below, unsure what to say. Whilst I understood what he had said, it didn't change anything.

"I'm sorry to hear that, David. But, if your relationship is as strong as you say it is, why was she so threatened by me?" He turned back to me, his face expressionless. My gaze not leaving his, I pressed on. "It seems to me that your wife can see what you continue to deny."

We stared at each other for what felt like an eternity. I watched as realisation flooded his eyes, as the tension around his jaw increased, as the colour returned to his face. I didn't move, refused to look away as he stared at me. Eventually he turned back to the window, resting his hands on the sill as he looked out.

"Emily."

"David." I almost whispered his name. Tentatively I took a step towards him. He inhaled deeply.

"Emily. Get out."

I stopped, staring dumbly at his back. His voice was still soft. He didn't mean it. I took another step.

"Did you not hear me?"

The gruffness I had heard last night had returned, tainting his otherwise calm voice. I hesitated. He was vulnerable, raw, and whilst I knew he was hurting, he was also ready.

"Yes…"

"Then why are you still here?" He turned to me. His chest was heaving, inches from mine, his hands clenched by his side. I looked up at his face. His blue eyes were brighter than ever as he stared down at me. He swallowed, the tension in his face making labour out of the simple gesture. "Get. Out."

"But…" I didn't know what to say, but he cut me off before I had chance to find the words.

"Emily – now." He looked at the door behind me then back at my face, a flicker of his eyebrows adding to the menace in his voice. I stared back, frozen by his fury.

"Get out!"

I stumbled back at the force of his voice. His red, contorted face scared me, repelled me. I hurried out of the room towards the exit. I needed air, and fast. I flew down the stairs, knocking into someone in my blind haste as they entered the building.

"Emily. What's wrong?"

It was Fran. Of course, it had to be. I looked at her face, a blur of red lips and eyeliner. I pushed past her and onto the street.

"Emily…"

"Leave me alone."

I didn't look back as I hurried down the street, my arms folded and prickling with cold. People muttered and sucked at their teeth as I barged past them, but I didn't care. Finally I came to a green amongst a row of Georgian townhouses. I spotted a bench unoccupied by the street drinkers who seemed to dominate the park and sat down, my folded arms pressed against my churning stomach. I closed my eyes against the sun doing little to warm my shivering body yet blinding me with its light. Gulping at the air with ragged breaths I rocked gently, the movement soothing me. I tried to make sense of what had just happened, but my thoughts, my feelings, my memories of what had occurred in the last twenty-four hours were too disorganised to order in my mind. I looked around desperately, hoping to see David stride across the park towards me to apologise, to tell me I was right, to tell me he loved me. The group of tramps gathered around the bench opposite were staring at me in silence. I looked down at the floor, anything to avoid their gaze, pitying me despite their own circumstances.

In my pocket, my phone beeped. I scrabbled it out desperately only to find Fran's name flash up on the small screen. I was about to ignore it when I remembered where she was, who she might be with. Hastily I opened the message.

Emily, where are you? Eric's looking for you. Is everything okay? Here if u need me x

My stomach lurched again. My emotions were in too much turmoil to face the complaints of our oversized service manager, no doubt about my supposedly poor performance. The thought of having to listen to him tell me what we both knew was a pack of lies was too much for me to bear. I looked back down at my phone and quickly tapped out a reply before tentatively getting to my feet and walking out of the park. When I got back to the office Fran was outside, waiting for me with my bag. As I approached she rushed forwards and gave me a hug.

"Emily, hun, you look like death warmed up. You want me to go home with you?"

I smiled feebly. She had proved useful in my hour of need, but the thought of spending a second longer with her than I had to was more than I could bear.

"No, I'll be okay. Thanks for packing up my stuff for me, though, I really appreciate it."

"No problem, hen." She passed me my bag and began helping me into my cardigan.

"It's okay, I can manage." My tone was harsher than I had meant it to be, but when I looked back at her face she was smiling at me sympathetically.

"Okay, Emily. But let me know, you know, if you feel like you can't."

She hugged me again before turning back to the office, giving me another reassuring smile before she disappeared through the door. I stood motionless in the middle of the pavement as I digested what she had said. She thought I had lost the plot, that the pressures of the job, of Eric's witch-hunt, of my relationship with David had finally got the better of me.

David.

The jostling of a passing pedestrian brought me back to my present reality. I looked up at the building in front of me. As I slowly began to walk away I felt a pang in my chest. I desperately wanted to work things out with him, but there was no way I was going to be able to with Eric on the prowl. No, it would have to wait. Hopefully time would give David the chance to reflect upon what he had said to me and to finally stand up to his manager. Passing through the barriers at the tube I realised that, if he didn't, I could very easily be without a job within a week. As I stepped onto the escalator and descended to the platform, the thought rested heavily on my chest. And I knew there was only one person who could release its pressure.

42 – David

"Here you go."

I looked up, blinking. Eric smiled down at me as he placed two steaming cups of tea on the table between us. I smiled back, a wave of gratitude almost overwhelming my composure.

"Thanks, Eric."

"Anything for my old mate Dave." He groaned as he lowered himself into his seat. I took a sip of the scalding liquid and grimaced.

"I added a teaspoon of sugar. Figured you might need a little pick-me-up."

I looked down at my mug with a frown. The hand holding it was shaking slightly.

"A shot of brandy would have been better, but I appreciate the sentiment."

Eric chuckled as he lifted his own mug to his mouth. I watched him as he slurped his tea.

"Ah, that's better." He placed his mug back down carefully and smiled at me again, his eyes searching my face. "So, are you sure you're ready for this?"

I stared back at his face. We had sat opposite each other like this numerous times before, looking at budgets, discussing service delivery, chatting about our children, but never before had I felt so grateful to have him as my boss – and my friend. I took another deep breath as, yet again, I struggled to keep my emotions in check.

"As ready as I'll ever be."

"Good man. Now, remember, I'll take the lead, I'll just need you to verify some points for me if she tries to deny them. If you need to take a break, though, just say. Alright?"

I nodded again.

"Gotcha."

"Good. Now you finish your cuppa and I'll give duty a call to see if she's here yet."

He patted me on the shoulder before wandering over to his desk. I watched him as he dialled the extension.

"Alright, Susie. Is Emily in yet? Oh, okay. Great. No, it's okay, I'll come and fetch her when we're ready."

He carefully replaced the receiver and looked over at me.

"She's here. Just nipped to the ladies."

I nodded dumbly. I hadn't seen her since Eric had suspended her on the grounds of harassment, and I didn't know how I was going to react to seeing her again. Gill had still not quite got over her unannounced visit despite my attempts to explain that Emily was... what? Crazy? Deluded? What had been most challenging was admitting that I had known she had a thing for me but had failed to put an end to her fantastical ideas before things got out of hand. I closed my eyes at the thought of it. It took a special kind of idiot to get into this situation, and an especially egotistical one at that. And I had managed it perfectly.

"What?"

I looked up. Eric was watching me, his frown a mirror of my own. I managed a smile.

"Nothing much. I was just thinking about how much of a mess I seem to have got us into. Sorry."

Eric's eyebrows shot up before he succumbed to a throaty laugh.

"Sorry? Well, I'm sorry too, son, but even if I wanted to I don't think I can blame you for it. Not this one anyway." He chuckled again as he turned back to the chaos of his desk.

"Well, I feel partly responsible. I was her manager after all. And I should have dealt with it better…"

"Should've, would've, could've," Eric interrupted. "At the end of the day I don't think any of us realised quite what was going on in her head and, even if we had, it would have always been difficult to deal with. God knows I've never been in this situation before. But then I'm not as handsome as you." He turned to wink at me and looked at his watch. "Right. I make it two minutes to. Are you ready?"

I looked down at my tea before downing the dregs and slamming the mug back on the table.

"As ready as I'll ever be."

"Good. Now let's get this over with then I can buy you a proper drink."

I watched him as he shuffled out of the office. His back was clearly bothering him but, in true Eric style, he wasn't letting it stop him. Since giving up alcohol he hadn't let anything stop him, not the prejudice his past had provoked, not his difficult home life, not his failing health. I shook my head in awe of the man who had so easily taken me under his wing when I had joined the service and talked me into applying for my current role. Eric was always there for me when one of my middle-class crises reared its ugly head. He had a point; he had never got himself into this situation, for no reason other than because he wasn't stupid enough to. He was a true professional, whereas I, approaching forty and quite frankly panicking about it, had let my fear of grey hairs and a growing gut get the better of me.

"Okay, Emily, take a seat."

I glanced up, but couldn't look at her face. She was dressed in black, the fade of her trousers breaking up the uniform colour. She was even skinnier than I remembered, her elbows swellings in the middle of her arms, her collarbones protruding from her flat chest like a pair of handle bars. I averted my gaze to my own hands, resting on the table. Suddenly aware of their close proximity to her own, I shifted them onto my lap. I was glad of the barrier the table offered but wasn't about to give her the opportunity to touch me or, even worse, suggest that I wanted her to.

"Right. If it's okay with you two, I'm going to try and keep this as informal as possible. It's a difficult situation and I don't want to make it even worse by standing on ceremony. Is that alright?"

I glanced at Eric and nodded before returning my gaze to my lap. I heard her murmur a response and felt the hairs on the back of my neck prickle. Involuntarily I clenched my jaw.

"Okay. So, as you both know we are here to discuss concerns that Emily here has breached our code of conduct in relation to her professional dealings with two of her clients and also in relation to harassment of another member of staff. As you are also aware, myself and a member of our board have conducted an investigation into these alleged breaches and have interviewed you both, along with several other people, about the circumstances around them."

At the word "alleged" I found myself bristling again. Yes, so Eric was trying to be objective, but he knew as well as I did that we had gone beyond making allegations. He had hard proof – the emails that landed in my inbox from her on a daily basis, not to mention the handful of letters that had arrived at my home address, were more than enough. I took a deep breath and closed my eyes. He was right. I really needed to let him do the talking. I was in no fit state to deal with her myself. Yet another shortcoming. I almost snorted a laugh at the addition to my ever-increasing list. Maybe Eric should be disciplining me too.

"First of all I'd like to discuss the case of Stacey Duggan. When David and I have spoken to you about this you have admitted that you did not notify Social Services when Stacey disclosed to you that she was drinking again, despite being aware that her daughter had previously been on the Child Protection list. As you are aware this is a serious matter…"

"I didn't know I had to contact them."

The whine of her voice stopped Eric in his tracks. Tentatively I looked up at him. He was gazing at her, his eyebrows slightly raised. After a brief pause he turned to me.

"David, am I right in thinking that, when we met to discuss this, you confirmed that this had been covered in Emily's induction?"

I nodded. I didn't trust myself to verbalise a steady response.

"And that this was signed off by yourself and Emily?"

I cleared my throat.

"Yes, Eric. I believe you have a copy of it on your desk."

I stood up to retrieve it from the stack of papers, but Eric waved me back in my seat.

"It's okay, David." He turned back to Emily, his arms folded over his chest. "Emily, do I really need to show you this document?"

I looked back down at my hands, clasped together. In the silence that followed, I assumed she had indicated to the contrary. Eric took a deep breath.

"Good. Now, I think we have said everything we need to about Ms Duggan. As you will both recall, following this incident and the seriousness of it, Emily, you had your probationary period extended. Now, shall we move on to Alan Briggs?"

I felt myself zoning out as Eric went over her failings once more. My knuckles whitened as I considered the case. I had worked with Alan before, and knew he could be a nightmare. I also knew that, if she had admitted the difficulties she was having with him, we could have contacted his housing officer, the police and God knows how many other services he was known to and have prevented it from getting to this stage. But she hadn't.

"I had it under control, Eric."

"No, you didn't, Emily. You can't always work in isolation, you know, and there is nothing from your case notes that suggests you made any contact with any other services until he had been arrested. In fact, when your manager received a report about him being street active again, you as good as lied to his face when he asked you for feedback."

"I did contact his housing worker…"

"Not until it was too late, Emily."

I could tell from Eric's tone that he was losing his cool. Across the table from me I could hear her sniffling. I sat up in my chair and ran my hand shakily through my hair. Eric looked over at me and gave me a short nod. I acknowledged it before returning my gaze to my lap. My wedding ring caught my attention, and slowly I began twisting it around my finger, a cooling comfort in the stifling room.

"The problem is, Emily, that both these instances happened in your probationary period. One slip-up would almost be excusable, but two would suggest that perhaps you are not ready for a career in this sector. And then of course we received a complaint about the assistance you were offering Ian Jones…"

"I needed more training and support." Her voice was small, childlike. I wondered if she knew full well that it was a lie or whether she really believed what she was saying. Like what she had said about our "relationship". Eric sighed.

"David, can you confirm that Emily was offered a range of additional training courses following her induction as and when needs arose? And that she was also offered shadowing from a more experienced member of the team?"

I nodded again.

"And that this was discussed in supervision, of which the notes were signed off by Emily here?"

"Yes."

"And that, during supervision or at any other time, Emily did not request further training or assistance?"

I looked up at Eric and nodded again.

"That's correct."

Eric offered me a flicker of a smile before turning back to Emily. I dared myself to glance over at her. Her head was bent, her hair hiding her face. For a moment I felt sorry for her. I knew that, since our confrontation all those weeks ago, Fran had been trying to contact her, to offer her help to get the support she needed, but she had refused to even reply to her colleague's texts. But then I also knew, having worked with hard-to-reach adults all my working life, that there was no point trying to support someone who refused to acknowledge that they had a problem, that they needed help. That some people needed to work their way further into the pattern of self-destruction before they could accept that maybe they had a problem. And that, in the meantime, they would drag down the people around them, too. People like me.

"David?"

My head jolted up.

"Yes?"

"Did you have anything else to add?"

I hesitated before answering. I hadn't heard much of what Eric had just said, nor any last-minute excuses from Emily. I shook my head.

"Good. Now, I'm afraid that we have come to the allegation of harassment. I'm aware that this is a particularly sensitive issue, and I shall do my best to respect that. Emily, I understand from David that, previous to your visit to his home there had been some emails exchanged between the two of you about your feelings towards him. Is that correct?"

She was silent. I heard Eric take a deep breath.

"Emily, it would help if you could respond to my questions. I have a copy of the emails I refer to if that would help…"

"Yes, there were emails sent, but…"

"And throughout these communications, David made it clear to you that he did not return your affections."

Eric's abrupt interjection surprised me. I looked up at him again. He was gazing at her calmly, his hands clasped loosely on the table in front of him. He glanced at his watch.

"Emily, I know this is difficult, but I just need to establish the facts."

I held my breath in the ensuing silence.

"Well, he may not have admitted it in his emails, but he was more than clear about his feelings when we talked in person and on Facebook."

Her voice, clear and determined, almost made me jump.

"Okay, Emily. Well, David has provided me with access to your correspondence on Facebook and, it has to be said, whilst the tone was casual, there is nothing in there that appears to be much more than friendly banter."

"Not when you add it to everything he said and did in the office and when we went out after work. And you both know it."

Her voice was suddenly louder, her tone hardened. I felt blood warming my face as my anger began to rise.

"Emily, did David ever tell you he loved you or wanted to be with you in any way other than as colleagues?"

"He didn't need to."

I opened my mouth to respond and raised my hands to emphasise the point I had yet to make, but Eric waved me down.

"So you admit that he never told you he loved you. And did he ever ask you to visit him at his home address?"

Her thin laughter penetrated my ears like needles.

"No, he didn't. But I think he would have minded a lot less if I had turned up when his wife wasn't there. When he had meant for me to come over."

"What?" I couldn't stay quiet any longer. I looked over at her, my intention to avoid any eye contact with her smashed by the frustration I just couldn't keep under control. She was staring at me, her green eyes saucer-like in their dark sockets. When our gaze locked, she didn't flinch. Automatically I looked away, floundering, and turned to Eric. He glanced at me before turning back to her.

"What do you mean, Emily?"

She snorted a laugh.

"Well, don't you think it's a bit of a coincidence that I 'found' his address just hours before he disclosed to me that his wife was going to be away the following weekend?"

I stared at Eric blankly as I tried to decipher what she was talking about. Then, I remembered. She had been with me in the pub when Gill had told me she needed some time out after her miscarriage and was going home for the weekend. The same day I had been trying to sort out a refund on our gas bill, which had disappeared off my desk, I had assumed underneath the mountain of paperwork that dominated my workspace.

"Emily was with me in the pub when Gill told me she was going away," I said, steadily holding my manager's gaze. "A bill had disappeared off my desk that day too. I can only assume that's what she's talking about."

"You assume correctly, David. Terribly convenient, don't you think?"

I kept my gaze firmly on my manager's face as she spoke. The comfort and familiarity of his ruddy complexion and kind eyes kept me in check as I digested what she had just said. That when my wife was grieving the loss of our unborn child, I had wanted to be with her. That in some way she could replace what Gill had given me and could offer me something more. I closed my eyes at the thought of the pain etched on Gill's face when she told me she'd lost the baby, when she saw Emily draped all over me in our hallway, when I tried to explain away yet another letter scrawled in red ink on rose-scented paper. I felt sick.

"David, can you tell me, did you mean for Emily to find your address?"

"No."

"And had you hoped that she would come and visit you when Gill was at her parents'?"

"No." My voice cracked.

Eric gave me a short nod.

"Thank you. Now, Emily, having spoken with David's wife and other members of the team, they have verified what David has said about his relationship with you. David has admitted that he may have been flirtatious on occasion but that this is no different from how he behaves with other female staff members in social situations, and again this has been verified by other people."

Involuntarily my jaw clenched in angry shame. What a fucking idiot I had been. What Eric said was right; I was a flirt, and my ego fed off the attentions of our largely young and female team. Maybe this made me guilty, at least in part, for the emotional adultery I was being accused of. I closed my eyes against the pain on Gill's face, that night and many times since. Pain that I had so carelessly, selfishly inflicted.

"And, most importantly, there is nothing I have heard from yourself or anyone else that suggests that David regarded you any differently from any other member of this service, and in any way encouraged you to come to his home or pursue him in the way that you have continued to do since that particular incident. Do you understand?"

I kept staring at his face, an anchor in my emotional turbulence. I just wanted the meeting to end, for her to disappear. My mouth suddenly became dry. The thought of the pint Eric had promised me teased me with its promise of relief.

"Yes, I understand, Eric. Perfectly."

Her voice was mocking, childish. I felt my fists clench in my lap.

"And you understand why we have to let you go."

The question came out as a non-negotiable statement.

"Of course."

"Good." Eric took a deep breath and looked at me as he released it, his relief undisguisable. He smiled at me briefly before turning back to her. I could feel her eyes boring into me. I kept my own on my manager and my expression as neutral as I could.

"Well, I am of course sorry that this has been the outcome of your employment here, Emily, and wish you all the best in the future. I will, of course, send you a full copy of the investigation and include it in the names of independent bodies you can go to for further legal and employment advice..."

"There's no need, Eric." She was on her feet, the legs of her chair dragging across the black carpet. "I've had all the explanation and advice I need from you."

I watched Eric as he rose and stepped forwards but she was through the door before he had the chance to open it for her. As the door down to the street below slammed I heard someone cheer.

"That's enough," Eric bellowed, shutting the door behind a titter of laughter. I dropped my head to my hands, the anxious energy I had been carrying around with me all day suddenly gone. I felt Eric's hand on my shoulder again, reassuring with its weight.

"Alright, son. It's all over."

"I wouldn't count on it, Eric. Just because she doesn't work here anymore doesn't mean that she can't contact me still. God, I had a letter from her yesterday," I moaned into my hand.

Eric sighed.

"Well, you can still call the police, Dave. I'm sure they would be more than happy to give her a harassment warning in the circumstances."

I looked up at him. He was smiling down at me, but his eyes were full of concern. I smiled back. I owed him that at the very least.

"You're right. Hopefully I won't need to, though."

"Hopefully." He patted my shoulder again and straightened up, his other hand on his lower back. "Cor, that's better. I was seizing up sat in that chair for so long."

I laughed despite myself.

"I don't think it's the chair, mate. I think it's a lack of TLC. Have you been to the doc's about your back again or not?"

He groaned.

"Oh God, here we go. Let's go get that pint down you before you remember about that blood test too."

I opened my mouth to respond but was cut off by Eric's laughter. He grabbed the scuffed leather jacket hanging on the back of his chair and pointed at the door.

"Just go get yer coat. You've pulled."

43 - Epilogue

"Er, hello? Can I get my sandwich, please?"

I blinked and looked from the window to the man standing opposite me on the other side of the counter. He raised an eyebrow before turning back to his iPhone. Confused, I looked at the range of fillings in front of me, drying at the edges in their metal trays.

"It was egg mayonnaise."

His tone said it all. Dressed in his flash suit with his manicured hands, he saw me as no one, just another minion put on this planet to serve him in between his business meetings.

"Of course, sir."

I grabbed two slices of white bloomer and absently slathered them with margarine as I glanced out of the window. David hadn't been out of the office since he had arrived at 9.23 that morning. It was now after one and he was late getting away for lunch. Quickly I spooned a mountain of egg onto the bread, squashed it down and added the top slice. I looked out the window again. No sign.

"Emily. Can we have a bit of focus, please? We have a queue here."

I nodded, not bothering to turn to look at my new boss. I kept my eyes on the entrance to Drug and Alcohol Action as I wrapped my lumpy work with greaseproof paper and handed it to my customer.

"Ten out of ten for presentation," he muttered. I didn't bother responding.

"Emily! Bacon and avocado on ciabatta, with salad. Now, please?"

I pushed a loose strand of hair off my face with my forearm and sliced open a roll, ignoring Sam's authoritative tone. She was younger than me and certainly no more qualified to work in the sandwich shop, but seemed to take great pleasure in telling me what to do.

"In a ciabatta roll? For fuck's sake." Although the expletive was said under her breath, it was certainly loud enough for my boss to hear. Whilst so far the greasy-haired Italian had tolerated my distractedness, I didn't want to push it. If I lost this job, the chances of me getting another at such a convenient location were next to non-existent.

"Yep. Sorry!" I said brightly as I rectified my mistake. I forced myself to concentrate, only looking across the road once the girl with braided hair had her lunch safely in her hand.

He was there.

I froze as I watched him walking towards Mornington Crescent, his hands in his jeans pockets, his head down. His hair was being swept out of his face, his white shirt pressed against his torso by the breeze that was keeping the otherwise warm day pleasantly cool. He still hadn't looked up when he was out of the limited line of vision my position allowed. In fact, I hadn't seen his face clearly since my first week at Luigi's. It was on my third day that I saw him crossing the road and walking towards me, his phone clasped to his ear. He had stopped dead in the middle of the pavement when our eyes had locked, his expression of surprise morphing into one of pain. His discomfort had satisfied me. He knew that the lies he had told Eric and his wife had saved his skin at the expense of my own, that his betrayal was not just to me, but to himself. Jostled by passersby, he had quickly moved on, glancing at me again as he hurried away.

"God, I'll do it myself, shall I?"

Sam pushed past me to grab another ciabatta roll. I staggered slightly to keep my balance and looked over at my colleague. Her rosy cheeks were getting redder by the minute.

"Sorry, Sam. Lou, what's next?"

My boss met my gaze over Sam's messy knot of auburn hair. His droopy eyes did little to hide his dissatisfaction. I smiled brightly, confident that my hard work in between my periods of distraction would keep me in his good books. He shook his head as he turned back to the till.

"One chicken and sweetcorn on granary, no salad, if not too much trouble?"

My back was to him before he completed the sentence, my hands working at double speed as I meticulously made the sandwich. I handed it over to my customer with a smile.

"Have a nice day," I called after them before turning back to Luigi. He nodded his head in approval before barking the next order. As I worked, I kept an eye on the clock hanging above the queue of hungry workers. I didn't want to miss David when he returned to the office. Whilst he had been clearly avoiding me, he knew where I was when he was ready. I didn't know how long it would be until he was, but I knew it would happen one day.

I just had to wait.